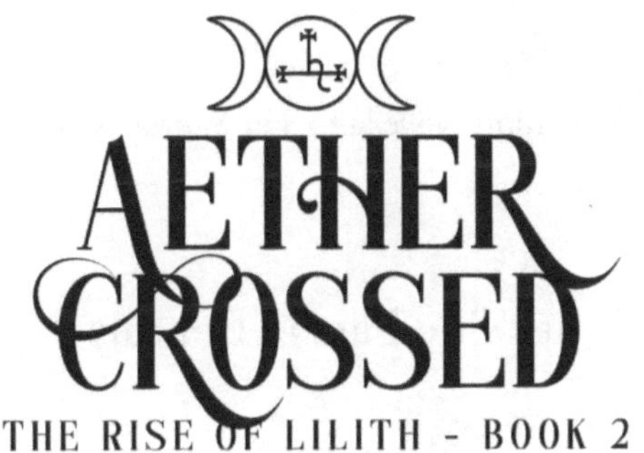

AETHER CROSSED

THE RISE OF LILITH - BOOK 2

Also by Megan Haskell

The Sanyare Chronicles

The Last Descendant

The Heir Apparent

The Rebel Apprentice

Guardian: A Companion Novella to The Sanyare Chronicles

The Winter Warrior

The War of the Nine Faerie Realms

Forged in Shadow

Quenched in Secrets - Coming Soon!

The Rise of Lilith Series

Aether Bound

Aether Crossed

The Author Wheel

(Non-Fiction for Writers by G.C. Boris and M. Haskell)

Publish: Take Charge of Your Author Career (Second Edition)

The Author Wheel Quick Guide Series:

Productive Writing Habits: How to Set Goals You'll Keep and Make the Most of Your Writing Time

Understanding Your Genre: How to Write What Readers Want

Planning a Novel: How to Activate Your Imagination and Develop a Story You Can Write

Learn more at www.AuthorWheel.com

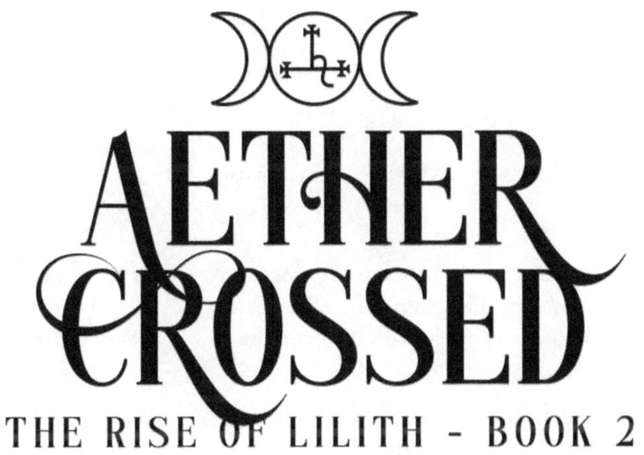

AETHER CROSSED

THE RISE OF LILITH - BOOK 2

MEGAN HASKELL

ISBN (Paperback) 978-1-950307-08-1
ISBN (eBook) 978-1-950307-07-4
ISBN (Audiobook)

Published by Trabuco Ridge Press
22365 El Toro Road #129
Lake Forest, CA 92630

Edited by Kim Peticolas
Cover Design by MoorBooks Design
Chapter Header Art by J. Kurnas Design

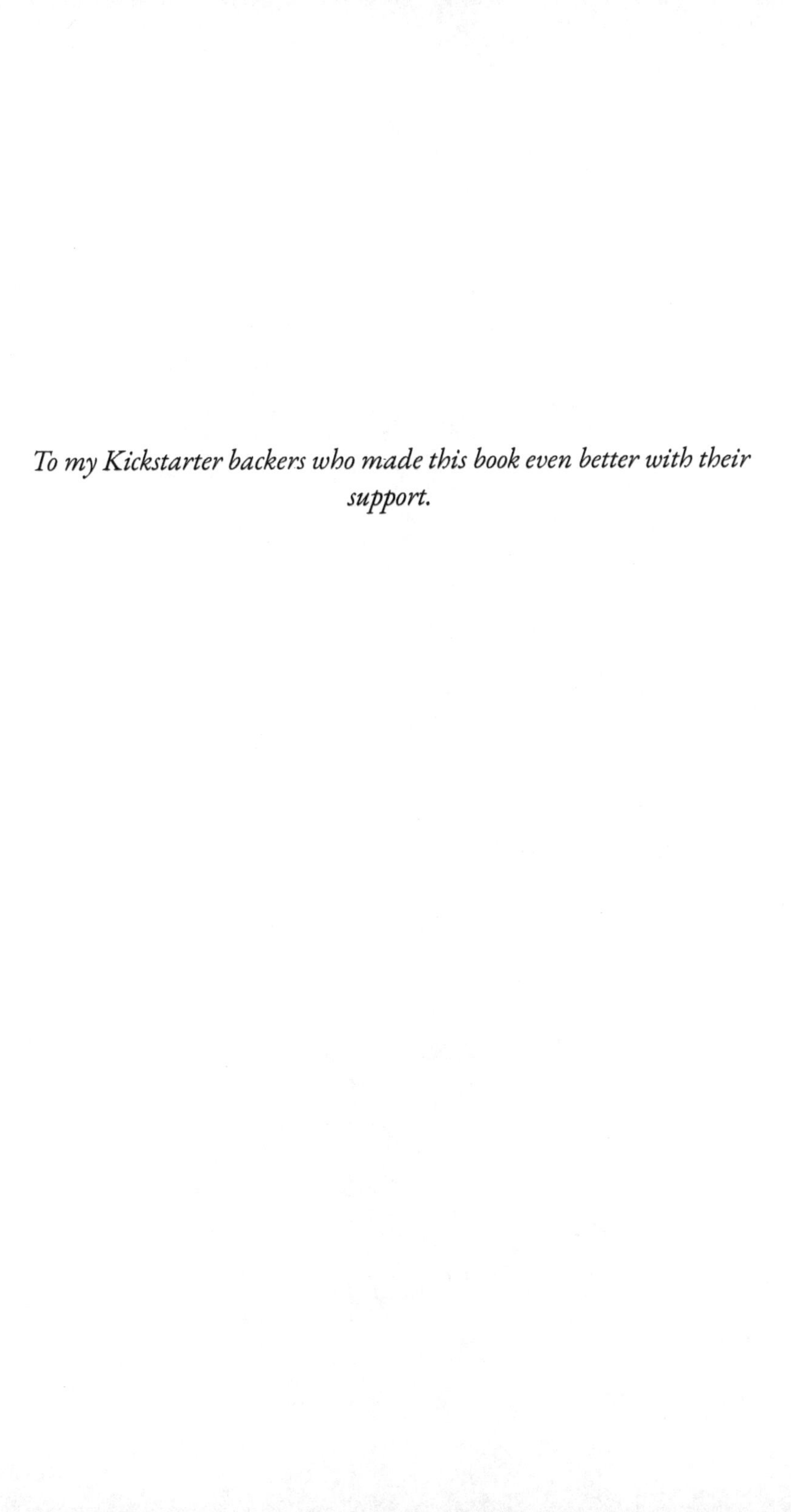

To my Kickstarter backers who made this book even better with their support.

Prologue

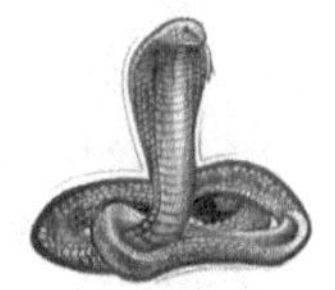

Apep, the Great Devourer, god of chaos and destruction, eater of souls, enemy of light, and generally foul-tempered snake, slithered through the black halls that served as tomb and temple.

"Ssshe banished me! Me!! As if I were nothing more than a newborn godling, fresh from the misssts of Heaven. Have I truly become ssso weak?" Apep asked.

The woman who had come to visit stroked the head of her black hound, who growled softly from the depths of his throat. "It's not as if you have cultivated any kind of following. How do you expect the humans to feed you their Aethereal energy if you do nothing to tempt them?"

"Tempt them? Tempt them! I am not a servant to mortals; it is the other way around. They ssshould fear me. Fear what I can do. What I *will* do if they fail to recognize my power."

"And what would that be?" Hecate asked. "Your myths have been buried in the depths of the desert sands. Even in your height, you were little more than a whispered fear, a horror story to scare the children into good behavior."

"How dare you speak to me this way? I am a warrior. A king! I was once the greatest of the godsss."

"And then the humans saw you for what you were, not a deity to be worshipped, but a monster to be defeated. In this modern age, there is no room for fantasy. They wish a rational explanation for all things. They shine the light of science and technology into the shadows to defeat the monsters that crept through their night-mares in ages past. They no longer need our false explanations. Your time has passed, my friend."

"I refussse to wither and fade. You have done it. You have found your strength in the modern age. It is why I called you here today."

"Yes. You called, and I came, but not because you demanded it. I came to warn you. Stay away from the daughters. They are mine."

"Ssshe must pay for her insolence. Ssshe will face the dark and tremble. And they all will learn why the ancients feared the dark."

The dog's growl deepened. The single torch that lit the space around the goddess of witchcraft, demons, and the underworld sputtered, its light making the dark paintings on the walls dance a macabre ballet.

"I have plans for her. If you interfere, you will regret it."

The goddess in red disappeared with a pop of displaced air, taking her hell hound with her. Apep slithered through the room where she had been, coiling his tail around the wicker and wood chair she left behind. He squeezed. Wood cracked and splintered.

He would not be reprimanded like a naughty godling. He would not bend to her whims. No. He was the Great Devourer and all would fear the shadows he wrought.

But first he must find and activate his avatar.

Leaving the remains of the chair behind, Apep traversed the secret tunnels and hidden causeways of his demesne, making his way to the edge of the Abyss. His red eyes pierced the darkness and called in his shadows. They had been multiplying. He was pleased to see their eagerness. They were ready.

The mortal realm had no idea what was coming.

Chapter 1

Friday night and the Trident was packed. We'd thrown open the windows and turned on the overhead fans with their fake palm fronds, letting in the breeze to cool the sweat and releasing the music to draw in the crowd.

Silas's voice wrapped around me as I worked, mixing drinks, and chatting up the customers at the bar. The band was hot, the blast of their horns and the rhythm of their Southern California ska sound keeping the customers dancing and the party thriving. Summer in Laguna Beach.

I smiled, enjoying every minute.

Silas caught my gaze from beneath his ratty old fedora and winked. His mouth lifted sideways in a half smile even as he leaned forward into the mic. Butterflies thrummed in my stomach. I couldn't help the sappy smile nor the heat that blasted my cheeks. I was way too old for a teenage crush, but my eyes kept drifting to the stage anyway.

"Sweet Jesus, Lil. You two are so *cute*." Virginia nudged my shoulder as she set down her tray of dirties to move the glasses to the bus bin. "It's like eatin' a spoonful of sugar every time I look at 'cha."

"Yeah, well, it's better than walking into the alley to find your friend practically swallowing her boyfriend whole."

Virginia blew a lock of hair out of her face and grinned. "Not my fault that man's a demon in bed."

I winced at the unintentional reference to my secret skill. Virginia couldn't know the demon wasn't her boyfriend. In fact, she was the one with a vaguely serpent-shaped, fuchsia-colored lust demon riding her shoulder. The creature flicked its tongue at me and smiled. I wasn't going to interfere. She was enjoying herself, and apparently, so was Ben, the drummer and her boyfriend of the last month. It was the longest relationship she'd ever maintained. No way was I ruining that for her.

"Two more Zombies for table eight," she said, ordering the next round for the girls in the corner nearest the stage. "That'll be their limit. They're already getting a little feisty."

I glanced toward the scantily clad women draped with yellow demon auras, laughing and cheering and wobbling on their high heels as Silas started up the next song. It was one of my favorites, a fast-paced, horn-forward melody that you couldn't help but move to. I bobbed my head to the music as I measured out the juice and alcohol for the drinks.

"I'll take another one, too," Surfer Jeff chimed in, drawing my attention back to the counter. "It's a good night, tonight."

Jeff was right. It *was* a good night. Wall to wall people laughed and shouted over the music, jostling together in the one-handed shuffle of dancing without spilling their drinks.

"The band's on fire," I said as I lifted the shaker over my shoulder.

I poured the contents into a glass, added the orange, cherry, and pineapple flag, and slid it over to Jeff. As a regular, he got priority.

"I hope not." Jeff bit the cherry off the fruit skewer garnish. "'On fire' is commonly used to mean really successful or unstoppable, but if something goes up in flames, it's destroyed. I like them too much to want them incinerated."

I grimaced, but Virginia beat me to the response.

"That's dark, Jeff," she quipped as she put the fruity drinks on her tray. "Way to kill the mood."

Jeff shrugged as Virginia wound her way back through the crowd to the women in the corner. The two blondes didn't even glance at her as Virginia set their drinks on their table. Their eyes were all for the guys on stage. Not that I could blame them.

Taking advantage of a momentary pause in orders, I started prepping more flags. I was almost out of garnish, and with a set break coming up, I had to be ready for a sprint. Sure enough, as I was sliding the last of the cherries onto my skewers, the music ended, and Silas's voice broke over the crowd.

"Thirty minutes, and we'll be back!"

Conversation picked up, the canned playlist launched over the speakers, customers headed to the bar, and within moments I had five tickets backed up on my station. Even as my hands flew across the bottles, my body hummed with awareness of the man wending his way through the crowd toward me.

"Great show tonight," Surfer Jeff beamed at Silas, sliding over a few inches so my trombonist could squeeze in.

"Thanks, Jeff." Silas pushed his hat back and leaned his whole body across the counter with a wide grin. "Hi, Lil."

His teasing smile brightened his face and sent my heart into twirly little pitter-patters. Annoying. Yet I couldn't help the lift of my own lips. I also couldn't look at him directly for fear of forgetting where I was in the drink mix.

"Hi, Silas."

His hand snaked out to grab one of my just-made skewers and I half-heartedly swatted it away. He grabbed my fingers instead.

"I need those." I laughed, referring both to the flags and my hand. "Fruit is for customers."

Silas squeezed my fingers and ran a thumb across my knuckles. "I bet you could make that drink one handed with a blindfold on."

I met his playful gaze and lifted an eyebrow. "Maybe, but not fast enough for this crowd. You guys have them all hot and bothered."

"And you?"

"No comment." My lips twitched as I playfully suppressed my smile. "Can I have my hand back now?"

Silas tipped his head to the side and gently pulled my arm forward to kiss my knuckles before releasing my fingers. "Oh, I suppose, but only because I want a Blood and Sand before I go back on stage."

The butterflies were dancing a jig by now, but I managed to nod my head. "I think I can make that happen."

As I turned back to the shaker, Silas grabbed the skewer he was originally after and bit the cherry off the end.

I rolled my eyes.

"What?" He asked, faking innocence. "Now I'm a customer. You can take it off my drink."

He slid back to the floor and leaned his side against the counter, facing Surfer Jeff and the mingling crowd, giving me his profile. I couldn't help my surreptitious glances any more than I could stop the waves from lapping at the beach a few hundred yards from our front door.

Silas was unassumingly gorgeous, in a nerdy band-geek kind of way. Lean, but not scrawny, his well-worn jeans hung across his hips, while the collar of a white t-shirt peeked out from beneath a vintage Hawaiian shirt. Stubble dusted his chin, making him look like he'd just rolled out of bed and climbed on stage.

That may or may not have been an accurate representation. We'd only been dating a few weeks and hadn't made it to overnight visits yet. It was hard to open up, to let someone else in after more than a decade of false friendships and family who distanced themselves after discovering my little secret.

Do you really think you can hold his attention? A worm of doubt whispered through my thoughts. *He could have anyone he wants. Why would he stick around to wait for you to warm up? He'll abandon you, just like all the others.*

The only person who'd been a constant in my life, who had supported me through everything without running away at the first sign of trouble, was Ezra. My brother was my rock.

But Silas had been my anchor, calling me home from the Aether when I'd been drawn to Aegir's Hall. His music had kept me rooted—*he* had kept me rooted—when the gods of the ocean had tried to bind me away from my home. He hadn't flinched when I told him of the demons or my extra sensory sight. He hadn't run.

How long can that possibly last? the voice whispered again. *You are nothing. Just some bartender. You can't give him what he needs. You're broken.*

My hands slowed. I wasn't broken. I was different. A Daughter of Lilith. I would not change myself to please someone else.

But what is a Daughter of Lilith, really? You don't even know.

I didn't. Grams had asked me to visit, but she hadn't pushed. She said I needed to recover. And it had only been a few weeks since my return from Aegir's Hall. We hadn't had time. *I* hadn't had time. I had to work, and my hours were not exactly normal.

You neglect even those who try to help you.

The air felt heavy. Oppressive. The bustle of the bar felt distant, muted. The pop beat piping through the speakers felt subdued. A sickly sweet smell, like rotting fruit, wafted across my nose as a shadow slithered into my peripheral vision. I struggled even to lift the shaker over my shoulder.

You've spent your life hiding. No one knows you. No one sees you. You are insignificant. If you left, no one would notice.

"You okay, Lil?"

Silas's warm brown eyes came into focus in front of me. The weight bearing down on my heart lifted. The shaker picked up speed as I finished the last of the drink orders.

"Yeah, of course," I deferred. "My thoughts just drifted there for a second."

Silas smiled, but the worried crinkles at the corners of his eyes gave him away.

"Really. I'm good." I poured the Rum Runner into its designated glass and slid it down the bar to an older gentleman with a bald head, thick beard, dad bod, and smoky-green sloth demon riding his shoulders.

"Two minutes. I got you." I smiled half-heartedly as I started Silas's Blood and Sand.

Silas looked like he wanted to say something, but I turned away to work the blender. A shadow, thin and sinuous, wound through the top shelf bottles on the back wall. When I tried to focus on it, the shape disappeared.

A soft chuckle drifted through the back of my brain.

Who do you think you are, puny mortal? Untrained. Abandoned. Alone. The voice was insidious, breaching my mental defenses and digging into my psyche, riffling through my innermost fears.

While the blender churned, my hand drifted to the athame hanging off my belt in a sheath at my side. The ceremonial knife— a gift from the goddess Hecate—warmed at my touch. I'd only used it a few times since my return from Aegir's Hall, but I'd carried it with me every day. It felt comforting for some reason, and it was small enough that I could pass it off as a kitchen tool if anyone asked. No one had.

In truth, the athame channeled my ability to interact with the demons from the Aether. Virginia's lust demon was just one of the elemental minions I'd encountered. There were others. They came in all different shapes, sizes, and persuasions. The bar tended to attract the party influencers: lust, passion, freedom, irresponsibility, addiction, and euphoria. Every once in awhile we got a jealous fighter or a vengeful lover, but those were pretty rare.

I didn't think I'd ever seen a shadow demon play hide and seek like this. Most of the minions attached themselves to an individual and stayed with that person until they got what they wanted or found better prey. This one seemed more interested in sowing discord, traveling between individuals rather than staying with any one person.

Go away. I thought toward the shadow, keeping my hand on the knife. *I will not listen to your lies.*

The voice chuckled again. *Are they lies? Or simply the truth you fail to acknowledge?*

I stopped the blender and turned my back on the demon and its evil suggestions. I wouldn't give it the satisfaction of a response.

I see you, Daughter of Lilith. I know you. The voice faded as if moving away into the distance. It was probably too much to ask that the thing would leave the bar entirely.

Chapter 2

"You sure you're okay?" Silas was due back on stage, but his warm brown eyes held concern as he took his drink from my hand. Our fingers brushed and the last of the oppressive weight drifted away.

Silas had my back. He knew what I was, and he didn't flinch away.

I dipped my chin to say yes, then tilted my head toward the stage. "You'd better get back up there before a riot starts." The rest of the band was already picking up their instruments.

Silas's eyes narrowed. "Fine. But I'm taking you out after closing. You need a break."

"Out? How about we stay in?" My eyes widened and I pressed my lips together between my teeth as my cheeks heated. What was I thinking? "I mean, I'm pretty tired. I'm not sure I'm up for a party."

Silas lifted an eyebrow and squeezed my hand. "A cuddle on the couch it is, then." He leaned across the counter again and pulled me forward. It was awkward, but he somehow managed to reach me. His lips brushed against mine, softly, but with promise. "I'm up for anything, so long as you're there," he whispered before pulling away.

His smile held hope and joy as he pushed his hat back down onto his head. With one last wink, he turned and threaded his way toward the stage.

"Now, who's on fire?" Surfer Jeff quipped.

I rolled my eyes and ignored him, putting my hands back to work while my thoughts circled around the idea of Silas in my tiny studio apartment. I didn't have a couch.

Thirty minutes later the band was rocking, and the party was back in full swing. The Zombie girls had finished their drinks, and it showed. Loose limbed and squealing, they were bouncing around like bunnies on crack—bunnies who wore pushup bras.

The men in the crowd watched with rapt attention and skeevy grins. It was almost as bad as a tennis match, but instead of turning their heads side to side, their eyeballs bounced up and down in time with the ladies.

I snorted my amusement and shook my head. If only everyone else could see what I saw. Yellow party demons bubbled around the women's heads like poofy chef's hats with earmuffs, bouncing in time with their propped up cleavage. If the men could have seen that, they would be rolling on the floor laughing instead of struggling against pants-related embarrassment of their own.

Surfer Jeff, still on his stool, raised an eyebrow. "Something funny?"

I nodded my chin toward the Zombie girls with a grin. "I think I'm going to have to cut them off."

"If I wanted that kind of entertainment, there are better places for it. Like Hooters."

"Is Hooters even still open? There used to be one off the 405, but I thought it got shut down."

Jeff shrugged. "Not my scene. I learned my lesson years ago."

"Wife number two or three?"

"Does it matter? I just hope those youngsters know what they're getting into. STDs are no fun. Trust me."

I grimaced and glanced back at the Zombie girls. I hadn't really noticed, but they kept skootching closer to the stage. It wouldn't be the first time drunk girls decided the band was fair game, and I doubted it would be the last. I wouldn't exactly say the guys were used to it, but it seemed to come with the territory, at least a bit.

It didn't mean I had to like it.

Do you really think you can hold his attention? Why would he wait for you to warm up? He'll abandon you, just like all the others.

The shadow demon's hollow words rang through my mind, even though the creature was nowhere in sight.

Silas was a catch. I was . . . a challenge. At least, that's what I had been raised to believe. I'd started to come around to a different point of view, but those deep-seated fears loved to linger.

Up until recently, I'd done my best to fade into the background, out of sight and mostly out of mind. I'd hidden my scars —internal and external—and kept myself separate from the others.

Except . . . Silas had seen me. He'd drawn me out of my shell, then anchored me to the world when the Aether threatened to overwhelm and wash me out to sea. Without him, I would still be stuck in Aegir's underwater underworld, drinking mead and playing supplicant to the megalomaniacal ocean god.

The shadow snake was nothing more than a liar, playing on old fears. I was wiser now and could see it for what it was.

Silas wouldn't abandon me. He knew exactly who and what I was. I wouldn't devalue his faith by letting false fears persuade me otherwise.

Distracted by my thoughts, I bumped into our barback, Ferghus, who was collecting the dirty dishes from around my station.

"Sorry," I mumbled as he grabbed a couple of abandoned glasses on the counter.

Of all of us behind the bar, he was the most mobile, moving in and out as need arose, though he tended to favor Ty's bottle acrobatics and female admirers over my sedate regulars. He was also the youngest of the crew—barely twenty-one—and a wiry beanpole that could slide into the gaps without disrupting the bartender's flow.

All the same, I took a small step back to get out of his way since I wasn't working on a drink at the moment. As I did, a shadow moved across the floor in my peripheral vision, hovering in the darkness near our feet. When I turned to look, it was gone.

So the shadow demon was still here, or maybe there was more than one of them. They were leaving me alone now, which was great, except I had no way of knowing who their next target would be, or how it would manifest. I couldn't hear *people's* thoughts, after all. Only the demons, and only when they were loud enough to hear. All I could do for now was watch for the shadows and wait.

Patience was not my best virtue.

And unlike the neon yellow demons bouncing around the Zombie girls' heads, the shadows were harder to spot.

A new customer caught my attention, drawing me away from my speculation. A mousy woman wearing a UCLA sweatshirt and no makeup, with thin lips and thick glasses, lifted her fingers in a hesitant wiggle-wave. She lifted the menu off the counter.

"Is Tempest's Mead any good?" she asked.

"One of my favorites. Do you like your drinks a little sweet?"

Her nose wrinkled. "I was trying to stay away from the juices."

"The Mead doesn't have any. It isn't as sweet as a Rum Runner or Fog Cutter, but it does have honey liqueur and sherry, so it has some sweetness to it. If you want something more refreshing than sweet, you might try the Spa Water. I invented it myself."

She scanned the menu, her lips moving subtly as she read the list of ingredients. She tapped the counter with her right pointer finger. "Sure. I'll try that. I like tequila better than rum anyway. And a Mai Tai for my . . ." She paused and glanced over her shoulder with a grimace. ". . . Mother."

A woman with auburn hair that billowed around her head sat in a booth near the window, watching the Zombie girls with a frown of disapproval. When she caught me looking, her eyes narrowed.

"Sure thing," I replied after waiting a beat too long. I'd had mother-daughter pairs come in before. It was usually pretty cute. They got all dressed up for a bonding night. Ms. Mouse and her mom didn't fit the mold. "If you want to go back and sit down, I'll send the drink over with Gabi. She's the server working your table. She's usually quick to greet new customers, so I'm surprised you had to wait." I commented as I started muddling the cucumber, syrup, and lime together in the shaker.

The woman pressed her lips together in a weak smile. "We didn't see any servers, so we thought we had to order at the bar. That's alright anyway. I'm already here." She tapped the counter again and looked away.

I shrugged. As I poured in the tequila, movement in my peripheral vision caught my eye once more. The shadow demon slid beneath and between the holes in the rubber floor mat, snaking closer to Ferghus's toes.

Go away! I thought at the thing, but there was no response and no change in its slithering motion. It was like a puddle of oil in water, smooth and shiny and constantly moving. My hand twitched, wanting to reach for the athame again, but I couldn't draw Ms. Mouse's attention to the blade. I had to finish her drink first and get her back to her table.

Ferghus came back around with the dish bucket, this time headed for Ty. The shadow lunged out of the darkness beneath the counter and latched onto Ferghus's foot.

Ty stepped to the right, a bottle flipping through the air. The shadow flung itself toward the bartender like a whip, tying the two men together with some sort of Aethereal web. Ferghus stepped to the left. The shadow demon sprang back like a rubber band, pulling Ferghus toward the center station.

Before I could say or do anything to stop it, Ferghus stepped on Ty's toe. Ty grunted, missed the bottle catch. The bottle hit the edge of the dish bucket. Ferghus's grip slipped. He made a grab for the plastic lip, but the bucket was too heavy. It fell to the ground with a crash. Several glasses broke and the bottle of rum shattered in a wet mess across the floor.

"What the hell!" Ty shouted. He never shouted at Ferghus. He adored the kid who idolized his every move.

The shadow expanded like a balloon and split in two, half wrapped around Ferghus's foot and the other half climbing Ty's calf.

Ferghus was already picking up the glass, but his movements were slower than usual, almost lethargic. His head hung low as he mumbled an apology and pulled a dishtowel from beneath the counter.

The demon had latched on. It was the only explanation. My own hands had slowed as my fears and insecurities rose to the surface under the influence of the shadow.

I hurried to finish the mousy woman's Spa Water. I needed to zap that demon before it could drain the joy from Ferghus's job.

"Want me to leave a tab open?" I asked as I set the second drink in front of the woman. I was itching to move on, to free Ferghus, but I couldn't do that in front of watching eyes. I needed her to leave.

"The void is calling," she murmured, her eyes glued on Ferghus.

My eyebrows lifted in shock. "Excuse me?"

Her lips twitched ever so slightly, but she said nothing as she continued to stare at Ferghus with unblinking eyes.

Out of habit more than fear, I leaned away from her. Thanks to Grams's intervention, my secret skill was still a secret, at least with the crowd in the Trident. Silas was the only person here who retained the full and unadulterated memory of the shark-topus man and the attack on the bar, or my involvement in any of it. They'd all forgotten their short stint in the undersea underworld of Aegir's Hall. But they'd supported me before, and I was almost totally certain they'd support me again. That said, I didn't feel the need to test that theory just yet.

"Are you okay?" I asked, pretending I had no idea what she was apparently seeing. I couldn't spot any indication that she was a Daughter of Lilith, but if I were being totally honest, I wouldn't know how to spot a Daughter anyway. I'd thought Grams was just an old lady until she approached me. Was this woman the same? How many of us were there? If the woman could see the shadow demons, I needed to know.

"Are you—"

"Keep the change," the woman abruptly tossed three twenties on the table, shot me a too-wide smile, and grabbed the drinks. She was gone before I had a chance to ask anything else.

I glanced back down at Ferghus, still cleaning the mess with hunched shoulders. I'd failed to banish the shadow demon that attacked me, but it had at least left me alone. With the mousy woman gone, I could try again. At a minimum, I could keep it from feeding off my friends. Maybe then it would go away for good.

I scanned the customers at the bar. No one was watching. Even Surfer Jeff had turned his chair toward the stage to watch the Zombie girls' shenanigans. It was the perfect opportunity.

This time, I drew the athame from its sheath at my hip and pressed my thumb into the triple moon design inlayed into the handle. I turned my attention to the energy that flowed around all living things. Lilith's sigil acted as the focal point while the blade itself was the conductor of my . . . magic.

I hated that word. I wasn't some witch, casting spells and crafting potions. But I had to do what I could to help. For the second time that night, I wished I'd spent some time training with

Grams so I actually knew what I was doing, but I hadn't, and I didn't, so I could only do my best.

I stepped up to the small cutting board on the counter, holding the knife out as if I was simply going to chop some more garnish. When I was sure I wasn't being observed, I pointed the small blade toward Ferghus.

Go away. I thought toward the demon I could barely see. *Return to your demesne.*

There was no reaction. If anything, it got worse. Ferghus glanced up at Ty, but the other bartender didn't even spare him a glance. He was too busy chatting up a tall red-haired guy with a curled and waxed mustache and perfect coif on top of his head. Probably the customer who's drink Ferghus had interrupted. The shadow demon spawn that had attached to Ty's leg had disappeared, even as the one on Ferghus grew stronger. Ferghus's shoulders slumped. His knee hit the ground. The shadow was larger, darker than before. It hovered over his shoulders like a heavy winter cloak, weighing him down into the floor.

With one hand still holding the athame I kneeled next to him, pretending to help clean. My mother—Rán—had told me that to counter the Aether, you had to find the opposing element. With Aegir, god of the ocean, fire had opposed water. What would it be for a shadow? Light?

It was worth a try.

Careful not to touch him—the last thing I needed was to fall under the shadows spell a second time—I traced Lilith's sigil with my mind's eye and focused my energy into the blade.

Shadow demon go back to where you came from. I imagined a ray of pure light shooting out of the tip of the athame like a laser scalpel from some sci-fi movie. With that image in mind, I sliced the shadow from his body.

The demon hissed and recoiled, peeling back from Ferghus's shoulder. With an eardrum-shattering squeal that only I could hear, it popped out of existence, leaving Ferghus alone.

Chapter 3

"Thanks," Ferghus mumbled as I placed a piece of broken glass in the bucket. The shadow was gone—for now—but I could see that its affects still lingered. His normally cheerful and energetic demeanor was subdued, and a thin film of gray energy remained draped across his shoulders.

"Are you okay?" I wondered if there was something else going on, something more than just a simple mistake of a dropped dish bucket. I put my hand on his shoulder, surreptitiously attempting to wipe away the shadow's remains, but nothing budged.

"Fine." The barback wouldn't look at me. Instead, he glanced up at Ty again. It was possible I was wrong, but I could have sworn there was longing in his eyes.

"Ty's a solid bartender," I murmured.

"Yeah." Ferghus's lips pulled down as he picked up the dish bucket. "Thanks for the help."

I watched him shuffle toward the tiny kitchen in back. The demon was gone, but the negative energy remained.

Unable to do anything else for him at the moment, I returned to my station and wiped up the small splashes of liquor and juice. My thoughts turned to the mousy woman sitting in the corner with her mom. The women weren't talking. They hardly looked at each other. Ms. Mouse stared at her Spa Water with an empty expression while her mother continued to watch the crowd with a sneer of disgust. Who were they? What had the girl actually seen?

I couldn't know, and I didn't dare ask. They were unknowns. Better to remain invisible and anonymous. For now, at least.

A shout from the stage drew my attention. The Zombie girls had climbed on the platform to dance with the band. Their arms were up in the air, waving—maybe flailing was the better word— as they shouted and shimmied. The neon yellow demons on their shoulders pulsed in time to the music.

Seconds later, some of the guys in the crowd started egging them on. They had their own demons to contend with, puffed up electric blue macho demons, in fact. Testosterone central.

This was getting out of hand. It was like the demons were on a rampage. More than usual, anyway.

The taller of the two women shimmied her way to Silas, who smiled and kept singing. He leaned in, and then away, weaving to the music.

My hand clenched on the handle of the knife. They weren't touching, but she certainly looked like she wanted to. She was probably itching to put her hands all over him. *My* trombonist. He was *my* goofy fedora-wearing band-geek hottie.

You are nothing. Just some bartender. You can't give him what he needs. The shadow demon's words whispered through my mind as the overhead lights dimmed and stuttered.

I glanced at the floor where I'd last seen the demon to make sure it was just a memory and not a revisit. A flicker of movement on the far side of Ty caught my attention, but then disappeared beneath Bruce's station.

As if sensing my agitation, Silas glanced in my direction and smiled reassuringly. He wasn't flirting with the girl. He was a performer. He was putting on a show. I blew out a breath, trying to calm my raging heartbeat.

The woman leaned forward, shaking her shoulders—and her cleavage—side to side. I growled in the back of my throat, but I was too far away to do anything.

Silas leaned away but kept the smile up. He couldn't help it that his eyes drifted to the deep V of her neckline. He was a hot-blooded male. Hell, even I couldn't help looking a little, and I had never been bi-curious.

Unfortunately, the woman seemed to take that as an invitation and shimmied herself even closer, until the only thing between them was Silas's trombone. When he lifted the instrument to his lips for the next solo, she slid up behind him, pretending to grind on him from behind, her miniskirt riding up her thighs to show off the flower-print panties underneath.

"Bruce!" I shouted. She'd taken it too far. He was a musician. A performer. A professional. I knew that. But he was also my boyfriend and the bar was about ready to combust.

"On it." The big, tattooed Samoan flipped up the end of the bar and waded out into the crowd.

The shadow demon stretched across the floor from the bar toward the gathered masses and grasped Bruce's ankle. He stumbled.

The lights flared, then blacked out. A woman gasped; a man shouted. The band's amplifiers popped, and the music screeched to a halt. A thump and a crash of cymbals and the lights sprang back to life.

Shadows raced back into hiding like cockroaches from the light, finding refuge in the crowd. Now that I knew what I was looking for, I spotted dozens of them hiding in the darkened gaps beneath shoes and in the spaces between.

Bruce was on the floor clutching his head. Blood dripped from a small cut on his scalp. He shook it off and stood, pushing his way through the mob to get to the stage. One of the shadow demons split in two and wrapped itself around his waist like a belt. Bruce growled something up to the stage and grabbed at crop top's ankle. One of the blue demon macho men interfered, shouting something about laying hands on a lady. The new guy took a swing at Bruce, who was forced to let go of crop top or catch a fist to the face.

Without any music, the girls turned to the crowd, leaning over as they laughed and taunted the audience, begging for more encouragement. The neon demons on their shoulders had blossomed into halos around their upper bodies. Once more the lights dimmed, and the shadow demons attacked. This time, they went for the girls on stage.

"Dion!" I shouted.

Our door bouncer came running in but paused at the edge of the crowd to look at me with one raised eyebrow. He'd only been working a few weeks at the bar, taking the place of our former bouncer, Carlos, who'd quit after the incidents of a month ago. Dion, however, was more capable of handling the demon influence. After all, he was a demigod himself, the half-human son of the primordial god of the ocean, Aegir.

"Get in there and do something!" I yelled.

"You do something!" he shouted back, even as he wrenched people out of the way to help Bruce.

But what could I do? I had no idea how to handle this madness. I'd never experienced anything like this before.

Silas and the band moved out of the way, toward the back of the stage, leaving the Zombie girls to their madness. Crop top bumped into her friend, who tripped on a cord and knocked over the mic stand. Flower-panties recovered and shoved crop top away, saying something I couldn't hear over the bedlam. Crop top visibly snarled and shoved back. Between one beat and the next, the girls were clawing at each other's faces. Hair was pulled, nails were used like claws to tear at skin. A couple of college-aged frat bros started chanting encouragement, adding to the furor, even as Bruce was wrestling with a heavyset, bearded man I didn't recognize.

The shadows twisted around the Zombie girls' legs, climbing

up their bodies. They hissed at the neon yellow party demons on the women's shoulders. The neon demons puffed up and hissed back, like cats on the defensive.

Meanwhile, the women clashed in a tangle of red painted claws and heavy heels. With each scratch or pull, the shadows seemed to grow larger, taller, encompassing more of the women's bodies and moving ever upward toward the neon demons.

I'd never seen anything like it. It was as if the demons were battling for supremacy, but the women had no idea what was going on. No one did, even as they jeered and taunted and encouraged the fight.

The serpents were gaining strength, and with that strength, their voices grew louder and more insistent. Competitive jealous rage burned through their essence, the desire to consume and destroy overpowering the more playful desire to let loose and have some fun.

The women rolled into more of the band's equipment, scattering mic stands and knocking an amp off the riser.

Between one blink and the next, the shadow demons struck, lunging for the yellow demons on their shoulders. The yellow demons lurched to the side but weren't fast enough to get out of the way. Like boa constrictors on the hunt, the shadows swallowed the neon demons whole.

Pulsing in time with the neon demon's dance, the shadows grew even larger.

The women's movement slowed. They slid to the floor. If I hadn't known better, I might've said they were just too drunk to maintain the effort, but I did know better. The demons that had been influencing them were gone, and the shadows had taken their place. Now they, too, were slowly being consumed.

Unfortunately for them, the crowd didn't settle even after the girls disappeared from view. If anything, the chaos grew worse. It had turned into a veritable mosh pit, and we didn't have the space for it. The girls were about to get trampled.

"I'm calling the cops!" Ty shouted over the mayhem. I

nodded my understanding. We needed help. Bruce and Dion were being swarmed, and the crowd was only getting rowdier.

The shadow demons hovered over where I assumed the girls had fallen, lashing out at anyone who got close enough to touch. Each time they did, a piece of the shadow broke off and multiplied, growing larger and more powerful as they ate away at the person's essence. If you've ever seen one of those videos of bacteria multiplying under a microscope, then you know exactly what it looked like.

Silas and the band's drummer, Ben, ran toward the front of the stage to pull the women out of the way.

"Stay away from them!" I shouted, but they couldn't hear me. They bent down. The shadows reared up. They disappeared from view. I couldn't see what was happening. Couldn't see them behind the surging mass of humanity.

They didn't reappear.

I had to do something. The shadows were taking over, taking control. I'd never seen demons multiply like this. As the shadows spread, first chaos, then unconsciousness followed. It was as if the shadows riled up emotions, then drained them of that energy.

I couldn't let it continue. I was still holding the athame. I pointed the knife at the chaotic crowd.

"Goddess help me," I whispered, channeling my will down the length of the sharp and shining silver metal. I couldn't do it on my own. I didn't have the knowledge or the power. I needed Hecate's help. She'd helped me before, I prayed she would help me again.

Once more, I imagined the laser beam of white light erupting from the end of the blade.

"Back to the Aether." I murmured, pressing everything I had through my hand and into Lilith's sigil. "Go back to the demesne from which you came."

Energy erupted from my core, spiraling down my arm and out through the knife.

A flash of blinding white light jolted the room.
The demons squealed as if in physical pain.
I staggered against the edge of the bar.
When my vision cleared, they were gone.

Chapter 4

Blinking away the afterimage of the athame's blinding light, I struggled to make sense of the scene. The shadow demons were gone, but the affects hadn't been limited to the minions of the gods. The entire standing-room-only audience was no longer standing. They'd been knocked over like bowling pins. Even Bruce and Dion were sitting on the floor, rubbing their heads and groaning.

Ferghus emerged from the kitchen as Ty and I rushed out to help however we could.

"What happened?" Ferghus asked.

I shook my head. I didn't know how to answer or explain.

"Cops are on their way," Ty murmured as he headed for Bruce and Dion. The three of them would get people up and moving, and mollify them with a fresh drink.

I was more concerned with Silas and Ben. They lay on the floor next to the Zombie girls, the four of them out for the count.

"Oh my gawd!" Virginia screeched. "Ben!"

I got there first, relieved to see the guys were still breathing. Silas had fallen across the edge of the stage, his hands on flower-panty's shoulders. Ben mirrored him on the other side, one arm draped over crop top. It looked like they had tried to pull the women up onto the stage, safely out of the way, or at least safer.

The shadow demons had done their work fast.

The women lay slumped against the stage riser, heads lolling at an angle. They also still breathed, but I didn't waste any mental energy on them. I was more concerned with my trombonist.

I gently rolled Silas over and brushed my fingers through his hair. His ever-present fedora had been knocked from his head and the imprint of the hat band made his hair twist in odd little whorls. His eyes stayed closed. "Silas," I whispered. Not a twitch. My eyes clouded with tears.

A sobbing Virginia shook Ben's shoulders, trying to wake him. When he didn't budge, she sat close and wiggled his head and shoulders into her lap.

"Wake up, baby," she crooned. "Wake up."

It was all my fault. I'd been too slow, waited too long to intervene. The guys hadn't had a chance. They hadn't been able to see what was really going on. They'd had no idea what they were facing.

I should have stopped the demons sooner. I should have banished them. Banished them all. Damn the consequences. I'd let my own fears and insecurities hurt my friends.

"You are a sorry excuse for a Daughter of Lilith," a voice hissed from behind me.

At first I thought it was another demon attack, but a hand clamped down on my shoulder to spin me around. The shock cleared my head and tore me out of my self-loathing.

"You might as well have unleashed a nuclear bomb in this place. Invoking a goddess?" Ms. Mouse's mother glared down at me, her expression filled with unrestrained fury as she thumped her clenched fists on wide hips. "Never have I witnessed such a fundamental lack of control and abuse of power all at once. A disgrace!"

Ms. Mouse smirked at me from behind her mother's shoulder.

"I don't know what you're talking about." It was the only thing I could think to say.

The older woman rolled her eyes. Maybe fifty-five years old, she wasn't even as old as my own mother, and yet I felt like I was getting a rude reminder of what maternal disapproval felt like.

"You are going to come with me. It's about time you learned what it really means to be a Daughter of Lilith."

Her grip tightened on my shoulder. Scowling, I yanked my arm out of reach and stood tall. "I have no idea who you are or what you're after, but I'm not going anywhere with you."

The woman rose to her full height—maybe five foot two— and puffed out her chest. Given that I was at least five inches taller, she still had to look up at me, which reduced the effectiveness of her glare.

"I am Brigitte LeClaire, First Sister of the West Coast Coven."

"I don't care if you're Mother Theresa. People are hurt. So you can either help or get out of the way."

The woman's head lurched back, as if she'd been struck. "Well, I never . . ."

I ignored her and returned to Silas's side. Virginia was still sobbing over Ben, and the Zombie girls hadn't moved.

"Did they hit their heads?" Bruce pressed a wadded up piece of cloth to the cut on his scalp. A smear of blood swept across his cheekbone. He was the one who'd hit his head, but he wasn't complaining. At least he was conscious.

"Are you okay?"

"I'm conscious," he replied, echoing my thoughts. "What happened?"

"I don't know. They won't wake up, and I'm afraid to move them."

"The police will handle the sons and daughters of Eve. You have to come with me," the woman interrupted.

"Back off, lady!" I pointed the athame toward her while keeping one hand on Silas. I hadn't even realized I was still holding the goddess blade.

"You wouldn't dare use that on me," she sputtered.

I clenched my jaw, breathing out through my nose. I focused on the steady rise and fall of Silas's chest beneath my palm, taking comfort that he was still breathing. Whatever the shadow demons had done, it couldn't be permanent. He was alive.

I turned back to Bruce, trying to get a handle on the situation. Silas and Ben and two of our customers were lying unconscious on the stage. Bruce was bleeding, and he and Dion had been swarmed by the unruly crowd. A crowd that had been under the dire influence of the minions of the gods. Then this woman and her daughter stood there acting as if they had some sort of authority over me.

I was barely keeping it together, but Silas needed me. Somebody needed to take control. "Was anyone else hurt?"

"They do not matter!" The woman's hands flew up into the air. "You are a danger to yourself and others. You must come with us. Now. Before it's too late."

"It's already too late!" I exploded. "Get out of here! Go away! Go back to wherever you came from!" My chest heaved. So much for keeping my cool.

"Come on." Bruce held out his free arm to usher her away from the stage. "Your drinks are on the house but it's time you left."

"This isn't the last you'll see of me," the woman shouted over her shoulder as she unwillingly left the area. "You are a Daughter of Lilith, and you will join our coven or fall."

I snort-laugh-sobbed and dropped my head to Silas's chest as tears soaked into his shirt. "Wake up, Silas" I whispered. "Wake up."

His heart beat steadily in his chest but there was no other response.

Chapter 5

The antiseptic smell of the hospital burned my throat as I sat in the waiting room with my head in my hands. After the cops had cleared out and shut down the bar, I'd borrowed Bruce's truck to get here as fast as I could, calling Grams on the way. She said she'd be here as soon as she could, but given that she had to be well over eighty years old, didn't have a car, and lived in a secluded cabin in the hills on a winding road with no name, I wasn't sure how long that would take. A ride share would have a hard time finding her.

The doctors wouldn't tell me anything about Silas's condition except to say that he was stable and with the doctors. I wasn't family. Wasn't listed as an emergency contact. I didn't have any rights when it came to his care.

I felt useless. Worse, I felt responsible. I had been too slow to act. There had been so many demons in the bar, Aethereal minions only I could see, and I'd done nothing to contain or control them. They had overwhelmed the ignorant customers and consumed their energy. I could have done more. I should have.

And now Silas and Ben—and the Zombie girls—paid the price.

"Wallowing won't help anyone or anything, you know," Grams chided.

I lifted my head to look at the woman who wasn't related to Silas by blood, but still claimed him as her own. Blue-gray eyes gazed at me with sympathy from beneath soft gray hair that had been left free to float around her shoulders. Her arms were crossed loosely over her chest, holding a burnt orange and blue patterned shawl over a loose white maxi dress.

I could hardly face her, the woman who Silas looked up to more than anyone else in his life. How could I bear it?

"It's all my fault. I didn't stop them."

Grams sat down in the chair next to mine and wrapped an arm around my shoulders. "My dear, you can't blame yourself. You've only just been introduced to the Aether. You did what you could with the skills and experience that you have."

"You weren't there." I should be comforting her, not the other way around. She should hate me, rail at me, shout accusations . . . something. Instead, she squeezed me tighter.

"No, but as old as I may be, I still remember the early days, when I was just coming into my power. It's not an easy thing."

"I could have done more." I knew I could have. I'd had Hecate's athame in my hand. "I froze."

"Perhaps. But second-guessing ourselves is never productive. Assess. Learn. Move forward."

"I don't know what I'm doing. I don't even know what I don't know."

"This is true for all beginners. And despite your power, you are just beginning."

"I don't have any power."

"Keep telling yourself that and it might be true. In the meantime, I need an update on Silas. Would you like to come with me?"

Grams stood and held out her hand, inviting me to join her. When I hesitated, she shook her hand at me.

"Come on, dear. We need to find out the truth, see what's

really happening. These idiot doctors won't have a clue." As always, her words might be scathing, but her tone was gentle.

I placed my hand in Gram's surprisingly strong grip and let her pull me to my feet. The trip to the nurse's station was quick, and with a few kind but firm words, we were soon through the automatic doors and on our way to Silas's room.

The doctor met us at the door, clipboard in hand.

"You're the emergency contact?" She asked, glancing at her notes without meeting Grams's gaze. "Lillian Ayers?"

I glanced at Grams, realizing this was the first time I'd ever heard her actual name and surprised that it was so similar to my own. She'd always told me just to call her Grams, it's what Silas called her, so I did.

"Yes, dear. That's me. May we see Silas?"

"Of course." The doctor pushed open the door and let us precede her into the room as she continued to review the chart. "Silas remains unconscious, but so far the tests have been inconclusive. There's no brain damage or indication of a head wound. Vitals are strong and stable. Our best guess at this point is that he took or was given some kind of party drug. We've taken some blood, but it will be a while before the toxicology reports come back."

My brain tuned out the doctor and Grams as I approached Silas's bed. My trombonist lay pale and still in the hospital bed with its guardrails and beeping machines. They'd taken off his ever-present fedora, of course, but his hair still maintained the imprint of the hat band around the sides. Sheets covered his body from the armpits down, but I could see the top of the hospital gown at his shoulders.

"He's so still," I whispered. Silas was always moving, always brimming with energy. To see him lying here so quiet . . . It seemed like he was gone, only the shell of his body remained.

I reached out to touch his hand but withdrew before making contact. I didn't want to know if he was cold. This wasn't him. He wasn't really there.

Grams approached my side and wrapped one arm around my shoulders, while the other grasped Silas's hand as I couldn't.

"His song is faint," she replied, keeping her voice low. "But there's hope for him yet. He's not lost forever."

I swallowed the lump in my throat, desperate for Grams to be right. "How do you know?"

The elderly woman's smile was peaceful as she closed her eyes. "Just listen. Feel your connection to him. It is a bond inside you, loose yet, but present. Do you feel it?"

I took a shaky breath and closed my eyes, copying her movement. "I can't feel anything but the room around us."

"You must go deeper, dear. Use all your senses but aim them inward."

I squeezed my eyes tighter, *willing* myself to see the connection.

"Now think of Silas," she urged. "Look for the thread that ties you to your anchor. His sound is unique."

I tuned my thoughts to my trombonist. A vibration hummed at the base of my sternum, just above my diaphragm. I mentally looked down. There, softly shimmering, was a thin line that extended out into the darkness. Harder to see than fishing line, I could feel it more than see or hear it, but it was there.

I started to reach for it, but Grams stopped me with a word.

"If you break the thread, he will be gone forever, lost in the abyss to be consumed by the nothing."

My eyes snapped open. The older woman was staring at me with both pride and sadness. "You are his anchor now."

"I can pull the line. I can bring him home."

Grams shook her head slowly. Sadly. "Apep holds him. Your bond isn't yet strong enough for a game of tug of war with the gods. If you pull, the line will snap. But there is another option." She reached out and brushed a few stray hairs off his forehead. "He's a good boy. Strong. Solid. He'll make it back to us. Just you wait and see."

She patted him on the cheek and smiled. I still couldn't touch him. Despite her reassurances, he seemed too lifeless. I didn't want to remember him this way. I'd think of his wink and his smile, the way he kissed my knuckles and stole a fruit skewer from the garnish tray. That was Silas.

Grams straightened and gave my shoulders another squeeze. "The doctors will take care of his body for us. Now we have to get home and get some rest. We have work to do in the morning."

"Work?" I asked bewildered. "How could we possibly work through all this?"

"Not here, dear. There will be time for more explanations later. For now, let the doctors do their jobs. You need rest and so does he. You'll come home with me and stay the night in my guest room." Her words were firm, uncompromising, while my thoughts swirled through the misty depths of my brain.

I *was* tired. So tired. But how was she so calm?

A weight pressed down on my shoulders and my eyelids drooped.

"Come on, dear. Let's get you to bed."

I let the older woman guide me out of Silas's room without complaint. It seemed I didn't have much choice.

Chapter 6

Sunlight peeked around the edges of my blackout curtains.

No, not my blackout curtains. These were shiny dark blue instead of the matte dark gray in my apartment. The blanket that twisted around my legs and waist was not my lightweight down comforter.

I rolled over on my back and gazed up at the golden chandelier that hung over the bed. Memories of the night before roared through my head.

I was in Grams's guest bedroom. She had insisted and I'd been too tired and stressed to object.

I pushed myself up to sitting and glanced at the tiny golden analog clock on the nightstand, sitting primly next to the winged lady-lamp holding the world. It was only ten in the morning.

Given my bartender hours, I was pretty used to sleeping through the day, so what had woken me?

Voices wafted into the room, along with the heavy scent of cinnamon and coffee.

Grams had a visitor.

Other than me and Silas, I had never known Grams to have a visitor. She liked to be alone, living in the wilds—or as close as you could get in coastal Southern California, tending her herb garden and listening to the birds in the canyon. She did not like company. Which might explain why the women sounded forcefully pleasant.

"I see you're still baking up your concoctions." I could hear the patronizing smile in the woman's voice even without seeing her.

"It is hard to break old habits. Don't you agree? Would you like a biscotti?" Grams replied.

I grinned. Saccharine sweet, yet with a titanium core, that tone of voice only came out when Grams was truly irritated.

The woman sniffed. "No thank you. You know perfectly well that much cinnamon disrupts my abilities. It will take days to recover from the stench."

"Ah, yes. I'd forgotten how sensitive you are to smells." Grams's voice sounded louder than necessary. If I didn't know better, I'd say she intended for me to hear.

"So tell me about this girl."

"Lil."

I froze, listening intently. They were talking about me. Why? Who was this woman that Grams clearly didn't enjoy?

"Yes, Lil. The events at that bar last night lead me to believe she's entirely untrained." The voice sounded familiar.

"Not entirely, no."

"She clearly didn't even know the basics of Aethereal manipulation. There were minions running amok all over the place. Including multiple shadow thralls, which were given free rein to grow and reproduce."

My groggy brain finally caught up. Ms. Mouse's Mom. That's who was talking. But how did she know Grams? How did she know where to find me?

"And why didn't you assist?" Grams asked.

The woman sniffed again. "I had to see what she was capable of."

"And did she handle it?" A tink-tink of a spoon against a cup, Grams stirring the cream into her coffee.

"She invoked the goddess! Of all things." The woman's outrage felt flat to my ears, like she wasn't nearly as shocked as she wanted Grams to believe. I'd bet Grams already knew that though.

"So she handled it."

"She needs proper training. She needs to join the coven."

Grams snorted. "Bind herself to your merry little band of conformists? I think not."

"You do her—and us—a disservice. She's naturally powerful but she needs training. Your abilities are waning, we all know it. You can't give her proper instruction. You can't guide her through the intricacies of the Aether. She needs her sisters."

Uncontrollable fury washed through me. I rose from bed and strode past the modern chef's kitchen into the doily covered living room where the red-headed harpy perched her smug derriere on the couch.

"You!" I pointed a tense finger in the woman's direction. "Who the hell do you think you are? Coming to the bar, trying to force me away, and now you're here? Are you *spying* on me? Abducting me?"

The woman's lips pulled up in what could have been a smile, if it hadn't looked so smug. "Well, hello."

I spun to face Grams. "Who is she and why on earth are you listening to her?"

Grams's lips twitched with suppressed amusement. "Good morning, dear. I am sorry we woke you so soon." The look in her eyes suggested she wasn't sorry at all. She'd intended me to wake and overhear their conversation. Somehow, I was sure of it.

Remaining in the safety of her kitchen, Grams poured me a cup of coffee and set a still-warm biscotti on a small blue plate, pushing them across the granite-topped peninsula and toward me. "Why don't you have a seat?"

I narrowed my eyes, but took my place on the offered bar stool, strategically located between the two older women. I didn't say anything as I blew the steam off the cup and took a sip.

The red-haired harpy sniffed but remained seated on the wood-framed antique couch. Her own cup of coffee sat on a doily covered side table, within reach but seemingly untouched.

"Well?" she finally demanded. "We haven't got all day."

"All will proceed as is required," Grams murmured, catching my gaze as she took her own sip of coffee. "However, I suppose it is appropriate that I officially introduce you. Lil, I'd like you to meet Bridget, another Daughter of Lilith."

"It's actually pronounced Brizh-eete. In the French way. B-r-i-g-i-t-t-e. And I am not just any old Daughter of Lilith. I am First Sister of the West Coast Coven." She pressed her lips together in an offended sneer.

"We've met," I replied shooting the woman a glare. "And I'm still not impressed."

Deep-seated anger burned in the woman's eyes, but Grams was quick to interrupt.

"Brizh-eete—" Grams emphasized the correct pronunciation so hard I almost snorted coffee out of my nose, which would have hurt. And been a waste. The coffee was really good. "—would like to speak with you about your training."

"Or lack thereof." The woman lifted her chin and faced me directly. "As your mother abandoned you and bound herself to Aegir, she is no longer able to train you in the ways of the Daughters. She has abdicated her mother-given responsibilities, not that she seemed keen on upholding her role anyway. And as—" She paused to curl her lip disdainfully. "—Grams's abilities have begun their decline, I would like to offer you my services as a mentor and invite you to join the coven, where you will gain mastery over your Lilith-granted skill."

I took a bite of the melt-in-your-mouth deliciousness of the biscotti. Crunchy on the outside but tender on the inside, Grams's biscotti were perhaps the best breakfast pastry I'd ever eaten. That single bite instantly calmed my nerves and centered my more rational brain.

"No." I'd gone from volcanic fury to icy determination. I had no interest in this woman or anything she might have to say.

Grams held her mug in front of her lips to hide her amusement.

With her hands clasped lightly in her lap—I noticed she still hadn't taken a sip of her coffee—Brigitte continued as if I hadn't said anything.

"Your situation is dire. Even worse than I feared. You should have been inducted into our rites as soon as your abilities manifested. However, I will try to elucidate the basics. You will find out more when you join us."

"I said, no. I'm not going anywhere with you, and I'm certainly not going to become your apprentice, or whatever. I have Grams."

Brigitte huffed and rolled her eyes. "Grams is not enough. She can't even cross the veil anymore. You need the coven."

"I don't even know what that is," I replied.

"Have you taught her nothing?" Brigitte's glare could have melted the ice caps.

Chapter 7

Grams stirred her coffee with slow turns of the spoon. "Have I taught her useless rules and formal structures? No. Practical applications? She's learning those just fine. She's a quick study, in point of fact."

Brigitte wiped the corner of her mouth with a finger as she sniffed again. Her gaze darted around the room before landing on something behind my shoulder. I turned to look, but there was nothing there.

"Well, now's as good a time as any to learn the formalities of being a Daughter of Lilith," Brigitte turned to face me more directly. "Your *Grams* might think our ways are confining, but the coven was created to support and educate, not constrain. The West Coast Coven, of which I am First Sister," she pressed an open palm to her chest, "is a group of like-minded women descended from the Great Mother Lilith, as you are. We meet monthly to discuss the activities of the Aethereal elementals on Gaia and share tactics on dealing with their incessant incursions into our region."

I caught Grams rolling her eyes in my peripheral vision, but Brigitte didn't seem to notice.

"When necessary, we band together to protect our communities and each other from elemental influence. New members must be sponsored by a senior sister, then complete a minimum five year apprenticeship before being appointed a full member of the coven. Most of our apprentices are sponsored by their mothers, and join when their abilities manifest, but this is an unusual situation, which is why I'm here myself, in person."

Grams glanced at me from under lowered lashes, still stirring. "Lil only just recovered from her ordeal in Aegir's demesne. She can hardly be expected to present herself to your circle."

"Actually, her venture into the Aether is all the more reason to begin immediately," Brigitte snapped, then took a deep breath before returning her full attention to me. "Most apprentices lack the ability to travel the Between without a guide, but that makes you all the more enticing to the elementals. If last night is any indicator, you and everyone around you are in a great deal of danger."

I sucked in a sharp breath just as I took a bite of my biscotti. A crumb caught in my throat. The ensuing coughing fit had both older women looking at me with concern.

"Danger?" I pounded my fist against my chest, trying to clear my airways while choking on biscotti and words.

Brigitte's gaze was intense. "Yes. Danger. Like that boy, that son of Adam that you refused to leave behind yesterday. He's in an Aethereal coma, or didn't your *Grams* tell you?"

I glanced at Grams, who took another sip of her coffee with forced insouciance.

Had she lied to me? I thought back to the hospital and our conversation at Silas's bedside. As best I could remember, she hadn't said anything about Silas's condition, except that the doctors wouldn't know what to do. Of course, that implied that *she* did. And she'd said she would explain everything.

I lifted an eyebrow in her direction. If ever there was a time, now would be it, but Brigitte continued spewing verbal manure.

"A son of Adam is hardly worth the attention of a Daughter of Lilith, of course, but then, you can hardly be expected to know your worth given your upbringing. Yet another reason you should be with your sisters."

My shoulders tensed. "Silas is more than just *some boy*." The words erupted with more force than I intended, but this woman brought out the worst in me. "He is my anchor. He called me home from the Aether. Twice!"

Brigitte's lip curled with distaste. "And isn't that a sad state of affairs? To rely on a *man* to save you? To bring you home? Your power was strong enough to knock over every single person in that sad little bar of yours, and yet you think you need a penis to tie you to this world?"

I gritted my teeth as Brigitte tsked in disapproval.

"Men are at best bedmates and playthings. They are unnecessary for success in this life. Your sisters will give you all the support and strength that you need to stand on your own two feet."

My jaw dropped and I couldn't help turning to Grams to back me up. "Aren't you going to say anything? Silas is your adopted-ish grandson."

"He is. And he's a good boy, that one. He doesn't need me to defend him any more than you do, dear. You are fully capable of making your own judgments and decisions."

"Look," Brigitte interrupted. "The minions of the gods are already gathering, hoping to influence you to their side. You should have been raised with this knowledge, but since you weren't, we must bring you under the protection of the coven and train you in the Lilith-given strengths of your sisters."

Brigitte wasn't wrong. I did need training. Last night had made it clear that I needed more than a few minutes with my deadbeat mother to figure this stuff out. I couldn't continue to put my job—not to mention my friends—at risk. I was a liability until I could control the demons and keep them from attacking.

But I wasn't about to give up Silas. Not for a second did I think he was worth less than Brigitte's *sisters*. He was my anchor. My connection to this world. He made me feel alive in a way that no one else ever had.

All I knew about Brigitte was that I really wanted to punch her in the face. She'd been at the bar, watched the demons wreak havoc, and done nothing to help me. She might know more than I did, but she had only used that knowledge to serve herself.

"That bar was *littered* with the influence of the gods," Brigitte continued her monologue while I stewed. "You're like a magnet for them. No, you're more like a bright light, drawing the moths and denizens of the dark to your porch. We need to teach you to be a bug zapper instead."

"Bug zapper?" I asked, brow furrowing.

"Oh, please," Grams scoffed. "You and I both know perfectly well the gods and their minions aren't inherently evil. Sometimes they can be quite useful."

Brigitte's lip curled again. It seemed it was her base-level expression. "The gods and their minions are our tools, not the other way around. If she can't learn to banish or control them, she will be doomed to suffer her mother's fate."

I shuddered. Although my mother—Rán—and I had kinda sorta made amends, I had no desire to be bound to the service of a megalomaniacal Aethereal being and used like a battery for his goals.

"Based on what I saw last night," she continued, "there's no time to lose. She's a risk to herself and others."

Grams didn't seem convinced. "Lil has handled herself just fine. She has spent the last fifteen years protecting herself and her brother, learning how to co-exist and discern the good from the bad."

"Discern the good from the bad? Do you hear yourself?"

Brigitte's voice rose, but Grams, as always, remained placid.

"Do you? You seek to control and conform, but that is not the way of our Great Mother. We are the protectors of the wilds, the keepers of the balance."

"Balance cannot be achieved if the Aether is allowed to overwhelm and control humanity."

"That's not what balance means."

Brigitte tilted her head back to stare at the ceiling and release a deep breath. "I don't want to entertain this argument again." She turned to face me once more. "Clearly, you have some power. The fact that you returned from Aegir's Hall at all suggests you are strong-willed and instinctively able to manipulate the Aether. However, you are as yet untrained, your abilities under-developed. The West Coast Daughters of Lilith can teach you control and expand your skillset beyond what you could do on your own."

I tilted my head to the side to study the woman. "I have Grams."

Grams smirked from behind her coffee cup, but Brigitte was quick to quash it.

"Grams is no longer in her prime. I am. She cannot walk the Between. I can. Her tactics and lore are from a bygone era, when the Daughters of Lilith could hide in the wilds as hedge witches and soothsayers. She does not live in the modern world, surrounded by humanity and the endless temptations of the Aether. You do. You need skills she no longer, and perhaps never, possessed."

Brigitte unzipped a small hip bag at her waist to pull out a card. She stood and held it out to me. "Please consider joining us. We meet tonight."

"I have work tonight." The excuse flowed through my lips before I'd framed the thought. I had no intention of going anywhere with this horrid woman.

Brigitte pressed eyes closed in an exaggerated, frustrated, slow blink. "Work is immaterial."

"Not with Southern California beach rents," I mumbled as I took the card from her outstretched fingers. I made decent money, but that didn't mean I could skip one of the best tip nights of the week.

"The meeting takes place in the Aether. Follow the sigil on the card to find us. I hope to see you there."

With a swish of diaphanous skirts, Brigitte swept out the front door.

Chapter 8

Grams flopped onto the couch and pinched the bridge of her nose. "That woman is insufferable!" she spat. I'd never heard her so angry, even when the woman in question was spitting venom at her. "Thinks she can order everyone around. Including me. Even in my own home!"

I glanced at the front door, worried that Brigitte might still be hovering outside, but Grams shrugged away any concern. "Even if she's still here—and I doubt she is—she can't hear anything. She's like a bloodhound—barely able to see, her hearing mostly gone, but she can smell a lie ten miles upwind. It's why I always keep cinnamon biscotti on hand. The spice is her kryptonite. Between that and the coffee, she should be essentially blind."

"Where did she go? How? I didn't see a car."

Grams waved a hand through the air, keeping her eyes closed. "She'll probably sniff her way through the Between. Show pony. Always trying to prove her superiority."

"Who is she? I mean, really?" I asked.

Grams shrugged. "She is who she says she is, First Sister of the West Coast DoLs."

I laughed, coming around the couch to sit in the overstuffed easy chair where I could face her.

"The West Coast Dolls? Do they wear pink jackets and burst into choreographed song and dance?"

"Ha! That would be less annoying."

"But what do they *do?*" I asked.

Grams's face scrunched as she looked up and to one side in thought. "I told you there's a network of Daughters of Lilith, right? That we all keep tabs on each other and help each other out when needed."

"I think you called it a loose organization."

"Yes. Well, Brigitte and a few others decided we needed to have more structure, that the loose organization should be tightened up. Over the last fifty years or so, groups have been forming, binding themselves into circles or covens. I think they got the idea from the Wiccans. Anyway, they've become regional organizations, mostly for linguistic and logistical reasons, though apparently, they've now formed an international oversight committee to advise them all. Brigitte is on that board, as well."

"And you're not part of it?"

Grams scoffed. "No, dear. I can't stand organizations. I once tried to join the PTA for Silas's high school—I wanted to honor his grandfather and support the music program—and I didn't even make it through one meeting. I have no desire to bind myself to anything or anyone. I prefer to honor the old ways and the intentions of our Great Mother."

"So I shouldn't go with her? Join this coven thing?"

Grams tilted her head to the side in thought. "I never said that. The woman is insufferable, but then, I find most people barely tolerable. You have to decide for yourself."

"She's not wrong about the demons last night. There were dozens of them, of all shapes and sizes. I don't know which gods they served, but it had to have been more than one."

"I know, dear." Grams patted me on the hand.

"And Silas . . ." I swallowed down the tears that once again rose to the surface. My voice cracked as I whispered the rest. "It was my fault."

Grams frowned. "It's not your fault, but it is your problem."

I covered my face in my hands, the last of the anger from Brigitte's intrusion draining away in my despair. "What do I do? How do I fix it? How do I help him?"

"Them, dear. Silas and the others have been consumed by the shadow thralls and exist in an Aethereal coma. Their core essence —their soul or aura—has been split from their physical form and become lost in the Aether. The doctors can keep their bodies alive, but if their essences can't find a way back to their bodies, they'll never wake. Their energy will be pulled apart, bit by bit, consumed by the abyss."

I stood and paced the length of the room, from the counter to the front door and back, pulling my hands through my hair. "I let this happen. I didn't stop them."

"Admittedly, it would have been better had you acted sooner, but as with all things, it will work out as it should in the end."

"How can you be so calm about this? Silas is in a coma!"

Grams shrugged. "What will be has been and what has been will be. Tell me, why did you wait so long to act?"

I crossed my arms over my chest and stared at Grams. "I didn't know what to do."

"You had the athame." Grams stared at me over the top of her mug, her eyes daring me to dig deeper.

"I didn't want anyone to see me waving a knife around, talking to myself and acting weird, adding to the chaos."

"Before that. When the shadow thrall first attacked you."

"How did you—"

Grams waved a hand through the air, dismissing my words before I'd finished the sentence. "Never mind that. What did you feel?"

"I didn't feel anything. I was numb."

"Maybe at the end, before you freed yourself, but what was the first thought?"

My arms dropped and I slumped down in the cushioned

armchair as I thought through the shadow serpent's words. "I'm not good enough. "

"Lies. The shadow thrall fed you lies, and you believed them. Why?"

I didn't answer. I couldn't. For one thing, Grams wasn't my therapist, and I had long ago decided I hated therapists anyway. But the truth was, the question hit too close to the heart.

After a few beats of silence, Grams pressed her lips together in a knowing smile. "Fear will bind you. Control you. Instead, you must take control. Find your path through the chaos, through the mess, to achieve your purpose."

"I have no purpose."

"We all have a purpose, dear."

I thought about that for a moment but couldn't come up with anything.

"Back to Silas, what do I do?"

Grams frowned. "As much as I hate to say it, there are things Brigitte and her sisters can teach you that I am perhaps less well equipped for these days. I cannot follow the Aethereal threads, but the coven will help you sense them. They will set you on your way. But remember that you walk your own path. No one can bind you against your will, but once bound, you may find escape difficult."

"Binding? Like my mother?" I shook my head. "I don't want anything to do with that."

"You are not your mother. The coven may be able to help you follow the thread to find Silas and guide him home." Grams paused for a deep breath. "Go. Talk to them. Learn what you can. But keep your eyes open."

"I wasn't kidding about work. I can't skip out, not after the days gone in Aegir's Hall." Not even for Silas. Chaz had been watching me like a hawk, double checking my register and all my log-ins. If I was even a minute late, I would hear about it. He was going to be mad enough that he had to book another band.

"That won't be a problem, dear. Remember, time is

immaterial."

"That doesn't make sense."

"Neither does the Aether. When you take your break tonight, you'll visit the coven. When you return, don't think about how long you've been gone. Instead, focus on the time you want to return to. You might even still get your break if you handle it right."

I looked at the card Brigitte had given me. It felt heavy in my hand. The thick, plain white cardstock was blank except for a silver geometric design embossed in the center. No words. No dates or locations. Just a five-pointed star with the lower case "h" looking symbol of Lilith's sigil in the center.

"What is this? It doesn't tell me anything. How am I supposed to even get there?" It was all so confusing. I'd only known about the Daughters of Lilith for a couple weeks and yet they seemed to expect me to have this all figured out already.

"That's the coven sigil. Just like Lilith's sigil that I gave you on that bar napkin, it will help you focus your energy and connect with the Aether at the right place and right time. When you're ready to go, focus on the card. Trace the symbol with your mind's eye like you did my little drawing. It won't be hard. Then when the meeting's over, you can concentrate on the Trident to bring you home."

"Will that even work without Silas's music to guide me? He's my anchor." My heart raced at the thought of being lost forever in the realm of the gods. I would not become my mother. I wouldn't.

Grams interrupted my spiraling anxiety. "It's Saturday. Won't Ezra stop by with Aegir's daughter?"

"Probably."

"Call him. Make sure of it. The two of them can be your focus to find your way home." Grams took in my incredulous expression and patted me on the shoulder. "You'll be fine, dear. You have enough of a connection to that place to tie you to this realm and enough personal strength to accomplish your goals."

Chapter 9

Packed with summer tourists on a beautiful Saturday afternoon, traffic on PCH was practically at a standstill as I approached Main Beach. It usually made me glad I didn't own a car and could walk to work. Walking gave me the time to appreciate the little city that sparkled with every California cliché in existence. Except today.

Today, my own gloom overshadowed the festive atmosphere.

As I stood at the corner waiting for the light to change, the weight of all I'd learned, of the consequences of my failures, weighed heavy on my mind.

A mom holding the hand of a little girl in pigtails pushed a stroller filled to the brim with toys and towels next to me. The dad stood at her side with a cooler in one hand and beach chairs on his back.

It was an afternoon outing in the making, but all I could think about was how my own mother had abandoned me, and my dad had convinced me for years that I was mentally ill. Now, even though I knew my visions were real, I doubted myself so much I had let the one person I cared about besides my brother get hurt by the shadows only I could see. Silas was stuck in that narrow, railed bed, alone and lost in the darkness of his own mind.

A runner in a bright pink sports bra panted up behind us, her ponytail bobbing as she jogged in place. Guilt added a new layer to my misery. I hadn't been on a run in at least two weeks. Yet another person I'd let down. My brother was still training for his next paratriathlon, and I was supposed to be his spotter. I'd been pushing him off with flimsy excuses. Sure, they felt true when I said them—I really was tired, and work was wearing on me—but the truth was I didn't want the reminder of Aegir's Hall. I didn't want to remember Ezra transformed by the god of the ocean or wonder if he regretted once again losing the use of his legs…even if they hadn't exactly been human.

I shoved my hands in my pockets and crossed the street with the crowd headed toward the beach. A co-ed volleyball game had drawn an audience to the sand courts, and nearly every bench was filled with spectators, while the playground swarmed with little kids like ants on a log.

I couldn't enjoy any of it. I had failed. Again. The people I loved kept getting hurt.

Brigitte said she could teach me things, and even Grams agreed, but would it be enough? Would she even really help, given her obvious distain of anyone who wasn't a Daughter of Lilith?

I didn't know, but in the end, it didn't matter. I had to find a way into the Aether, a path to Silas, and the coven meeting was the best first step.

With that decided, I called Ezra and explained everything that had happened in the last twenty-four hours.

"So what's the plan?" Ezra asked when I was done.

"I'm going to this coven thing. Brigitte said the elementals couldn't be allowed to overwhelm and control humanity. Therefore, it follows that they have to help me bring Silas home. I just have to convince them."

"Good. And the more you can learn from them, the better prepared you'll be. And who knows, maybe you'll make friends. Socializing is good for you."

I rolled my eyes at my big brother's unasked for advice, not that he could see me on the other end of the phone line. "Anyway, I need you at the Trident tonight. With Silas—" I paused, trying to control the emotion that threatened to drag me under again, "—unavailable, I need an anchor to focus on when I'm ready to come home."

"Not a problem. Tempest and I were planning on it, anyway. We'll just head over a little early."

I blew out a relieved breath. "Thanks." I could always count on Ezra to have my back.

Ezra rolled up to the bar, his slim wheelchair maneuvering around the tables and customers with surprising grace. Tempest was with him, her bouncy blonde ponytail perched high on her head, perky despite the tension that pulled the corners of her eyes.

"Are you sure this is the best idea?" she asked, keeping her voice down as she glanced nervously from side to side. Like me, she was a Daughter of Lilith, but her other half was sired by the primordial god of the ocean, Aegir. She and her brother, our bouncer Dion, had been raised in the Aether, knew its secrets, and its dangers.

"Ezra filled me in on what happened, but it's risky to walk Between. Now that they know who you are, the gods will be watching for you."

"Maybe that's why there were so many minions in the bar last night." I replied. "Everyone here is at risk because of me. My choices are to join this coven thing so I can learn how to use and control my abilities, or walk away, and I can't leave Silas to fade into the Aether!"

My voice rose and Ezra gripped my hand where I wiped the low accessibility counter.

"I've been hiding too long. I can't hide anymore. People are getting hurt," I finished in a quieter tone.

"You're doing the right thing," Ezra murmured.

"But we don't know who these women are," Tempest argued. "How do you know you can trust them?"

"I don't. Even Grams was cautious. But what choice do I have?"

Tempest ignored the question. "I should go with you. You could bring me across. I can help."

"I don't think that will work. Even if I wanted to, the invitation was for me. Brigitte had some pretty strong ideas about the gods and their influences . . . I don't know what she'd think about you or what she'd do if you just showed up."

Tempest's attention caught on something over my shoulder and our conversation paused. Ty sidled up, drying a glass.

"Bar's pretty quiet tonight," he said, voice subdued compared to his usual high energy bottle-tossing performance. "I guess everyone heard what happened."

I dipped my chin in a rough nod, unable to come up with a response. Ezra patted my hand.

"How's Silas? You went to see him at the hospital, right? And Ben?"

I swallowed down the pain. "Yeah. Still unconscious, last I heard. The doctors wouldn't tell me much, though."

Ty glanced around the mostly empty, quiet bar. The boss hadn't been able to book another band, and without the live music, there wasn't much draw compared to the other bars in the city. The customers looking for a party would head to one of the other nightspots instead, and the more sedate regulars rarely ventured out on Saturday.

"Why don't you head home? You look a wreck."

"Thanks for that," I replied, dryly. It wasn't as if I'd had much time or inclination to do more than put on a clean shirt before coming in to work. Even my makeup was a day old and smeared around the edges. But it didn't matter. I was on thin ice and couldn't afford to lose my job. "I can't though. Chaz is watching my register like a hawk. If I leave early, I'm pretty sure he'll fire me. Why don't you go, though? We don't all need to be here."

Bruce was down at the other end of the bar, chatting up a solo customer about growing up in Hawaii. Ferghus had called in sick, but even two of us was probably too many.

"You sure?" Ty asked.

I nodded. The younger bartender put down the glass he'd been drying and wrapped me up in a hug. "It'll be okay, Lil. Silas will come around. You'll see."

I swallowed, choking down the emotion. He was right. I was going to make sure of it.

As Ty closed up his register and headed out, Ezra eyed me, warily. "So what's the plan?"

"I'm going to take my break soon. I'll need you to stay here to act as my anchor. I guess, try not to move around too much? That way I can pinpoint you better." I'd done it in the Aegir's Hall by visualizing Bruce's tattoos and making him stand next to some easily identifiable scenery. I could do that even better with my own brother and the bar I knew better than the back of my hand.

"We'll sit at the table over there," Tempest replied, pointing to a square two-seater near my station, somewhat hidden in the shadows and out of the way. A rope net hung loose on the wall overhead, with a plastic octopus tangled in the webbing. It was as good a target as any, I supposed.

"Good. Thanks. What do you want to drink? My treat." It was the least I could do since they were using their date night to help me.

Tempest glanced at Ezra with a significant look I couldn't read. "Just a tonic water and lime, for me," she said.

"Same," Ezra added.

I lifted an eyebrow.

"We can't sit here getting drunk while you travel into the Aether."

"If I can't go with you, then the least I can do is stay vigilant here." Tempest glanced over her shoulder toward her brother on the bouncer's stool at the door. "Dion will be on watch, too."

"Thanks. Just . . . stay close." I didn't know what else to say, or what to expect. Grams had made it all sound so easy, but now that I was getting ready to intentionally cross by myself, my nerves were jangling.

I gave the bar one last swipe with my rag as my brother and Tempest took their positions. I patted Bruce on the shoulder as I passed behind.

"I'm going on break. Be back in fifteen."

The big Samoan shot me a thumbs up as I walked out the back door.

Chapter 10

The sound of the bar's canned music dimmed as I shut the alley door for my break. I glanced to either side, but the little bistro table we used for breaks was empty and no one was skulking around outside. That was a relief.

I pulled the embossed white linen business card from my back pocket and gazed at the inlaid silver design. All I had to do was use the image to focus my energy. That's what Grams had said. Brigitte hadn't said anything at all about *how* to get to the coven meeting, just that the card would lead me there.

Skeptical, but without any other choice, I had to try.

I blew out a breath through pursed lips and concentrated. *Stop, look, listen.* That had been the advice, and the method to traveling within the Aether at Aegir's Hall. It couldn't be so different to use it to get there.

Taking a seat in the delicate metal chair, I rested my forearms on the table while studying the pattern. I could do this. I could work the magic.

I closed my eyes and envisioned the symbol from behind my eyelids. The pentagram glowed a soft white. I traced it with my mind's eye. Where my attention traveled, the sigil burned brighter. In the center, Lilith's sigil sparked with light. I continued to mentally trace the image as I looked for my destination on the other side of the Between.

I imagined Brigitte, with her wild, copper-red hair. It was tied into puffy pigtails on either side of her head. She wore a navy blue jumper tied around the waist with a paisley patterned cloth—maybe silk?—belt. She clasped her hands behind her back as she waited for others to arrive.

The space around her was gray, and kind of foggy, but lit from the floor by the same sigil as had been printed on the card. Like a mosaic crest inlaid into the entryway of some celebrity mansion, the design was the signpost greeting new visitors. Shadows twisted through the fog of the perimeter, dancing like leaves in an autumn wind.

The mousy woman from the bar—Brigitte's daughter—stood slightly behind the older woman on her right side. As before, she wore thick rimmed glasses and no makeup, baggy jeans, and an oversized sweatshirt. It was hard to determine her age. She could have been ten years younger, or a few years older than me, it was hard to say. Her sullen posture made me think younger, though.

As I watched, another woman arrived, this one with a tight-curled pixie cut and wide set eyes. Her smile was genuine as she held her hand out to Brigitte.

"Welcome," Brigitte greeted, clasping the woman's hand between her own two palms. *"I'm glad you made it. We have news today."*

"Nothing bad, I hope?" the woman replied. Her voice was resonant, but kind, her body language open. I immediately felt drawn to her breezy energy as she stepped forward to shake Mousy's hand. The younger woman's lip lifted in a half smile as she shyly touched the other woman's fingers.

I followed my senses into the Aether.

And landed on my butt.

Cheeks heating, I stood and dusted off my rear-end, not that there was any dust in this . . . space. I wasn't sure what to call it. It wasn't a room, but neither was it outside. It was more like a void, the boundaries indiscernible yet continuously shifting, as if we were sitting in the middle of a campfire but there was no heat or flame or smoke. Rather disconcerting, really.

The pentagram design on the floor pulsed and then dimmed, the white glow illuminating the faces of the women around me then casting us all into twilight.

"Well, hello," the Pixie woman smiled.

I returned the grin, but Brigitte interrupted before I could say anything.

"Ah. Good. You managed to get here. I wasn't entirely certain you had the skill, but I suppose it proves my invitation was deserved."

My smile slid off my face, and even Pixie frowned. Mousy glared at the floor and hunched even further in on herself, like a teenager angry at the world. She couldn't be that young since she'd been in the bar, and I didn't know what I could have possibly done to her to earn that kind of loathing, but she made it clear I was not welcome.

I shook off the odd feeling as two more women arrived. Identical blonde-haired blue-eyed twins, one had her hair pulled back in a messy braid, the other left hers free to hang nearly to her waist but for a white daisy tucked behind her ear like a nineteen-seventies hippie. They moved in eerie unison, stepping toward Brigitte together. They glanced at me curiously as they passed to greet the elder stateswoman of the group.

"Brigitte," they intoned together.

Brigitte clasped the hands of Hippie first, then Ms. Messy-Braid. "Welcome, sisters."

The twins stepped back to greet Pixie, and then finally Mousy. It seemed there was a hierarchy to this circle that I didn't yet understand.

The twins stood opposite each other on the points of the pentagram, mirrored on either side of Brigitte. They stared with curious expressions.

"Who is this?" Hippie asked.

"I'm Lil," I replied.

Brigitte shot me an irritated glare. "I will explain everything once the rest of our sisters arrive. It should just be a moment."

As she finished that statement three more women arrived, each greeting Brigitte and the others in turn. When that was done, they took positions at the points of the pentagram, with Brigitte at the top of Lilith's 'h.'

"We begin with praise of the Great Mother Lilith, that she may bless our circle of sisters."

"Praise Lilith," the women intoned.

I tried to keep a bland smile on my face, but I couldn't help thinking this was sounding more and more like a religion. Or a cult. Even in the institute, where they preached a higher power and the benefits of prayer as meditation (or meditation as prayer) I'd held back. It wasn't that I didn't believe in spiritual energy—I could see the demons on everyone's shoulder, and I'd met at least a few gods in person—but I wasn't about to worship someone or something I *couldn't* see. Especially when I didn't know their motivations. If there was an all-powerful singular god or goddess, they didn't seem too interested in protecting me, so why should I devote myself and my energy to them? It just never made much sense.

Still, I wouldn't insult these women by saying so.

"We bind the circle with the strength of the elements," Brigitte continued.

"Earth," Hippie said. She placed the flower on the ground within her section of the pentagram. A gentle rumble rocked beneath my feet. The triangle that had been outlined in white filled in with the loamy green color of soft spring grass.

"Air." Pixie untied the scarf from around her neck and tossed it into the air where it floated upward, unaided, to hover above our heads. Her section of the sigil began to glow the pinky-purple of the setting sun.

"Water." One of the last women to arrive took a vial from a cord around her neck, uncorked it, and poured it over her point of the pentagram, which turned the shifting, swirling blue of the ocean.

"Fire." the second twin drew small votive candle from the pocket of her cardigan and set it inside her section. With a snap of her fingers, the flame burst to life and the sigil burned a fiery orange-red.

"Spirit." Brigitte finished by pricking her finger with her own athame and letting a single drop of blood fall across the final section of the pentagram.

At first, nothing happened. The drop seemed suspended millimeters above the floor. It was only a half a heartbeat, but unlike the rest of the women, the sigil didn't immediately take the offering. I wondered if anyone else noticed. Maybe it was normal.

The drop fell the remaining distance and splashed within the top triangle of the pentagram. A rich gold spread out from the offering in slow waves, mimicking the beating of a giant heart. Every third or fourth beat, the heart stuttered, and the gold dulled, but then recovered on the next beat. At last, the liquid gold reached the edge of the central pentagon.

With a burst of light, all of the colors around the pentagram bled down the lines to Lilith's sigil in the center, shifting and swirling together in an iridescent rainbow that made my eyes hurt if I looked at it too long.

Brigitte lifted her hands in front of her, palms up. "We thank the Great Mother Lilith for her blessing and her gifts and swear to use them for the benefit of the balance."

"We swear," the rest of the circle intoned, as did Mousy.

"Now that the circle is bound, we may speak freely," Brigitte said, once again clasping her hands behind her back. "I called this meeting to discuss the disturbances in Laguna Beach and Lil's failure to control her territory."

I bristled at the insult, even if it wasn't entirely misplaced. I hadn't been able to control the events at the bar, and I regretted every second of it. It was why I was here. The *only* reason I was even remotely interested in dealing with Brigitte and her attitude.

I needed to learn what I could from these women so I could find Silas and bring him home.

At the same time, it wasn't my fault, and no one had told me it was "my territory." I couldn't meet their expectations if I didn't know about them.

"Isn't Grams still in the area? She's been the protector of the beaches for the last hundred years. Surely she has something to say about this?" Pixie asked.

Hundred years? That couldn't be possible. Grams was elderly to be sure, but she couldn't be much over eighty.

"Grams is on the decline, as you all must be aware. She can no longer hear the spirits to banish them."

"That's not true," I interrupted. "Grams may not be able to cross to the Aether, but she can still hear and speak with the demons. I've seen her do it."

I'd been half-dead when she'd invited Mnemosyne to change people's memories, but I still remembered the purple clouds filtering through people's heads after I'd returned from Aegir's Hall.

"Then that suggests an even worse dilemma, that she's given up and is allowing the spirits free rein. In either case, the region is unstable and Lil, though old enough to be of use, is untrained. I have brought her here to sponsor her into the coven so we can teach her our ways."

"Welcome, Lil," Pixie smiled. "I'm Becks."

"I'm Agatha," Hippie said, "and my sister is Agnes." Ms. Messy-braid dipped her chin in greeting.

The water wielder was next. "I'm Aadhya, and my daughter and apprentice is Pria."

I turned toward Mousy as the final member of the coven. She hunched deeper into her sweatshirt and glared without speaking for a few heartbeats, until Brigitte turned and gave her a look of exasperated encouragement.

"I'm Wendy."

"My daughter," Brigitte added. "She has been apprenticing

with me for the last eight years. Sadly, her abilities are weak, and she is still unable to stand as a senior member of the coven."

Given what I'd seen at the Trident, I found that hard to believe. The younger woman had been quick to see Ferghus's distress.

Brigitte took a deep sniff before turning back to me. "Lil, please stand in the center of the circle over the Great Mother's symbol for the questioning."

My brow furrowed and I took a step back. "The questioning?" That sounded ominous. "No one said anything about an interrogation."

Becks smiled gently. "Not an interrogation, just an interview, so we can get to know you better and find out if you would be a good fit for the coven."

I shook my head. "I'm not here to join the coven. I'm not going to bind myself to your circle or whatever." I wouldn't make the mistakes of my mother. "I'm only here to learn how to find my boyfriend and bring him home."

The women looked toward Brigitte, who curled her lip in disapproval. "Lil has connected with a son of Adam, who is in an Aethereal coma as a result of her inability to control the minions in her region."

"Of course we'll help," Becks said. "You are our sister, even if you are not part of the coven."

"But to help, we must first know what you are capable of and where your allegiances lie," Brigitte added.

"So long as you understand I won't be bullied into anything."

"Of course not," Brigitte snapped. "Grams has put such ideas into your head. We do not coerce our sisters."

"So long as we're clear," I replied. "My only motivation is to find Silas and bring him home."

"You are welcome here," Becks added.

Her voice soothed my nerves and after glancing again at each of the women around the circle, I stepped across the lines and into the center of the pentagram.

Chapter 11

I expected to feel something different, but nothing seemed to change. I shrugged it off.

"We begin with earth," Brigitte lifted her palm toward Agatha on her left.

I turned to face the blonde woman, curious at the formality of the situation.

"Our Great Mother is our foundation, the fertile ground from which we all spring. We trace our ancestry through the maternal line, yet your mother is not here to stand with you."

"Is there a question somewhere buried in that?" I asked.

"Where is your mother?"

"Bound in Aegir's Hall." The words felt pulled from my mouth, as if compelled. "She serves as Rán, goddess of the ocean after a failed attempt to sever the Aethereal bonds from my body."

The women glanced at each other around the circle, worried furrows buried between their eyes. "If her mother fell to the influence of the elementals, then she is likely to follow suit." I glanced over my shoulder to find the voice. Agnes, the fire-wielder, crossed her arms over her chest in a belligerent stance behind me.

"That is always a possibility, no matter who our mothers are,"

Becks replied. "But why would she sever your bond to the Aether?"

I turned to face her and the space of air. "I believe she wanted to protect me, to give me a 'normal'—" I paused to frame the word in air quotes, "—life not tied to the elementals and their minions. But I am not my mother. I am who I am, and I will not change who I am to please another."

It was an important distinction, one that I hoped they understood to mean more than just the Aether. I wasn't going to change myself to fit the coven, either.

"You see? She has already claimed her voice." Becks smiled. "However, our emotions resonate from Earth to Aether, creating vibrations that affect all creation. What is your greatest happiness and your greatest fear?"

As she spoke, a giant shadow seemed to swim through the fog behind her back, like a whale in dark water. No one else reacted so I ignored it.

Once again, the words felt pulled from my soul. "My greatest happiness is my place at the Trident, my greatest fear is losing it."

Brigitte scoffed. "That bar? Surrounded by sons of Adam and daughters of Eve? You no more belong there than you belong in a circus, holding seances and telling fortunes. To them you are nothing more than a freak, an insignificant outcast. With us, you will never have to explain yourself. You will become so much more."

I glared at the poofy-pigtailed red-head. I don't know what circus she was going to, but it was fifty years out of date. "They are my friends. They gave me a family when I needed one. They helped me in Aegir's Hall and stood up for me when I returned. I won't abandon them, Silas least of all."

"You were very nearly swallowed into the void because of them."

"Actually, it was the reverse. They were taken into Aegir's Hall by his son and greatest minion, the half-human child of Aegir and the first Rán, who was also a Daughter of Lilith. They were taken because they stood between me and that minion. I was only able to send them home with Grams's help."

I glared at Brigitte in challenge. The Daughters of Lilith weren't all-powerful. They were just as susceptible to the influence of the elementals as the rest of humanity, if not more so. She could set herself apart and above everyone else, but it was a hollow pedestal, bound to crumble under pressure.

Aadhya, the water-bearer interrupted our silent exchange. "Every boat must take harbor in a storm. It is good that she found safety amongst them. But a boat may still crash against the rocks if there is nothing to hold it in place. Who, then, are your anchors?"

"My brother, Ezra, and Silas, whose music calls me home."

"You claim sons of Adam as your anchors?" Agatha asked, aghast.

"They may be sons of Adam, but Ezra is my brother and therefore also a son of Lilith. And both have been more supporting and understanding than any other person in my life, including my own mother."

I turned to Agnes, ready for the next question.

"Fire is the energy that gives us purpose. What do you fight for?"

"I fight to live my life, the way I choose to live it, each and every day. I fight to protect those who have protected me."

"You seek independence from the elementals. This is good," Brigitte said.

"No, that's not what I said—"

Brigitte interrupted before I could explain any further. "Our power is of the spirit, manifesting differently in each of us. How does your power manifest?"

"I see the demons of the gods and hear their whispers. I taste their influence and smell their intentions. I walk the Between and exist equally in Earth and Aether."

I had no idea where the words came from. They felt true, and yet I had never experienced taste or smell, at least not noticeably. But then, I had been able to drink the mead in

Aegir's Hall and smell the decay of the shadow spirits, so maybe it was true.

A gasp from Agatha. "You carry all five senses of the Aether?"

Brigitte smiled and nodded, knowingly. "She will be an asset to the coven. I promise you that. I will train her personally."

"I told you before, I'm not here to join the coven. I only want help finding Silas and bringing him home. Grams said you could teach me to follow the Aethereal threads, whatever that means. Silas and I are connected. I can feel him." I clenched a fist over my sternum where our bond hummed.

A rumble vibrated through the sigil beneath my feet. As I glanced down, I noticed hairline fractures crackling through the iridescent glow.

"Do you see that?" I asked no one in particular. "Something's wrong."

"Nonsense," Brigitte interrupted. "I smell nothing out of the ordinary."

The other women looked at me, questions in their eyes.

"The colors are fracturing."

"Colors?" Aadhya asked. She closed her eyes and tilted her head to the side in contemplation. "I taste the salt of the sea mixed with the brightness of lemongrass, with layers of crisp char and frothed cream. The flavors are clean. No bitterness at all."

Another tremor rolled beneath my feet. One of the cracks widened, zig-zagging its way into the golden section of spirit. A shadow larger than the whale rose above Wendy's head.

"Watch out!" I shouted as the shape morphed from a blob into the head of a cobra. I was pretty sure I recognized that head.

I sprinted toward Brigitte's apprentice but slammed into some sort of invisible barrier.

"Let me out!" I pounded the barrier with the side of my fist. "Don't you see it? Apep is going to swallow your daughter to the void."

Brigitte held up a hand and smiled sadly. "Even the most

fundamental aspects of the rites of Lilith are beyond your understanding. We will fix that. You will see when you join us."

"I already see plenty, and I'm not joining the coven. Apep is here, hovering over Wendy, and you're too self-absorbed to notice." Another deeper crack broke through the golden section of the pentagram. The liquid gold began to drain away, into the darkness of the space beneath us, whatever it was.

"I hear it now. The void is calling. The elementals know we're here." Becks whispered. Her head turned left, then up. "The circle is broken. Our protection is gone." Her gaze snapped toward Brigitte. "What have you done?"

"We are in neutral territory, outside of any demesne," Brigitte snapped. "They will not reach us here."

"Apep already has," I replied, determined to make her see the truth.

"We cannot remain. I must protect my daughter," Aadhya said. She pulled her daughter beneath her arm.

Brigitte slashed her hand through the air. "No! We're not finished! Lil must join the coven. We cannot leave until it is done."

Aadhya shook her head. "I'm sorry." She spat on the ground. The pair disappeared. The blue section of the pentagram returned to neutral gray.

The color began to bleed out of Lilith's symbol. The barrier in front of me softened, feeling like a balloon instead of a glass wall.

The red of Apep's scales began to glow through the gray fog that surrounded us. His tongue flicked out as he tasted the air.

"We will not risk the void," Agnes declared. She bent to blow out the candle as Agatha picked up the flower.

"The Great Devourer would gain too much from our power. We must all retreat."

"Agreed," Becks said, snatching her scarf from the air. "We can reconvene somewhere safer."

The three women left the circle and the barrier dropped. I rushed forward to tackle Wendy as Apep's head came down for the strike. We rolled out of the way. I thought of the Trident and my brother, imagining him sitting at the table with Tempest. We fell through the Between and into the bar, leaving Brigitte to fend for herself against the Egyptian god of chaos and destruction, the void snake, the devourer of light and life.

I hoped she survived.

Chapter 12

Wendy scrambled away from me, knocking over a chair in the process.

"What did you do!" She demanded.

At the same time, Ezra hissed "Lil!" His gaze jerked around the room. "You're back?! But I just saw you walk out the back door. What happened? And who's this?"

I blinked hard, trying to gather my bearings. "She's a . . ." I hesitated for a moment, ". . . new friend. The daughter of one of the coven sisters."

The bar was almost exactly the same as I'd left it. Bruce was chatting up a customer at the far end of the counter, his back to us. Another couple held hands over the table in the corner near the empty stage, completely oblivious to everything and everyone except each other. I tuned my ears into the music, pretty sure the speakers were still playing the same song.

Time really did work differently between Earth and Aether. That was probably all for the good in this case. I'd done as Grams suggested and managed to return to the Trident before my break was even over. At least Chaz wouldn't get on my case for missing work or ducking out early. The last thing I needed was another interrogation, or accusation that I was off on a bender.

I stood and held out my hand for Wendy. "You probably don't want to be sitting on that floor. We mop every night, but it still gets pretty sticky."

Wendy grimaced but pushed herself up to standing without touching me or my proffered hand.

I shrugged. I had no idea what I'd done exactly to deserve her irritation, but I *had* tackled her to save her life. I decided I wouldn't take the rejection personally.

"What did you do?" She demanded.

I rocked back on my heels. "I saved your life. Or your essence. Or something."

"What happened?" Ezra asked again.

Tempest pursed her lips into a deep frown. "I can smell the void on your skin," the blonde woman murmured. The knowledge in her eyes burned through the last of the fog in my brain.

"Apep attacked the meeting."

"The gathering of the circle," Wendy corrected. "I can't believe you don't even know the correct terminology."

"Excuse me, princess, but I'm new to this," I snapped. Okay, so maybe I was taking her bad attitude a *little* personally.

The mousy young woman crossed her arms over her chest. "Clearly."

"I saved your life! You could at least be grateful."

"You didn't save my life; you broke the circle!"

"I was trying to protect you. Your mom wasn't listening. No one was. They didn't see him, didn't understand, and didn't believe untrained little ol' me could possibly know what I was talking about. But I've dealt with Apep before. He nearly swallowed me whole once, and I wasn't about to let that happen to anyone else; not if I could help it!"

Every muscle in my hands and arms tensed as the adrenaline once more rushed through my system. I was vibrating with pent up emotion.

Ezra wheeled his chair out from behind the table, putting

himself directly in my line of sight. "Pause," Ezra interrupted. "Start from the beginning."

I took a deep breath, recognizing the wisdom of Ezra's advice. Four counts in, hold for four, out for four, hold again, and in. Then I was ready to talk.

"I made it to the meeting. Just like Grams said I would. It wasn't too hard."

"You fell on your butt like a toddler learning how to walk," Wendy argued.

I closed my eyes and gritted my teeth, doing everything I could not to scream. "As I said, I made it. Everything seemed to be going fine, although the interview took me by surprise, but something went wrong."

"Yeah. You broke the circle," Wendy insisted.

I threw my hands into the air. "That can't possibly be true! I didn't do anything."

"Then how did the shadows find their way inside?"

Obstinate and accusatory, the little mouse pushed all the wrong buttons. Not meek like I'd first assumed, she was a harpy circling overhead, waiting for the opportunity to strike.

"How should I know? Your coven was supposed to help me, not fall to pieces."

"Doesn't matter." Wendy sliced a hand through the air. "I have to go back. I can't stay here, in this . . . place." Wendy's lip curled as she gazed around the room.

"Isn't your mom your group's First Sister, or something? Doesn't that make her pretty powerful?"

Wendy's eyes narrowed. "What does that have to with anything?"

"I'm sure she escaped. She just had to pop through the Aether like we did." I replied, purposefully keeping my voice light and nonchalant. Brigitte had made a point of saying Wendy wasn't strong enough to stand in the circle, so I had to imagine it would rankle that with all her training she couldn't do what I could naturally. Maybe it was petty, but I couldn't help myself.

"You make it sound so easy." Wendy practically growled the words.

"Stop, look, and listen. It's the one thing my mom actually taught me about the Aether. Of course, it had been unintentional. But still. I just needed an anchor."

"Which was my job," Ezra chimed in. "But you still haven't explained anything."

"Right." I paused for a breath and propped my hands on my hips. It was time to demand answers. I didn't know how the circle functioned, or what Brigitte could have done. All I knew for sure was that the seal had cracked and Apep had been ready, waiting to strike. "What happened up there? Or out there. Or down there. Wherever." I shook my head, trying to clear my jumbled thoughts. "What happened in the Aether?"

"How should I know?" Wendy snapped, repeating my words back to me. "That's never happened before. The sigil should keep us safe. The circle is supposed to be a boundary that the elementals can't cross. They shouldn't even be able to sense us within the Aether. It disrupts their influence."

"I didn't notice a circle in the sigil."

"It's not *in* the sigil. You really don't know anything, do you?" Her voice was simultaneously condescending and immature. It annoyed the hell out of me.

I clenched my jaw for a half a second just to keep myself saying something I knew I'd regret. "No. I don't. Brigitte wasn't wrong when she said I'm untrained. I've been alone with this stuff since I was twelve years old and told I was crazy. So explain it to me."

"As the leader of the coven, Mother prepares the circle before the sisters arrive. It is a binding in Aethereal space and time. The sigil is the beacon that leads us there."

"Then you can go back," Tempest said.

"No. The circle is broken. The sigil is no longer active."

"Okay. So your mom would have followed her anchor or whatever home, like we did."

"Like you did. You basically kidnapped me."

"You're not that much younger than me. I don't think it counts as kidnapping."

"Abducted, then. Doesn't matter." She crossed her arms over her chest in another belligerent shrug. This girl had to have been seriously sheltered to get away with that kind of attitude.

"So where would your mom have gone?" I asked.

"I don't know. We move around a lot."

"You don't go to UCLA?" I nodded toward her sweatshirt.

Wendy quickly shook her head. "We just visited. Mother says it's a waste of talent for someone like me."

What was implied but not said, was that 'someone like me' meant someone on the outside. Someone different. And given what I knew of Brigitte, someone superior to the rest of humanity.

I suddenly felt a kinship for this girl. We weren't really so different. Sure, her mother hadn't abandoned her, and had passed on the knowledge that I just now realized I'd been missing, but she'd still hobbled her. She'd placed her—and the rest of the Daughters of Lilith—on a pedestal above everyone else in the world. It was no wonder Wendy felt like she couldn't live up to the standard.

"Where were you last staying? Somewhere here in Laguna?" I felt like I was pulling taffy trying to get any information out of her.

"Our RV is parked in one of the beach campgrounds. Moro, I think?"

I nodded. "Makes sense. Not too far from here, and close to Grams." She'd probably walked home after meeting with Grams this morning which was why I hadn't seen a car. "I bet that's where she is. Hopefully she'll figure out that I brought you here and come looking."

"I'll walk. It's only a few miles."

I glanced out the window at the fading light. It would take her well over an hour to walk, especially because a good chunk of it would be uphill. By the time she reached the campgrounds, it would be long past dark and there wasn't much in the way of streetlights out that direction. I'd ridden my bike late at night before, but not along PCH and even still, it was different than walking around on foot.

"I'd feel better if you either stayed here until Brigitte comes to find you or let me call you a ride share."

"I don't need your help."

I shrugged. "Maybe not, but I still think you shouldn't walk alone after dark. Besides, do you even know where you're going exactly?"

"I'll be fine. I just need directions."

"We can give you a ride," Ezra offered.

"I said I'll be fine," Wendy spat. "I don't want your help."

Ezra lifted his hands in an 'I surrender' motion.

The glare Wendy turned my way could have peeled the skin off a grape. "I might not be as powerful as you are, but I can defend myself."

Powerful? As I am? "Look, I don't know what you're talking about. I just don't want to feel responsible if you get hurt. It's what I would do for any of my friends."

"I'm not your friend."

"You've made that clear. I still won't send you into the dark alone."

"It's not your choice. You have no responsibility for me."

"You know what, you're right," I snapped. I walked over to the bar to grab a napkin. With the pen I always kept tucked into the messy bun on the top of my head, I drew out the rough directions to the campground. "Good luck. Tell your mom I have no interest in the coven."

I'd find another way to bring Silas home.

Chapter 13

Surfer Jeff lifted an eyebrow as he sucked down a gulp of his Navy Grog, all while watching me rub an endless circle into the already spotless bar top. "Wanna talk 'bout it?"

"Not really." After Wendy left, I'd had to get straight back to work, my break time was more than up. Bruce had been fine with it, but I knew Chaz would check my logs tomorrow. Besides which, I needed some space to think. I couldn't talk about it all with Ezra. Not yet. I needed to figure out my next steps. I still needed to find Silas, and my only clue had stomped out of the building. She was my only remaining connection to the coven. I didn't know where else to turn.

"Family's hard."

I glanced at my brother. He and Tempest were still at their table, heads pressed together as they chatted. "Ezra's not so bad." Understatement of the year. There wasn't a better brother in the entire world.

"Ezra's great. It's the new girl you'll have to keep an eye on."

"Tempest?" I watched my brother's girlfriend for any sign of malicious intent. She *had* kidnapped him once. I thought that was over and done with now that she and her brother were both safely away from Aegir's Hall, but maybe I wasn't seeing things clearly. Maybe I was forgiving too fast.

"No, not the blonde. She's good for Ezra. I'm talking about the young one with glasses who left a little while ago. She's a tough bite to swallow."

"I guess. She's not my family though."

Jeff waffled his free hand from side to side. "Maybe not by blood, but she sure acted like your little sister. As Desmond Tutu once said, 'You don't choose your family. They are God's gift to you, as you are to them.' Sometimes God gifts us the family we need when we need it."

"I'm not sure God has anything to do with it."

"God, fate, karma, whatever you want to call it, it's real. It's how I met my second wife."

"The one who left you for a millionaire?"

"No, that was my third wife. The second one was the real deal."

"Then what happened?"

Jeff took a long pull on his straw. "She died. Car accident. Also karma."

"Oh. I'm so sorry. I had no idea."

The older man shrugged and tilted his head to the side, his salt and pepper hair catching the light ever so slightly. "Thanks. Twelve years, eight months, and twenty-seven days I've been without her. It's the real reason Diana left me. I couldn't get over my Gigi." He paused for another sip. "But enough about that. Your karma sister is going to need you. I can tell. The ones who are most defensive usually do. 'Course that's what you're good at, isn't it? Diagnosing people's core needs?"

I scrunched my face. Jeff saw too much. He might not understand it, but he still saw it.

Jeff shook his empty glass, the dregs of ice cubes rattling around the bottom.

"Ready for another?" I asked, ignoring his all-too-insightful question.

"Yes, ma'am."

I thought about Jeff's insight as I mixed up his drink. I still needed help to find Silas. I didn't even know where to begin. He was my anchor, and I could sense our fragile bond, but I believed Grams when she said I would break that connection if I pulled too hard on the string.

I needed someone with more experience to help. Someone who could put me on the path to wherever in the Aether he was being held. Grams said she couldn't do it anymore.

I needed Brigitte.

Ezra rolled up to the counter just as I slid Jeff's drink across the counter, Tempest at his shoulder. My brother got straight to the point. "You're going to have to find Wendy and Brigitte."

"I know." I wiped the counter.

"We're going with you."

"What?"

"I warned you the Aether was dangerous," Tempest said. "The elementals know who you are now. They've seen you and witnessed what you're capable of. You can't hide anymore."

"I don't *want* to hide anymore."

Tempest shook her head. "No. I don't think you understand. The coven is powerful. The elementals talk about them with both awe and fear. Rather than binding themselves to the service of a god, they bind to each other, and together they are more than the sum of their parts."

"Sisters," I murmured.

"Exactly," Tempest replied. "If an elemental found you, attacked you, in the Aether, in the midst of their circle, then something else is going on. The elementals can see you. They're drawn to you like a beacon."

Like moths to a porch light. I squeezed my eyes shut. "I'm putting everyone at risk." It was me, always me. I was to blame, even if no one wanted to admit it. This is what happened when I let myself get close to people.

"You have to go to Grams."

"She said she can't help."

"I find that hard to believe. She's a powerful Daughter of Lilith, proven by the fact that she's never been bound, either by one of the gods or by a coven. She exists outside the structure, as the original Lilith did, and as you do now."

"Outside the structure?"

Tempest gazed at me from beneath raised eyebrows.

"Right. Outside the structure." Except the coven had tried to bind me to their circle.

"So we go to Grams first thing in the morning," Ezra said. He lifted a hand to Tempest. "All of us. I have a feeling you're going to need the whole team."

Team. More than family, chosen as well as born, a network of connections that included my brother as well as the woman he claimed as his own and the mentor for us all, Grams. For once, I didn't feel alone.

Chapter 14

Ezra drove us to Grams's eclectic cabin in the figurative woods, his specially equipped van allowing him to connect his wheelchair to the frame of the car and drive with hands only. It still took longer to get in and out, but it gave him the freedom to travel. And since I refused our father's money and didn't have a car, he often played chauffeur.

Unfortunately, Grams's hundred-year-old porch had not been updated for accessibility. Without a ramp, Ezra was stuck in the driveway unless or until someone could help him up the three stairs to the front door.

We were debating the best method of tackling the problem when Grams opened the screen.

"I wasn't expecting you for another hour," she announced without preamble. With strength belying her age, she bent and pulled a metal ramp from the side of the porch and positioned it over the steps.

"Ugly thing, but my carpenter is still working on the custom wood ramp to install next to the stairs. Apparently, contractors are in high demand at the moment. But this'll do for now."

She gave the ramp a final tug and tested the balance. It covered the stairs entirely, giving Ezra a manageable incline to roll up and into the house.

"When did you get this?" I asked, striding up the black sandpaper and aluminum slope. I hadn't thought about it, but I certainly hadn't expected her to retrofit her house for Ezra, not when she'd only met him a few weeks ago.

"I ordered it the day after your return from Aegir's Hall, dear. I couldn't very well have Ezra dragging himself up my old steps on his hands."

"No, but—"

"Ezra is your brother, and secondary anchor. He is as welcome in my home as you are." She pushed open the screen door and ushered us all inside, Ezra leading the way and Tempest bringing up the rear.

"Thank you," he murmured. I could see the surprise and gratitude written across his face.

"You are welcome."

As we arranged ourselves in the doily-covered living room, Grams set to work making plates in the kitchen.

"Now, I imagine you're here about Brigitte."

"How did you know?" I asked.

"Hecate told me. The chaos snake was bragging about his capture of a powerful Daughter of Lilith, and she was worried it was you. I set her straight."

"You did?"

"Mm-hmm. It took a bit of digging, but I tapped into my network to find out what happened. Brigitte has always been too big for her britches." Grams passed around snack plates with scones. "Who wants coffee?"

We all raised our hands and Grams quickly set out mugs. I got up to help pass them around, but there was an extra on the counter.

"I think you miscounted, Grams." I held out the extra mug for her to put away in the cupboard.

"No, dear. We're waiting on one more. She'll be here soon."

Grams set to pouring the coffee from her French press without looking at me.

"Who?"

She finished her pour and smiled as she handed me a mug. The scent of perfectly balanced medium roast wafted on the air and my shoulders immediately relaxed. Grams was a connoisseur of good coffee, thanks to Silas. He had introduced her to my favorite roaster after tasting some of the brew I'd made at the Trident.

Before we'd even been dating, he'd been paying attention, noticing the details. It had only been a day since the attack and already I missed him terribly. He was too good for me. I was going to ruin it. I already had.

Angry steps on the porch knocked me back into the moment. The screen door burst open, and Wendy slammed into the room.

"You!" She pointed a finger at Grams, but her mouth dropped open when she saw me standing at the counter. After half a second, her eyes narrowed and she scanned the living room, taking in Ezra in his chair and Tempest sitting in the armchair next to him.

"I should have known. You're all in on it."

"In on what?" I demanded.

"Come have a cup of coffee and sit a moment," Grams forced a mug into Wendy's hands and gestured toward a counter stool. "You and Lil have business in the Aether, and you're going to need all the energy you can muster."

"I have to find my mother," Wendy protested. "She never came home after *she* destroyed the circle. It's your fault and you have to fix it."

"I didn't do anything to your precious circle," I replied. I might take the blame for the events at the Trident, if only because I didn't stop them soon enough, but I couldn't possibly have done anything to Wendy or the coven. I'd barely figured out how to get there. "My only goal is to find Silas and bring him home."

Grams tsked as she settled herself onto the couch. "Those two tasks are more related than you know. Hecate confirmed that it is Apep, the crimson serpent of the void, who has taken both Silas and Brigitte. The first was to draw Lil into the Aether. The second was a consolation prize when he failed to capture you." Grams shot me a pointed glare.

"Hecate? You converse with the elementals?" Wendy's eyes widened.

"Yes, dear. Has your mother truly kept you so sheltered?"

"Mother says they must either be controlled or destroyed. They cannot be trusted or bargained with."

"Your mother would also have you believe the descendants of Adam are inferior and to be avoided when at all possible."

"They cannot see the truth around them. They are too easily manipulated. Only our sisters are free from influence and control."

"But are they? That is the real question," Grams mused. "Regardless, you will need to ask Hecate for passage within the Aether. It will likely come at a price, but of all the elementals I've dealt with, she is usually the most reasonable."

"How do we get there?" I asked. I was as ready as I was ever going to be. I wasn't going to leave Silas stranded a moment longer than I had to.

"As with all things of the Aether, it's easiest if you have a focus. Then you do as your mother taught you: *stop, look,* and *listen* to cross the Between." Grams lifted a card from the small coffee table between the two rocking chairs. She flipped it over and held it out for me to see. In the center she'd drawn a maze-looking circle with three crescent moons attached to the perimeter. "This is Hecate's sigil. Like Lilith's sigil, it will help you focus your Aethereal energy and allow you to connect with the goddess. She's expecting you."

"I'm coming, too," Tempest declared. "I might not be an Earth-born Daughter of Lilith as you two are, but I at least can help navigate the politics of the gods."

Ezra grabbed her hand where it rested on the arm of her chair. "Isn't that risky? What if Aegir finds you?"

"He won't. Not in Hecate's Hall." She sounded confident, and she knew better than any of us what was at stake.

"Yes, this is good," Grams murmured. "Maiden, Mother, and Crone, the three aspects of Hecate. A good omen. One she will appreciate."

"Hey, who are you calling a crone?" I asked, trying to keep a teasing tone in my voice despite my nerves. Hecate had been helpful in Aegir's Hall but meeting her on her own turf was a different matter altogether.

"No, dear. You are the Mother. Wendy is the Maiden and Tempest is the Crone. You are the protector. Wendy is the explorer. Tempest is the sage. Together you might be strong enough."

"Strong enough for what? What do you see?"

Grams didn't answer. "Go now, before Brigitte is bound and Apep's power breaks its bounds."

"Mother would never—"

Grams cut her off with a sharp glance while holding the card out for me to take. "Unlike the other elementals, Apep doesn't require consent. He simply consumes. Hence his moniker, *The Great Devourer*. What is swallowed into the abyss is slowly digested into the entropy that fuels his growth."

In other words, Apep was dangerous. An elemental force that could consume the world and take everything back to the nothing before creation.

"I've seen it. His appetite is endless. He shotgunned entire barrels of mead at Aegir's Feast of Renewal." I paused as a realization set in. "Why would Aegir want to fuel the snake? Any of the gods, for that matter? Why would want to strengthen his competition?"

"Balance," Tempest replied.

I frowned. "Explain."

Tempest looked to Grams, but the elderly woman nodded for the younger to continue.

"Aegir is the primordial ocean. Apep is the endless abyss. Enlil is the storm that tears through the heavens and sparks new life. Each of the gods has a purpose, or a dominion, from which they gathered their earliest worshippers."

"Worshippers," Wendy scoffed. "More like witless groupies. They had no idea what they were dealing with. Still don't."

I frowned. "It's not their fault they can't see or experience the Aether."

"Ignorance is no excuse," Wendy insisted.

"Perhaps not, dear, but we are all susceptible to fantasy when reality is too hard to bear. Fear has always been a powerful motivator."

"And the gods didn't hesitate to use that to their advantage. My sisters loved to tell stories of entire civilizations destroyed because the elementals wanted to increase their influence or undermine their rivals. They thought it was funny, how gullible the humans were." Tempest crossed her arms over her chest, hugging herself as if fending off the cold. "There was even one about Apep, that he once tried to swallow the sun, and with it, the sun god, sending humanity into a violent panic that ended in worldwide mass suicides."

"That seems a bit . . . counterintuitive," Ezra chimed in. "I mean, if people were your source of power, why would you destroy them?"

"Right? Which was why the gods banded together to stop him before the madness destroyed everything and everyone. Eventually, they came up with a truce. They would each share some portion of their power so that none would be favored over another. That balance has allowed the human population to flourish along with the gods."

"It worked quite well, until people stopped believing," Grams interrupted. "As the imbalance grows, some will do anything to regain their strength. Which is why you must find those that

Apep has taken before their time and return them to their bodies. The abyss cannot be allowed to expand past its boundaries."

Tempest uncrossed her arms with a deep breath and straightened her spine. "I'm ready whenever you are."

Ezra grabbed her hand. "I'll be waiting for you."

Tempest smiled. "You're my anchor. Of course you will be."

She bent to kiss him, and my heart twisted in my chest as I thought of Silas, his faint song humming a sound only I could hear. I suddenly realized I cared less about the fate of humanity than I did my trombonist.

With a mix of envy and guilt, I tore my gaze away from my brother and his girlfriend to face Wendy. "Are you ready for this? Have you ever been to one of the elemental's demesnes?"

She shook her head and swallowed. "Mother says I'm not ready."

That sounded all too familiar.

I was saved from responding by Tempest's footsteps on the hardwood floor. She shot me a shaky smile. "Let's go then, before I lose my nerve."

Chapter 15

It felt weird standing in the middle of the living room about to go all woo-woo and bridge the spiritual realms. It didn't feel natural. I wanted dirt under my feet and a breeze across my cheeks. I wanted sun on my face and the smell of the saltwater to coat the back of my throat.

Choosing to follow my instincts, I left the house and stepped out into the grassy dirt yard. Tempest and Wendy followed, Grams and Ezra behind them. I kicked off my sneakers and pulled off my socks. Grams's cheeks creased, and her eyes twinkled as she watched me wiggle my toes into the dusty soil. I yanked my hair into a messy bun on top of my head and blew out a breath.

"Do you have the athame, Lil?"

"Of course." I patted the sling bag I carried on my hip.

At the Trident I could carry it on a sheath without anyone thinking twice. It was dark in there, and I did have to cut things pretty frequently, so I didn't feel too out of place. After all, even some grocery store employees carried box cutters.

But in public, during the day, I felt too noticeable with a big knife hanging off my belt. I'd found the hip bag was a perfect solution. Not only did it fit the athame, but I could wear it with anything, and it also held my phone, lip balm, and a few handy wipes in case I needed to wipe something down.

"Good," Grams replied. "When you reach the Aether, Hecate will put you on the path, but you must also follow your own instincts. Trust yourself, and your connection to Silas. Follow the line and you will find him."

I nodded and swallowed. I could do this. I *would* do this. It was easy. Follow the path, reel in the line, find Silas, and cut our way home. It was a simple plan, but it would work. It had to.

Holding Tempest's hand in my right, and Wendy's in my left, I closed my eyes. With the dusty ground beneath my soles and my face turned up to the midday sun, I felt the breeze coming up the hill, dusting my cheeks with the scent of the ocean. Earth, air, water, and fire. They grounded me in the present, but I needed to cross through the Between, into the Aether.

I'd placed Grams's card on the ground at the center of our little circle and now I opened my eyes to focus on the design. Starting in the center, I traced the circle-bound maze with my eyes, gradually moving outward to follow the curves of the crescent moons around the perimeter.

Holding the image perfectly in my mind, I once again closed my eyes. I paused all thought, letting my mind clear of all Earthly distractions. I started in the center of the now-remembered maze and drew the sigil behind my eyelids. The design began to glow, like an afterimage burned into my retina.

I thought of Hecate in her red dress and golden sandals. Her green eyes flashed with unspoken humor while she reclined on a Roman-style couch beneath the awning of the temple. One arm propped against the raised cushion to support her head, the other casually picked at a bowl of grapes on a small table in front of her.

Then I thought of her hounds, especially the one who had protected me against Apep in Aegir's Hall. The black Great Dane with the white starburst on its chest sat up from a pillow at her feet. He jumped to his feet and barked, coming to stand in front of Hecate protectively.

"Thank you, Brutus," Hecate commanded as a tanned, ring-bejeweled hand popped another grape in her mouth. "Quiet now."

The hound immediately sat and fell silent, but for the shush of his tail wagging across the stone floor. He whined, staring straight ahead to where I knew we would arrive.

"Come, Lil," Hecate smiled. "Step through and join us."

I took one last deep breath, squeezed Tempest's and Wendy's hands, then the three of us stepped forward in unison, toward the center of our little circle.

We fell through the Between and popped into existence in front of Hecate. I faced her between Tempest and Wendy's interlocked hands.

The goddess clapped her hands together and grinned. "Well done, Lil! I knew you could do it. And you've arrived not alone, but with your sisters. Your skills are already growing stronger. Excellent."

The three of us dropped our hands as Wendy and Tempest stared wide-eyed around the space. I probably didn't look much savvier myself.

We stood at the entrance to a grand colonnaded temple. Behind us, a horse whinnied, and I turned to see vast green hills blooming with wildflowers. A herd of horses galloped across a distant field, their manes and tails streaming behind them. A waxing crescent moon hung low and large in the sky, framing one of the horses as it reared up on hind legs.

I turned back to our host.

"Magnificent, aren't they? They came to me late in my classical period," Hecate commented. "Now they are part of my soul, carrying the fiery energy of battle."

She swung her legs to the ground, standing from her cushioned seat. With a flick of her wrist, the recliner and table disappeared.

The dog barked. "Yes, Brutus, you may greet our new friends."

Brutus lunged toward me as if launched from a spring-loaded trap. Wendy squeaked in terrified surprise, but his tongue lolled out in a doggy grin. Tempest side-stepped out of the way, and I braced myself for impact as he stood on his hind legs to put his front paws on my shoulders and lick my face. I chuckled, delighted by the antics, even if he almost knocked me over.

"Hello there, Brutus," I said as I scratched him behind his ears. "It's good to see you, too."

"He's missed you. You've been gone from the Aether for some time now."

"Have I? It doesn't seem like it from the earth side of things," I replied. I patted Brutus on his side and pushed him back down to four paws. He stayed next to me and nudged my hand for another pet, which I quickly obliged.

"Time works in mysterious ways," she replied, echoing Grams's usual refrain. Hecate tilted her head to the side and studied our group of three. A smile plastered across her face, but I couldn't tell if it was false or simply a mask to hide her thoughts. At last, she swung her left arm wide to usher us into the building. "Welcome to the Temple of the Maiden."

My feet moved without my conscious thought, as if drawn forward by some invisible force. When I would have resisted, Brutus nudged his head under my hand, guiding me up the stairs like a seeing-eye dog.

Inside the temple, the temperature dropped to the chill of a crisp spring morning. The ceiling soared above us, the vast stone roof held aloft by wide white columns. The floor, made of the same white marble, had been polished until it shone so brightly it reflected our faces. Behind the goddess, a giant statue of a young woman holding a basket of brightly colored living flowers smiled coyly down at us. She wore a circlet on her brow with a waxing crescent moon centered on her forehead. Her hair hung loose and appeared as if blowing in an unfelt wind.

Hecate placed her hand on the statue's big toe. "What do you think? Have I captured my likeness well enough?"

My gaze bounced between Hecate and the face of her statue. The stone woman did look remarkably like the goddess but wasn't an exact match. The face was rounder, the eyes somehow softer, even though they were made of stone. There was an innocence to the face that I didn't see in Hecate's unlined skin.

Even I knew better than to say that, though.

"She's a work of art," I replied.

Hecate laughed. The sound shifted from the throaty mature chuckle of a grown woman to the higher-pitched giggle of an adolescent. Her face transformed along with her laugh, becoming the exact match to the statue. "Very diplomatic of you, and worthy of the mother role you bear. But I am glad to see you brought a maiden representative with you." She nodded toward Wendy. "I am always thrilled to meet a new Daughter of Lilith."

"Grams said you would take us to my mother. To Apep's demesne." Wendy didn't even bother with small talk or the usual formalities.

Hecate lifted an eyebrow to study Wendy, but thankfully ignored the disrespect. "Innocence and ignorance and the intensity of youth." Her face transformed again, taking on the gentle lines and pointed chin of a woman only slightly younger than Grams. She turned her attention to Tempest. "And the youngest of Aegir's daughters, to act as wise woman and sage." Hecate's voice grated ever so slightly across the words.

"Lady Hecate," Tempest curtseyed. "We are honored and humbled to be in your presence."

"Well done, my dear, but no need for the formality. Lil and I go way back. Any friend of Lil's is a friend of mine." Hecate turned to face me once more, her figure returning to its original age. "Which places you in the role of mother, I suppose. Protector and champion, but not yet fully imbued with your power. You still have much to learn."

"You still haven't answered my question," Wendy interrupted.

"You didn't ask one," Hecate pressed her lips into an enigmatic smile and lifted one eyebrow, waiting for the realization to hit.

Wendy rolled her eyes in response. "How do we get to Apep's demesne?"

"That is the question, isn't it. One of them, anyway. You might also ask how to find your Mother and bring her home, if she yet lives."

I half-heartedly tried to hide my amusement at Wendy's discomfiture. I was so used to Grams now that Hecate's evasiveness hardly registered. I knew, as with all things, she'd get to the point when the time was right.

Hecate returned her gaze to me. "It is a good omen that you come in triple form. You will need the strength of the three to avoid the coming darkness."

My eyebrows shot to my hairline on those dire words. "Grams explained, did she not?"

"A little."

"I see. Well, come then. Let me tell you a story of an age that long ago passed into memory."

Hecate gestured forward into the temple and strode away, her golden sandals silent where our sneakers echoed around the marble space. She didn't bother to look over her shoulder or wait for us. She expected us to follow, and so we did, pacing clockwise around the base of the statue.

"There was a time when we, the elemental beings of the Aether, were only just beginning to understand our powers and our affinity for the mortals that called Gaia their home." Hecate's words reverberated ever so slightly around the room, lending power and prophecy to her voice.

"Affinity? Is that what you call it?" Wendy's strident, whiny voice was beginning to get on my nerves. For someone who had spent her life in her mother's shadow, she had gotten exasperatingly vocal and opinionated. "More like subjugation."

Hecate had far more patience than I did as she continued her story, barely giving Wendy the space to finish her sentence. "We each found our place amongst the worshippers. Some chose to align themselves with natural elements, like the sun or the wind or one of the seasons. Others found their place within the energy of the life cycle: birth, death, and renewal. Still others bound themselves to the emotions and desires of the mortals: war, cunning, love, or beauty.

"Over time, we found that our chosen alignment did more than influence the humans who gave us strength and power, it fundamentally changed who *we* were. We gained abilities that mimicked their Earthly origins. Our forms changed to fit the environment in which we fed, to fit the dreams and desires of the humans who worshipped us even as our spawn influenced those desires to our needs."

"Is that why Aegir took the form of a merman?" I asked. "Because he was the ocean god?"

"Yes. He focused all his influence in the realm of the almighty ocean, taking the souls of the drowned into his demesne.

"But Apep was always different. He never sought the love or worship of the humans. He was an agent of pure chaos and destruction, the Great Devourer who consumes the energy of all things. Even the gods. He is the embodiment of the cosmic abyss."

I shuddered. Hecate's words chilled me to my core. I'd almost gone there. Almost been swallowed into Apep's coils. The memory of the endless black threatened to swamp my senses.

"What was your alignment?" I asked, in an effort to change the subject and recenter myself. Besides, I was curious about the woman who had offered her help, unasked.

"I found my place amongst the women of the world, in all their ages and stages," Hecate surprised me by answering. "I have been associated with the moon as its cycle mimics so closely the female body, but also the earth as she is the mother of humanity, and the sea with its ever changing tides. My hounds have at times been the watchers at the door, and the hellhounds that haunt the nightmares of men. I have been a virginal innocent and a seductress, a protector of the home and a demon of the night, a crone, and a guide to light the way. I have had many faces and many names. All are me and none are me."

A new foot came into view, and I craned my neck up to see the face of the Mother, an exact replica of the Hecate that stood before us now. "The Maiden is my beginning, my waxing form. Her strength is her passion and her thirst for life as she grows into her womanhood." She gestured upward toward the second face of the statue. "The Mother is my prime. I am fierce and strong, able to bear and protect my children and defend my home."

Instead of the basket of flowers, this version of Hecate held a knife in her hand. A knife that looked eerily similar to the athame she had given to me in Aegir's Hall. The circlet on this woman's brow held a moonstone medallion shaped into a perfect circle. A hound sat by her side, her empty hand resting on its head.

Just as mine rested on Brutus's head now.

I turned away from the statue to look down the length of the Temple of the Mother. Instead of cold white marble, the long hall was built of warm polished wood with seating areas scattered around the space. A hearth big enough to fit a dining table contained a roaring fire, in front of which another hound rested while nursing a litter of puppies.

A tug on my sleeve had me turning toward Tempest just as Hecate disappeared around the edge of the statue's foot. We hurried to catch up.

"My third and final form is that of the Crone," Hecate continued her story. "The term has taken on a negative connotation over the millennia, but in its original meaning she was the wise woman or sage, not an ugly old hag."

I glanced up at the statue and saw exactly what Hecate meant. The woman was still beautiful, though creases lined her cheeks and curled around her eyes. An owl sat on her shoulder, the carving so realistic it almost appeared to be alive, except that it was made of the same white marble as the rest of the statue. The Crone held a lit torch in her right hand, its flames dancing in a gentle breeze. A set of keys dangled from her left hand, hanging just out of reach over our heads.

"The Crone's strength lies in her experience. She understands the many worlds and the many paths a life might take."

I glanced at Tempest to see her reaction. The blonde woman's face was serious as she listened intently to Hecate's words.

"This is all grand, but what does it have to do with my mother?" Wendy asked.

"If you wish to see your friends again, you must take the Crone's path. She holds the keys to the underworld where Apep reigns."

Chapter 16

Hecate's form shifted into the Crone. Her gown lengthened and drew up around her shoulders and head, transforming into a heavy cloak that wrapped her body. Her face slackened with age, and her shoulders stooped ever so slightly. She lifted her right arm and a torch burst to life in her hand. Her left hand turned palm up, and her fingers uncurled to reveal a single aged-bronze skeleton key.

"I will take you to the gates, but that is as far as I can travel."

"Can't you make Apep release Silas and Brigitte?" It seemed far-fetched, but still, I had to ask.

"And the others," Tempest added, her words a gentle scold. There were other lives at stake here, other souls. Ben and the Zombie girls had just as much a right to be rescued, but if I were being entirely honest, the only one I truly cared about was Silas.

I tested the delicate thread that bound us. It sang at my gentle touch, but the sound was growing fainter. Silas was fading. We had to hurry.

Hecate shook her head. "I cannot trespass on another's demesne without invitation. To do so would be to invite war. War we have avoided for millennia."

"But we can?"

"You are mortal, and Daughters of Lilith." She said it as if that was an answer. I wasn't sure I agreed, but I was starting to get used to the cryptic answers of the Aether.

"Then shouldn't we be able to just pop into his hall, grab Brigitte, and pop home?" I glanced at Tempest. "That's more or less how I managed in Aegir's Hall."

"I'm afraid not." Hecate's voice had shifted with her form and cracked with age. "Aegir invited you to his demesne. His minions led the way."

How did she even know that? I wondered.

"What about a sigil?" Wendy asked.

I glanced at the younger woman. It was a good question, and I was surprised by it. Maybe I shouldn't have been, given that she'd been raised to be a Daughter of Lilith from birth, but I was.

Unfortunately, Hecate was already shaking her graying curls. "As I mentioned, Apep was never worshipped by humanity, he was only ever feared. As such, the mortals tried to suppress his existence. He does not have a sigil on which you can focus to find him, as you did me. Your only path is through the boundaries between Aethereal demesnes, the crossroads of the gods." Hecate waved a hand to indicate the Temple of the Crone. "But it's up to you. The path to the underworld is not easy for those still living. There will be trials."

Unlike the bright and airy Temple of the Maiden, or the warm and cozy Temple of the Mother, the Temple of the Crone swirled with dark gray fog. A cold breeze swept past my face, pulling loose strands of hair toward the shadowed recesses of the room. The air was damp and smelled strongly of musty earth and mold.

A shiver cut a path down my spine. "What kind of trials?"

"That all depends on the path you choose, but I will not be the only elemental you will encounter. And even I cannot protect you from all the dangers on the road."

My breath was shaky, but there was no alternative. "We have to go." I murmured. I would follow the thread to find Silas. It would lead me to him. I would find him, and I would cut a path home.

Hecate's smile was gently condescending as she dipped her chin and turned toward the temple. "Do not stray from the path," she warned. "The creatures that live in these woods are not as friendly as Brutus."

"Well that sounds pleasant," Wendy snarked.

Hecate led the way between the marble columns, cutting a trail through the mist that grew thicker with each step and closed in behind us. Within a few steps we could no longer see the triple goddess statue. A few steps more and we could hardly see each other.

"Hold hands," I whispered, feeling the weight of the air on my soul. I held my left hand out to Wendy and my right to Tempest. "We can't risk losing each other in the fog."

"Seriously? What are we, Kindergartners?" Wendy sniped as I grabbed at her sleeve.

"Can't you feel them watching? They're everywhere." Tempest's hand trembled slightly as she laced her fingers between mine.

A low moan cut through the chill. I squeezed Tempest's hand tighter, and she returned the gesture.

Wendy rolled her eyes but didn't try to pull free. "Parlor tricks and mind games. Nothing *real* to worry about." Despite her brave words she shifted so she could grip my forearm.

"For someone raised in a coven, you should know better than to be so dismissive," Tempest snapped. "The Aether can hurt you just as easily as Earth."

"They're just shadows and ghosts," Wendy insisted, but her grip tightened.

"I do not collect the spirits of the dead as some of the others do," Hecate's voice was barely audible, the wind carrying it away from us, deeper into the temple. "But they may pass through this hall to their final rest. Or torment, depending."

"We'll be fine. Just stick to the path and keep moving. Stay together," I urged.

As we followed the glow of Hecate's torch through the mist, the marble columns began to change. Their forms lost the perfection of the artist's chisel. Rough edges and natural patterns in the stone began to emerge. Moss grew on the damp rock.

Tempest reached out a hand to brush the rough surface. "It's bark," she murmured in amazement.

I glanced to the side, unwilling to lose sight of Hecate, but needing to confirm with my own eyes. Sure enough, the columns were no longer made of stone. They were the trunks of trees, some sort of ancient pine, and the farther off in the distance they grew as wide as the giant sequoias in Yosemite.

An owl hooted from above. Wendy tugged on my arm and pointed up at the twilit sky. The giant grey bird sat on a branch almost directly overhead, watching us with wide knowing eyes. As soon as we caught its gaze, it spread its wings and lifted into the air, flying ahead of us along the path. "I don't think we're in the temple anymore."

"Come, sisters," Hecate called from ahead. "We're almost there."

Another dozen paces and the trees began to close in on us. The trail narrowed, barely visible as a thin, needle-covered track between the pines. Forced to walk single file, I let go of Wendy and Tempest and took the lead to push back the brush and bracken that stretched out from the deeper woods and snagged on our clothes and hair. When I turned to look back the way we came, the path was equally clogged with vegetation. There was no sign at all of the temple.

"This way," Hecate urged. "Quickly. There's no turning back now."

I couldn't see her form at all anymore, just the barest glow of her torch through the dense branches still swirling with fog. Each step grew more difficult. Thorns snagged on my pants, scratching at the skin of my ankles where they were exposed beneath the cuffed hem of my jeans. My bare arms bled from half a dozen thin red lines.

A growl issued from the brush to my left. I swerved right. My right foot stepped on a moss covered log off the path. A furry snout snapped at my foot, and I just barely managed to pull it out of reach. The animal disappeared back beneath the bush.

Tempest yelped from behind me. "Lil! I'm stuck!"

I paused, turned. Tempest was bent at the waist, one foot held aloft by a snarl of brambles. Brambles that hadn't been there a few seconds before. As I watched, a thorny vine snaked out from the surrounding trees and twisted through her hair, pulling at her ponytail. Every movement wove the sharp and sticky growth tighter into her blonde tresses, snarling them into a punishing tangle. Meanwhile, her left sleeve was stuck on a thorn the length of my palm, from tip of the middle finger to wrist.

Another blast of cold air swept past us. The mist formed a screaming face as it howled past. I shrieked and flailed, then tripped over a root that ripped up from the ground. I landed hard on my hip. Pain lanced through the bone. A thorny vine wrapped around my ankle, digging into the skin with vicious glee.

I yanked my leg back, tearing the skin. The vine held fast. Another snarl had me scrambling backward, but the vine was too tight. I couldn't break free. My ankle screamed in agony.

"Lil!" Tempest shouted again. I couldn't even see Wendy bringing up the rear. We were all getting stuck, the forest seeming determined to keep us from our destination.

"Hold on!" I stomped at the vine, using my heel to try to smash the fibrous material and make it let go.

"I'll push!" Wendy shouted from behind her.

"No! Wait," I replied, too late.

Tempest lurched forward. Her sleeve ripped, releasing her arm. The vine in her hair held fast, tearing out a chunk of blonde hair. She shrieked as she fell forward, and her legs caught on the brambles. The fabric of her black leggings tore, and a gash opened across her thigh.

I grunted, unable to move as she landed on top of me, her elbow knocking the wind from my lungs. Before I could take another breath, Wendy dove through the gap in the rapidly growing brambles and added her weight to the dog pile.

"I think this forest is trying to eat us," Wendy groaned.

I gasped and shoved at the women. "Get. Off. Me."

"Sorry."

Wendy rolled to one side, then Tempest shifted so I could sit up.

The vine had retreated from my leg, leaving a smear of red in its wake. The thorns had cut deep enough to draw blood from a cut across the side of my shin.

Wendy rubbed her forehead. A cut similar to my own sliced across her temple. Her glasses sat crooked across her face, one of the arms bent askew. She grimaced when she couldn't push them back up her nose.

Tempest looked even worse. Of the three of us, her wound was the deepest, bleeding freely and dripping onto the forest floor. Eyes wide and slightly shocked, she pressed her hands over the injury to staunch the flow. Half of her hair had pulled out of the ponytail, the other half stuck out in spikes and bumps. Leaves and sticks had caught in her tresses, and her shirt had ripped across her collarbone. She looked like some sort of wild woman.

I'm sure I looked just as bad.

I started to laugh. I couldn't help it. The forest had chewed us up and spit us out into a rough clearing, but it seemed to be leaving us alone for the moment, at least.

"What could possibly be funny right now?" Wendy asked.

"I've heard of Venus fly traps before, but not Hecate's people traps. Who knew the woods would be carnivorous?"

Tempest joined me with a chuckle. "Hecate's lady traps."

"Ew," Wendy groaned. "That sounds like some sort of gross euphemism."

My laughter buried itself in my belly. "Don't bother trying to pull out." I gasped.

Tempest snorted. "Watch out for the bush . . . es."

My laughter was uncontrollable by this point. "If you can walk straight afterward, you didn't do it right."

"Seriously?" Wendy protested.

"Shredded clothes are a sign of a good time." Tempest barely managed to get the words out between bouts of the giggles.

Tears streamed down my face, and I wrapped one arm across my belly, my abs aching.

"Are you done, yet?" Wendy stood, hands on hips, gazing down at us with disapproval. I'd seen that expression before. On Brigitte's face.

I sobered up on that thought. "It's better to laugh than cry," I replied, wiping the wet from my cheeks and swallowing the last of my laughter. "We're alive, and that's something."

"Souls are free to enter, but the living must pay the toll in flesh and blood." Hecate's voice startled me, and I spun around to find her. She waited for us at the base of a cliff maybe twenty yards away, her visage more stooped and older looking even than before. The mist of the forest swirled around a dark crack in the stone, flowing into and out of the cave as if the mountain itself was breathing.

"You could have told us that an hour ago," Wendy replied. "We could have pricked our finger or something. Didn't need all this messing about in the woods."

"If it were that easy, the path would be crowded with mortals seeking lost loved ones. I can't have that, can I?"

"All those mortals that can cross the Between?" Wendy asked.

Hecate's smile gave nothing away.

I dusted off my pants and stood, interrupting the staring contest between the goddess Crone and the mortal Maiden. "Right. Well. The path has taken its pound of flesh, so let's get cleaned up and get going."

I pulled three individually wrapped handy wipes from my hip bag and passed them out. Once clean, I pointed and flexed my toe to test the damage, then massaged my calf where the plant had tightened its hold. I was sore, but everything seemed functional.

Satisfied I wasn't going to have any lasting damage, I turned my attention to my companions. Wendy had missed a spot on her temple, so I wiped the last bit of blood from her face as she did her best to fix her glasses, grumbling the whole time.

Tempest had managed to stop the blood on her thigh, so together we limped toward the ancient goddess, while Wendy muttered at our side.

Hecate lifted her torch toward the hole in the mountain. "This mountain marks the end of my demesne and the beginning of the Aethereal Between. Once you pass within the cliff, there is no coming back."

I glanced back at the tangled mess of trees and brush, only to find the path had cleared and the fog had lifted. You could even see the marble columns in the distance. To return to the Temple of the Triple Goddess would be easy.

I turned back to the cave and a shiver of dread passed down my spine. To walk into the dark of the mountain would not.

Hecate seemed to pick up on my hesitation. "It is your choice."

"There is no choice." Wendy stepped through the arch without a backward glance. Three steps later, she disappeared from sight.

Hecate smiled indulgently. "I do love the impulsivity and fearlessness of youth." She waved a hand, and we followed Wendy into the passage.

Chapter 17

Three steps within the stone, my ears popped, and the path opened up into a cavern surrounded by gated tunnels. Each gate was made of what looked like forged iron, with a lock prominently located in the center, and a torch burning ominously on either side. I glanced over my shoulder and found our path now barred by the same gate and torches.

A pedestal marked the center of the room, a basin placed prominently on top. Hecate approached the basin and used her torch to light the oil inside. A flame burst to life, much like the opening ceremonies of the Olympic Games.

"Welcome to the crossroads of the Aether, one of few locations where our demesnes intersect enough to create a path. It is the only way to travel from one demesne to another without an invitation or a diviner's sigil."

She hung the key on a hook to the side of the basin and stepped back from the heat.

I turned in a circle, counting the gates. "Why are there only nine gates? I'm not a mythology expert, but there must be more than nine elemental beings."

"So there are," Hecate croaked, "but like spokes on a wheel, these are the nine that intersect here, now. One of them begins your path to Apep. Consider this your first trial."

"First trial?"

"You didn't think the journey would be easy, did you?" Hecate chuckled and faded from view, her final words echoing around the chamber. "The key will open any door, but it can only be used once. Choose your path wisely."

I gaped at the space Hecate had occupied. Like a puff of smoke wafting on the air, the woman left only the scent of her passing as she dissipated on the wind.

Wendy turned in circles her hands on her hips. "Well, this sucks. What do we do?"

I tilted my head to the side as I approached the nearest gate, reaching out to touch the cold wrought iron. The metal was rough under my fingers. "We choose, I guess."

"They all look the same."

I moved to the next gate over. Wendy wasn't wrong. The arch of the metal was bolted into the stone, leaving no room for anything bigger than a small dog—or, shudder to think, a large rat —to pass through. Simple, straight, vertical bars were welded into the frame, without any kind of ornamentation or sigil to identify where the gate might lead. The lock was placed directly in the center of the gate, but interestingly, I couldn't find any hinges.

"How do these things even open, anyway?" I asked the room.

Tempest leaned over my shoulder to peer at the lock. "It's the Aether. It probably dissolves like she did."

"Huh." It made sense in a not-bound-by-the-laws-of-physics sort of way.

Wendy—still standing near the blazing central pedestal— covered her eyes with one elbow and extended her other arm to point one finger at the wall while spinning in circles.

I yelped when she bumped the base with a toe. "Wendy, what are you doing?" I demanded. "You're gonna catch on fire!"

She stopped spinning and pointed at the gate three to our left. "We go that way."

I rolled my eyes. "That hardly seems like a good method to choose."

Wendy crossed her arms over her chest. "I don't see you doing anything."

"Grams said to follow the line. What did she mean by that?" Tempest asked.

Duh. "Right! You're right. I have a connection to Silas. I can find him. All I have to do is follow the string."

I closed my eyes and centered myself to find the connection. There it was, humming against my sternum. Barely visible, I could see the shimmering string against the dark of my eyelids. I was facing the pedestal, but like a video game guide, the string made a curve around the obstruction to pass through a gate on the far side.

"There!" I pointed. But, as I started to walk around the room, the string flickered toward a different gate. I turned, and once more the string changed direction to lead down a third tunnel. I slowly spun in a circle, and with each step, the line carved a new path.

I opened my eyes. "I think any of the gates will ultimately lead to Silas. The question is, which is the fastest and safest? There has to be some kind of indicator of where each of these goes. Maybe something carved into the stone?"

I strode to the closest gate and ran my hands around the opening as far as I could reach. I didn't see anything that looked intentional. It was all just rough worn stone. I couldn't even find any marks from a chisel or drill that would have explained how the tunnel was made. Then again, this was the Aether, so one of the elementals probably just "thought" it to make it appear. Maybe even Hecate herself.

"Do you smell that?" Tempest asked. She took a deep breath, even going so far as to stick her nose between the bars. "Smells like . . . rotting meat."

"No thank you," Wendy quipped.

"I don't smell anything," I replied. I peered into the depths of the tunnel, hoping for some kind of clue of where it might lead, but even my vision couldn't pierce the shadows.

Tempest moved onto the next opening and pressed her face between the bars as far as it would go. "This one smells like sunshine and wildflowers and late summer wheat."

"That's better, then," Wendy said. "Let's go there."

"We need to check them all. What else do you smell, Tempest?"

The blonde woman continued to pace the circle pausing to take a sniff at each gate. "Seaweed at low tide . . . Yeast and sawdust and maybe blood? . . . Wine, baking clay and some kind of flower I don't recognize . . ."

She took a big sniff at the next gate and physically gagged. "Sulfur . . ."

She hurried to the next opening and sniffed more cautiously, but then let out a relieved sigh. "Clean cotton, thank goodness . . . The back of your freezer . . ."

"My freezer? What's wrong with my freezer?" I asked.

Tempest ignored me, finishing with the last of the gates. "Running water passing over stone." She straightened from her final appraisal.

"Well, sulfur and rotting meat sound ominous. I'm not going that way." Wendy declared.

"We have to think like the elementals. What would Apep's demesne smell like?" I asked. "What do we know about him?"

"He's a snake, so a freezer is a no-go." Tempest said.

"Okay, but seriously. What's wrong with my freezer?"

"Nothing." Tempest shrugged. "It just has a very distinctive smell. You might consider one of those baking soda boxes."

"But somebody's afterlife is in my freezer? I think I would know."

Tempest chuckled. "I never said that. It just has the same smell."

"I'm going to have to work on that, then," I grumbled.

Wendy stamped her foot. "Can we get on with it?" She asked.

"Sure, sure. Not the freezer. I'm also going to rule out clean cotton, wildflowers, and seaweed. I don't think those would be a chaos snake's preference. We need to get to him as directly as possible."

"I think we came in through the river gate," Tempest added.

"Are you sure? I didn't see a river while we were there, and at this point I've lost track of the gates."

"Not a hundred percent, but I think so."

"So what are we left with?" I asked.

"Rotting meat (NOT going in there), yeast, clay, and sulfur (another no thank you)," Wendy replied, pointing to each gate in turn. She'd done a much better job than I had at keeping track.

"Maybe yeast, then?" I asked. "Apep drank multiple barrels of the mead at Aegir's feast."

Tempest shook her head. "Mead is made with honey and this one didn't smell sweet. I would have recognized it. And the underlying smell of sawdust and blood leads me think of soldiers or warriors or something. I don't think Apep has an army."

"And sulfur doesn't make sense. What would a snake want with rotting eggs?" Wendy asked.

"Snakes eat eggs sometimes," I replied, "but in this case I think you're probably right. Sulfur doesn't fit. So we're left with rotting meat and baking clay."

Wendy crossed her arms over her chest. "I told you—I'm not going into the rotting meat tunnel. I meant it."

"But he *is* the god of chaos and destruction and the endless abyss."

"None of those things sound like rotting meat to me. Chaos could be fire or lightning, but meat? Nuh-uh." She was adamant.

Tempest returned to the fifth gate. "Baking clay and some kind of flower . . ." her words trailed off as she took another deep breath, and another. "I don't remember Apep's story well, but I'm pretty sure he was at the prime of his essence during the reign of the ancient Egyptians. Maybe the smell isn't baking clay so much as hot sand?"

I shrugged. "I suppose it's as good a guess as any."

"Better than most. Especially because of that flower. I can't place it, which means it's something I haven't smelled before."

"Good. Great. Let's go," Wendy bounced forward to grab the key from the hook on the pedestal and joined us in front of gate number 5.

"I didn't realize your sense of smell was so precise."

"It wasn't until I followed you back to Earth that I realized it was better than human. I thought everyone smelled as I did."

I surreptitiously let my gaze slide over Tempest. She was showing more signs of being a Daughter of Lilith than a daughter of Aegir. I wondered if it was something about being in the mortal realm, or distance from her father. Maybe she was finally finding her true self. Maybe, now that Aegir couldn't drain her, she could develop into the person she was born to be.

Interesting thought for another time.

Wendy stuck the key into the lock on the gate and turned the handle. A click echoed off the cavern walls and a gong sounded from deep within our chosen tunnel as the gate dissolved in front of our hands.

I stepped back, Tempest's and Wendy's wide eyes mirroring my own. The other gates disappeared, the stone wall becoming seamless around us until our only option was to move forward toward the smell of baking sand and an unidentified flower. Whether we were right or wrong in our choice no longer mattered. It was the only way to go.

Chapter 18

We stepped into pitch black. The floor dropped out from beneath my feet. Wendy screamed. I flailed, smacking someone—probably Tempest—in the head. My foot connected with Wendy, who stopped screaming to yelp. We fell into nothingness.

Were we already trapped? Had Apep already won?

Wind rushed past my ears, and I twisted around to face into the pressure. I'd never been skydiving, but I imagined this must be what it felt like.

Wendy's screams died down as we continued to fall. I stretched out my arms to find the other women, hoping we were all falling at about the same speed. Tempest grabbed my hand and squeezed, but I couldn't find Wendy.

"I've got her!" Tempest shouted. I couldn't see her in the lightless space around us, but I was grateful she seemed to understand what I was trying to do.

My heart rate calmed as the initial shock of falling wore off. An odd sense of inevitability cocooned my mind. Either we were going to hit bottom—hard—without seeing it coming, and therefore blink into nothingness or whatever afterlife we were destined for, or we had been swallowed into the endless abyss and would be stuck here for eternity. Either way, we couldn't do anything about it until something changed. It was out of our hands.

The other women seemed to come to the same conclusion as one by one we fell silent and still.

"So . . . this is interesting," Tempest shouted over the wind.

"If by interesting you mean heart-attack inducing, sure," I replied. "Any idea how long it will last?"

"Nope."

"It has to end eventually though, right?" Wendy asked.

"This is the Aether. Anything can be made reality by the elementals," Tempest replied. "The demesnes are designed based on their whims."

"Buuuuttt . . . Lil, you can get us home, right?"

I thought of Silas, alone in his hospital bed.

The heart monitors and machines beep and whir as they keep the shell of Silas's body alive. He looks peaceful, but too still. He's lost the vitality that makes him a great performer. I want to brush the little twist of hair off his forehead. I almost step through the veil to go to him, to sit by his side and hold his hand as I should have done the night he was taken, but the door to his room opens. I freeze, stuck in limbo between Aether and Earth.

Grams enters with a nurse. She carries a clear plastic container filled with what looks like muffins.

"Here, dear," she says, turning toward the nurse in the doorway one step behind her. "These are for you and the other nurses to share. I can imagine how hard it is to stay up all night taking care of your patients. Someone really needs to take care of you, too."

"Why, thank you Mrs. Ayers."

"Call me Grams, dear. Why don't you take those out to the station while I get settled. I promise I won't touch anything. And I

made sure not to make anything with nuts in case anyone has an allergy."

"You're so sweet. I'll be right back."

The nurse turns to leave the room. Grams looks past my shoulder, or where my shoulder would be if I were actually there in the room. Her blind stare is eerie as she cocks her head to the side like a spaniel.

"Lil, my girl, you have to focus on the task before you. Don't get distracted and don't worry. I will make sure Silas's body is cared for." She waves her hand, shooing me away, and back to the blackness. I can hear the wind rushing around my falling body even as I hear her final words. "It's up to you to save him."

I blinked and came back to the Aether where we continued to fall into endless eternity. I could return to Earth at any time. There was nothing holding me here in this unpredictably terrifying realm. Silas couldn't play me home, but I could still cut my way through the veil between worlds.

"Silas is here. I'm not leaving him," I replied. There was no choice, no question. I wasn't going to fail.

"Then we have to find the path," Tempest said.

As if on cue, the space around us began to lighten. The echoing strains of laughter wafted around us. Pressure built in my ears. With a pop and a grunt, we fell to a sudden stop on a clay tile floor.

The laughter cut off abruptly. Silence deafened my ears.

"What the hell?" Wendy demanded, pushing herself up to sitting.

She, at least, had landed on her backside. I was face first on the floor, snorting a puddle of what smelled like red wine, my arms and legs spread akimbo. Tempest had been the most graceful, managing a cross-legged, almost meditative pose.

"Ow." I murmured, dryly, as I turned my head to the opposite side, away from the puddle and Tempest's composed figure. I almost kissed a sandal-clad foot.

I turned further, my gaze traveling up the heavily muscled leg of a perfectly coiffed man wearing nothing but a toga wrapped around his waist and over one shoulder. The man reclined on a cushioned bench, his opposite leg propped up to the side. I was lucky I didn't get an eyeful, but I was quick to turn my gaze up and away. He smirked down at me from a clean-shaven face. The cleft in his chin and bump on the bridge of his nose reminded me of a Roman version of Gaston. Coal-black eyes twinkled with mirth even as thick eyebrows lifted in surprise.

"What do we have here?" The man's cocky smirk could be heard in his voice.

We had landed in the center of a perfectly square room. Couches had been arranged in a wide circle around a pole in the center of the space, each occupied by a man or woman wearing a white toga, splattered with red wine. A few of the women giggled from behind wide ceramic cups, their edges painted with stylized eyes.

I quickly pushed up to standing, dusting myself off only to find it wasn't dust I should be worried about. My pants were wet, my tank top stained with red wine that had obviously been absorbed from the very messy floor.

I curled my lip. I was used to having liquor spilled on me, but this was ridiculous.

"Sorry for the intrusion." Tempest came to my side and gave the man a subtle bow. "We must have made a mistake."

The man leaned back and tilted his head to the side. "You are mortal."

He made it a statement of fact rather than a question. The people around us tittered.

"We're only passing through," I replied, taking in the crowd. They looked on curiously, but without rancor. If anything, we were the evening's entertainment. "If you can just point us to the exit?" I made it a question.

The man's deep chuckle resonated from within an overtly muscled chest. "Exit? Why would you wish to leave my symposium? You and your sisters should stay and join us."

"Thank you for your kind offer, but really, we must continue our journey," Tempest insisted

"And where are you going?"

Tempest glanced in my direction, but I shrugged, not sure what the right move was at the moment. Do we tell him the truth? Prevaricate to deflect our true purpose? Without knowing which of the elementals we were speaking with, and what his relationship with the chaos snake might be, it was hard to know the correct path forward.

"We're looking for my mother," Wendy said, answering before I could come to a decision. "She was taken by the chaos snake."

"Apep? He hasn't had the power to ensnare a Daughter of Lilith in more than a thousand years." More titters from the crowd, which seemed to have grown bigger as we spoke. Each couch now carried at least two or three people, with more standing in the background.

"Perhaps you can just point us in the right direction, then?" I asked. "We don't want to take any more of your time than necessary."

"Time? Time is a construct of the mortal realm. We of the Aether have no need of time. Our pleasures are endless."

It hit me then. "Bacchus? Are you the god of drinking?"

"Got it in one! And many thanks for your offerings." He winked.

I flinched. *Offerings?* I hadn't made any offerings to Bacchus. Or any of the elementals, for that matter. At least, not intentionally.

"Your lovely little bar is a wonderful feeding ground for my bacchae. But now you are here, and we can share a glass." Bacchus waved a hand and servants emerged from the back of the gathered masses carrying jugs and drinking cups. "We've decided to keep this party traditional, in the Roman way."

The scantily clad women wore little more than wisps of gauze tied lightly around their necks and bound with ribbon that twisted beneath their breasts and wrapped around their waists. One of them shoved a wide-mouthed ceramic cup with two handles into my hand, while another followed behind with a pitcher of wine.

Bacchus waved another hand and the room expanded, the couches moving ever so slightly farther away. A new, empty couch appeared behind us. As soon as we were seated and our cups filled, Bacchus lifted his into the air.

"To the Daughters of Lilith, who grace us with their presence. May they find pleasure in our fete and secure our future! Ya mas!" Bacchus shoved his glass higher into the air, splashing the red liquid over the rim and onto the floor.

"Ya mas!" The other patrons around the room mimicked Bacchus. It certainly explained all the puddles.

I glanced at Tempest, lifting my eyebrows. She returned the look with wide eyes but lifted her cup to take a sip. "When in Rome . . ."

I laughed just as I took a sip, and nearly choked. I sputtered and coughed as the wine burned the hair in my nostrils. My eyes watered.

Tempest pounded my back until I lifted a hand to stop the barrage.

"I'm okay," I coughed.

"Is my wine not to your liking?" Bacchus asked. Somehow he managed to sound offended while also laughing at my predicament.

"Sorry," I wheezed. "Just swallowed wrong. The wine is great." A big bold red that sucked the moisture out of my mouth, it was delicious but strong.

"Good. Good! Then you will stay and drink."

Wendy held out her glass. "I'd love a refill, if you don't mind."

Shocked, I gazed at her. Who chugged an entire glass of red wine? How? I mean, beer was one thing, and a shot another, but a full glass of wine? Especially *this* wine?

"Of course, my dear!" Bacchus waved his hand and the servant stepped forward. "We have enough stored in our cellars to fill the abyss, I'm sure." His lips curled in a knowing smile that set my nerves on fire.

"No, we really can't stay," I leaned over Tempest to stop the servant from pouring anything more into Wendy's glass. "She's young and enthusiastic, but—" I shot Wendy a significant look, "—we've lost our friends, *including her mother*, to the snake's appetite, and we have to find them."

Wendy's face fell. "Right. You're right."

Bacchus pushed his lips out and shrugged. "You are free to leave at any time. I can't stop you from returning to Gaia's mortal shores. Of course, your path would then end here."

"Our path?"

"Hecate the Crone started you on the route to the underworld, did she not? You made a wise choice coming to me. You'd have been lost in the Elysian Fields, asleep in the poppies, and the lava fields would have burned your mortal skin alive. We are much more entertaining, here."

I frowned, not understanding his meaning. "How do we reach Apep?"

The chiseled god put both feet on the ground and leaned his elbows on his knees. His face sharpened with a mercenary smile.

"If you wish to save your elder and your lover from the abyss, you must play the game."

Chapter 19

"The game?" I was so thoroughly confused. How did he know about Silas? I hadn't said anything about my trombonist, but somehow word must have spread. I didn't need further complications, but the Aether seemed to have been built as a maze, the gods intent on taking their toll from anyone who sought passage.

"Of course! Isn't everything a game?"

"No. Usually I ask a question and get an answer."

"How blunt and boring you mortals are." Bacchus took another sip of his wine.

"All we need is a path to Apep's demesne. That's it. We'll be out of your hair and our boring lives will be nothing for you to worry about."

Bacchus's eyes narrowed. "Tell you what, I'll make you a wager. I will answer your question if you can knock the plate off of that pole." He nodded his chin toward a contraption I'd hardly noticed in the center of the room.

I gazed at the device, eyes narrowed. Like any good carnival game, there had to be a catch. Was the saucer glued onto the pole? Was there some sort of King Arthur-esque sword of destiny thing going on here?

"Go ahead and take a look. There's no trick," Bacchus encouraged with a smug smile.

Tempest put her hand on my wrist. "It's never good to bargain with the elementals. They always have more information than you do," she warned in a whisper that I was sure everyone was still able to hear.

I nodded, understanding but unable to do much about it. We needed to move on from this place, and Bacchus was the only one we could ask.

I approached the pole and studied the design. It seemed simple enough. A wooden dowel had been set into a hole in the ground. Two-thirds of the way up, or thereabouts, a hammered metal disc wrapped around the pole. I tapped the disc with a fingernail, and it vibrated with sound, like a mini-gong or cymbal. That small touch made the saucer at the top of the pole wobble. I picked the plate up. It wasn't attached anywhere I could see, though this *was* the Aether, so anything might be possible.

I set the plate back on top of the pole. It took a few tries to find the balance point. "I don't get it."

"It's easy. From your seat on the klinē—your couch—you must use the dregs of wine from your cup to knock the plate from the top of the pole. Like so."

Bacchus emptied his cup with one large swig, then stuck his pointer finger through one of the handles attached to the side. Closing one eye, he took aim, spun the cup once around his finger, then flipped the cup over the top of his hand like the lid on a garbage can. I jumped back as a globule of wine launched out of the ceramic and into the air, striking the saucer and knocking it off the pole. The plate hit the metal disc below with a loud clang.

"See? Easy." Bacchus encouraged. "Now, your turn."

It didn't seem that easy to me, but what were my options?

"So if I knock the plate off the top as you did, you'll answer my question?"

"Agreed." Bacchus confirmed.

"And if I don't succeed?"

"Then you are welcome to remain here at our symposium for as long as you like." His grin was toothy and dangerous. It made me uneasy.

"I'll do it!" Wendy exclaimed. She drained her cup, and before Tempest or I could stop her, she was flinging wine across the room. She missed. By a wide margin. She frowned, pushing out her bottom lip. "Dang it."

"Alas, you failed. But please, join us for another drink. The party has just begun!" Bacchus flicked a finger and a quartet of musicians appeared with instruments in hand. They immediately struck up an energetic tune.

"Hold on," I called out. "The deal wasn't with Wendy; it was with me. That attempt wasn't valid."

Bacchus's smile widened. "Then you agree to the terms?"

"Yes. If I can knock the saucer off the pole, you will tell me how to move on from your demesne and find Apep. If not, we will return to the mortal plane."

"No. If you fail, you will share at least one more drink with us. *Then* you can return home if you wish."

I swallowed. I didn't like the phrasing of that. I imagined that, like Aegir, he would use our drinking to take our energy. I would just have to make sure I won. "Deal."

Bacchus clapped his hands. "Excellent."

One of the servant girls approached to refill my cup. I put a hand over the top to stop the pour.

"I'll just finish what I have here," I said.

"Nonsense. You must drink first. It's part of the game."

There's the catch, I thought. It's a *drinking* game. Hardly more refined than beer pong. But Bacchus should have known that as a bartender, my tolerance was through the roof. I wasn't a light-weight like Wendy. I had gone pro years ago.

Still, it was wine, not a shot, and not a beer. I needed to be conscious of the difference. So I sipped my now-full cup and listened to the tinkling music that played in the background.

The toga-wearing crowd had doubled in size, each with their

own cup. I had to laugh as I realized the eyes painted on the sides of the vessels were meant to be masks. As the cup emptied and the drinker tipped it higher and higher, the mug would cover most of their face. Painted tongues stuck out of mouths, eyes crossed, or wide smiles with bared teeth greeted anyone watching.

Tempest stayed quiet at my side, hardly touching her wine. I didn't blame her. Honestly, someone needed to stay sober, and it wasn't going to be Wendy. Her teeth and tongue were already stained red as she sloppily grinned around the room. At least one of us was having fun.

As I drank, another painting appeared at the bottom of my cup. With each sip, a little more was revealed until at last I could make out the scene. It didn't look Roman. If anything, it looked Egyptian. A boat filled with animal-headed people holding spears fought off a giant snake that seemed to be attempting to swallow the entire front end of the vessel. Several spears stuck out of its skin, like they'd been at it for a while.

I swallowed the last of the wine, leaving only a few drops and a bit of sediment in the bottom of the cup. "I'm ready."

The wine was swimming in my gut, but I ignored it. I'd had years of practice keeping my head clear.

Bacchus clapped his hands again and the music stopped. He leaned back on his couch, his left elbow pressed into the pillow at his side. "Go ahead, then," he grinned.

I twisted my head from side to side and rolled my shoulders back, stretching out the muscles that had become kinked from sitting so long. I stuck my finger through one of the handles to prepare for the toss. It didn't feel right. Unbalanced.

"Would you demonstrate, one more time?" I asked.

The crowd scoffed, but Bacchus held up both hands to quiet them. "Of course. You are new here, and this is, after all, your first attempt. There's a great deal on the line." White teeth flashed from between full, red-stained lips. The god took a deep pull from his wine cup. Without pausing to adjust his grip or give me time to see what he was doing, he spun the cup and flipped it over his hand. Another loud clang punctuated the hubbub of the room.

That hadn't been any help at all.

A server came forward to rebalance the saucer.

"Your turn," Bacchus grinned.

"Here goes nothing," I whispered under my breath.

I gave the cup an experimental twirl on my finger, testing the weight and balance. It was awkward, I'm not gonna lie. But the handle was smooth and turned easily, and the weight, though heavy, wasn't overwhelming.

My gaze flipped to the saucer on the pole. I needed to spin the cup hard enough to collect the liquid into one big drop, then fling it with enough force to bridge the distance to the pole, and land on the edge of the saucer.

I closed one eye. Stared at the pole. Opened it and closed the other. Squared my shoulders. Then turned sideways as if I was throwing a dart. Of course, I was still sitting on the couch, so I would have any power coming from my legs or stance. It was all in the arms.

"Get on with it already," a woman called from the crowd.

A few other spectators hushed her, saving me the hassle, but adding to the distraction.

It was now or never. I was going to do it, or I was going to fail. Gathering my courage, I spun the cup and flicked it over my wrist as Bacchus had done.

The globule of wine arced through the air. The crowd gasped. With a splat, the sediment hit the edge of the plate. Barely. The plate wobbled, once, twice. Everyone held their breath. I leaned to once side as if my motion would give the saucer the extra bit of momentum it needed to overbalance. I *willed* the plate to fall.

With a nails-on-a-chalkboard screech, the plate slid off the pole and hit the disc beneath like a gong.

"Yes!" I jumped up in the air. Luckily there was no wine left in my cup, or I would have splashed it all over myself.

Wendy, on the other hand, wasn't that careful. Wobbling to

her feet, she spread her arms wide, tossing wine across the white-toga clad ladies next to her and just barely avoiding dumping it over Tempest's head.

"Nice! Take that, Bacchus. My girl's gots game!" She threw me a sloppy high five.

I rolled my eyes, but Bacchus didn't seem to mind. If anything, he seemed to find it all secretly amusing.

"Nicely done! Congratulations!" He lifted his mug and took another sip. "You've earned yourself a question, so go ahead and ask what you will. I will answer."

Tempest tugged on my shirt. I looked down to where she was still sitting. "Be careful what you ask for," she murmured. "The gods are tricksters at heart."

I nodded. I knew this. Even Hecate had been playing a game. I considered the phrasing. "How do we exit this demesne to find Apep?"

It was as clear and concise as I thought I could make it, but Bacchus grinned as if I had walked face first into a screen door.

"Through the door, obviously." He pointed toward the wall across the room and to our right. The gathered spectators moved to the side, revealing a door I hadn't seen before.

"That wasn't there a minute ago, was it?" I asked Tempest.

She shook her head, her ponytail bouncing from side to side. "Nope. It's new."

I turned to Bacchus, his expression still unchanged. It made me nervous, that smug little smile, like he was just waiting for me to realize my mistake. Something was up. But until I knew what it was, I could play the game and be polite. He was our host, after all.

"Thank you for pointing us in the right direction." I bobbed in an awkward bow-curtsy-thing.

Wendy was already halfway across the room, so Tempest and I hurried to follow. The last thing we needed was to add another person to our search and rescue mission. Silas, Ben, the two girls, and now Brigitte were all depending on us. Sticking together was our only option.

I needn't have worried. As soon as we were close enough to see the door, I realized why Bacchus was so smug.

The door was locked.

Chapter 20

A keyhole couldn't have a personality, but if it did, this one would have been a bouncer at the door of the club rejecting us as not cute enough to get in: big and implacable.

Wendy put a hand on the door and tried to push it open, but I already knew it wouldn't budge. Bacchus wanted more from us.

"What the . . . ?" She asked no one in particular.

While I agreed with her sentiment, I knew better than to get caught up in the argument.

I turned to still-smiling Bacchus, who took a sip and gazed at me with a forced innocence.

"Where's the key?" I asked.

"Ah, yes. A key. You do need one of those to leave."

"So where is it?" I demanded.

"That's an entirely different question. I only promised to answer one."

The crowd around us laughed, all here for the spectacle, all knowing the prank in play. We were the butt of the joke, and Bacchus was going to draw out the entertainment for as long as he could. It was what he did. It was who he was. The god of wine and passionate revelry.

I suddenly remembered one of the stories my mother had read

to me as a child, a story of Bacchus in his youth. To the Greeks, he was a foreign god and had to earn his place in their pantheon. He was first worshipped in rural areas, where wine and viticulture dominated the landscape. But, when his followers brought him to Athens and put up a statue of him, the Athenians turned away. Bacchus grew so angry at this disrespect that he gave the men raging genital infections.

To be fair, she hadn't called it that—I was only ten after all—but the implication of scratching that one particular itch stuck with me.

I had to tread carefully. The god of this demesne would take his vengeance if we crossed him. I knew he had the key. Of course he did. Like Hecate, he had to willingly give us passage across his realm. Meaning, even if we arrived on our own—and no matter where we went next—we had to be granted the path forward by the master of the demesne. Otherwise, our only option was to return to the beginning of the maze: Grams's house.

"Tell you what, my lovely," Bacchus tilted his head and brushed his dark curls behind one ear with an elegant twist of his wrist. "Let's make another wager."

Wendy cackled with glee and clapped her hands as she bounced on her toes. "I want to play!"

"Wonderful!" Bacchus was quick to agree. "Come, come. Sit back down. Kottabos can be such a fun party game. There are so many variations to try. A little messy to be sure, but who doesn't love drinking wine? And I've got the good stuff."

As he spoke, the room around us shifted and expanded again. It was like a Hollywood camera trick, where everything around the character pulls back while he or she stays in place. Like Spiderman when he gets a Peter-tingle. Our empty couch and Bacchus remained stationary, but the other seated spectators slid backward, keeping pace with the walls. An aisle opened between our couch and the crowd, and four more empty couches materialized, one on either side of our couch and one on either side of Bacchus, creating two quarter-circles around the Kottabos pole.

"Here's the game." Bacchus reclined on his arm rest, holding his wine in his stationary left hand while his right gestured around the room. "We'll play on teams, the three of you against me and my two champions."

"That seems less than fair," Tempest interrupted. "I've never played this game, and Lil and Wendy have only attempted it once. Your champions, I'm sure, will be experts."

Bacchus waved his hand from side to side. "Can one truly be an expert at a game that involves intoxication?"

"I mean . . ." I started to argue, but Bacchus interrupted.

"However, to avoid any appearance of cheating, I will select champions who have already consumed several cups of wine. Does that alleviate your concern?"

"Not really," Tempest replied, "but I suppose it will have to be good enough."

"Excellent. Each competitor must remain on their own klinē, reclined like thus, for the entirety of the game." He waved a hand from his head to his toes. "If your elbow leaves the cushion, you lose a point."

That would make the game a lot more difficult, I realized. When I'd hit the target before, I'd been able to shift my body slightly to launch the droplet forward. Without that added momentum, the distance to the saucer seemed insurmountable.

"We will play three rounds. Each player will drink their cup of wine and attempt a throw. Each successful throw, that results in the plate ringing the gong, will earn a point. The team with the most points at the end of three rounds wins."

"What are the stakes?" I asked. This was the true crux of the matter for me. We needed to be sure this game would result in our passage out of here. No more tricks. No more evasion. Time might not matter to the elementals, but I was sure it mattered to Silas. I imagined him stuck in the chaos snake's coils and shuddered. The endless abyss was both hypnotic and terrifying.

Bacchus shifted on his seat. "If you win, I will give you the key and safe passage from my demesne to the next."

"Not to the next," I countered. "Direct to Apep's demesne."

Bacchus rolled his eyes. "That's not how the Aether works, my lovely. You must choose your path through the maze; I cannot choose it for you."

"Why not?" Wendy demanded. "Seems to me you have complete control of this place."

"Of my own demesne, yes. Of the Aether as a whole, no. It is an ever shifting, ever changing place. I cannot guarantee that my demesne will touch Apep's if the time comes for you to move on from here."

I took a deep breath and counted to five. "Fine," I replied after controlling my frustration. "Then *when* we win, you will give us the key and safe passage from here to the most direct path to Apep's realm, whatever that may be at the time of our departure."

"Such confidence," Bacchus hid a laughing smile behind his cup. "I like it." He lowered his cup to rest on his hip. "However, if you don't win, you will join the maenads and serve me in the mortal realm."

My gaze drifted to the gauze-wrapped servers who drifted around the room. Manic grins split their faces beneath wide blood-shot eyes. They drank as much as they poured, and spilled wine with every step.

"A Daughter of Lilith can't be bound against her will."

"True, true. But if you refuse and break our pact, I will send the maenads to your bar. They will infect your customers with hallucinations so vivid, they will tear their own eyes out to end the horror. Your drinks will become sour and repulsive to their tongues. Your bar will become a dark and dangerous place, attracting only the worst of the sons and daughters of Eve."

"You're mad."

"Precisely." Bacchus bared his teeth in a maniacal smile.

I swallowed. Silas needed me. Ben and the Zombie girls needed me. I had no other choice, and he knew it.

"Agreed."

"Then let us begin!" Bacchus lifted his glass. Two of the

servant girls appeared, each carrying a large pitcher of wine. "Vitus! You will be my second. And Felix, you will be my third."

Two men stepped forward. One was dark-haired and heavy-lidded, swaying ever so slightly side to side. He looked like he was about to pass out, a good sign for team Lil. The other man was blond, blue-eyed, and grinning from ear to ear. Apparently, he found our situation entirely too amusing.

"Take your seats everyone."

I took the middle seat on our side of the Kottabos pole, directly opposite Bacchus, with Tempest on my left and Wendy on my right. I leaned over to the side, positioning the oversized and rather stiff—but surprisingly comfortable—cushion beneath my left armpit and putting both feet up on the klinē to my right. Tempest and Wendy followed suit, but Wendy shifted around uncomfortably.

"Um . . . one problem," Wendy said.

"And what might that be, hmm?" Bacchus asked, ever the gracious host.

"I'm left handed."

"Couldn't you have said that a little sooner?" I hissed. Bacchus would be within his rights to enforce the left-arm arrangement since we'd already agreed to the terms.

Luckily, the god of wine was feeling magnanimous. "Not to worry, my lovelies. You may choose your side." He snapped his fingers and the couch flipped positions with Wendy still on it. She rearranged herself and settled.

"Now, if everyone is comfortable and prepared, we will begin. From this point forward, if your elbow leaves your cushion, you lose a point. I, of course, will act as referee on the matter."

"That sounds like a conflict of interest," Tempest argued. "An impartial third party should act as referee."

"My, my. You are taking this seriously."

"I know how you Aethereal elementals work," Tempest replied, non-plussed.

"Very well. Who would you suggest?" Bacchus made a wide gesture across the room.

"Hecate," I replied. I wouldn't trust anyone who was already here. They were under Bacchus's sway, under his control. If nothing else, they would also want to please and appease him.

Bacchus's laugh was loud and long. "Hecate? The guardian of the crossroads? Very well, you may have the witch, if you can call her to your cause."

It was my turn to smile. I knew Hecate, knew she was listening. I carried her blade.

Drawing the knife from my hip bag, I placed my thumb on the Lilith sigil in the handle. I traced the triple moon with my mind's eye. "Hecate, you are invited to Bacchus's demesne. Will you join us and act as referee for our trial?"

Bacchus's eyes twinkled from behind the rim of his wine cup. He didn't think she would come. I knew better.

We waited a breath. Two. She didn't appear.

I tried again. "Please, Hecate. We need your wisdom and guidance."

The hair lifted on my arms. Between one blink and the next, a hooded woman stood before us. I grinned in triumph. She'd come.

"Thank you for the invitation, Daughter of Lilith," Hecate crooned. "I would be thrilled to act as referee for this game of Kottabos. I was once a champion, you know."

"Hecate, you swore never to return."

"I swore never to return unless invited, Bacchus, dear. I was invited, was I not?"

Curiosity captured my attention. Logically, it made sense that the gods would have history. They'd been around for thousands and thousands of years. Particularly these two. But as far as I could recall, I'd never heard any stories that involved both Bacchus and Hecate. So where was this coming from? What was their beef?

The god of wine curled his lip in distaste. "Could you at least wear your maiden form? She is so much more fun."

"You think my maiden form more susceptible to your charms?"

"I simply do not wish to sour my wine with your disfigurement."

Hecate tsked in disapproval. "Your youth is showing."

"I'll take youth over the ravages of time," Bacchus sneered. "If you're planning to stay, stand over there." He dismissively pointed toward the gap between our two teams.

"As you wish," Hecate turned and winked at me from beneath her hood. As far as I could see, her face, though lined with age, was not in any way disfigured. Unless Bacchus was seeing something I couldn't, Hecate looked beautiful as ever. The triple moon goddess took her position as the servers poured our wine.

Bacchus lifted his cup into the air. "It's not a proper party without some music. Strike up the band!"

A stage appeared in the corner of the room. Four musicians climbed up and began to play a rollicking tune with drums, two stringed instruments I couldn't quite identify, and a double clarinet looking thing that sounded more like Irish bagpipes than anything I'd ever heard before. The musicians were fantastic, and the rhythm quickly lifted the energy level of the room. Within moments, the crowd was dancing, and conversations were back to normal levels. I didn't feel quite so much like a fish in a bowl. Or maybe a better analogy would be an underdog boxer facing off against the heavyweight champion in the Caesar's Palace amphitheater.

Yeah. That one.

Hecate's voice carried over the crowd like the bell that would start the round. "You may begin."

Chapter 21

The first cup of wine went down easy. Maybe a little too easy. I tried to pace myself, but Wendy guzzled the drink like it was her first glass of water after walking across the desert. She was twenty-one, and had been sheltered her whole life, but she was going to be drunk as a skunk before we even started the game.

Bacchus chuckled as he watched her over the painted-on eyes of his cup. "I see your friend knows how to have a good time."

I grimaced. I would have to hope her twenty-one year old metabolism and unpolluted liver could keep up with her thirst.

"Done!" She shouted, holding her glass up. "Extra point for finishing my wine first."

"I'm afraid that's not how it works, my lovely. But if you can plink the target, you'll get your point."

Wendy smacked her lips and grinned. "Watch me."

I held my breath. Just like in baseball, going first wasn't preferred. Bacchus now had the home field advantage both in the cheers of the crowd, and also the score. But it was too late to do anything about it.

Wendy hooked her finger through the handle. She closed one eye and stuck the tip of her tongue out of the corner of her mouth as she aimed for the saucer on the pole. She'd already made the attempt once and failed. Now she had another cup of wine in her system and even less coordination.

The cup swung. Flicked over the top of her wrist. A red droplet flew through the air toward the target . . .

And hit Felix.

Red wine splashed across his pure white toga. The dark-haired competitor looked down at his chest and back at Wendy, his half-lidded expression unchanged. Apparently, it was all part of the game.

I, however, groaned at the missed point.

Wendy slumped. "Damn. Thought I had it that time."

"Alas, you did not. And now I believe it is our turn. Felix? Since she tagged you, would you care to respond?" Bacchus asked.

The dark-haired drunkard tipped his cup up to finish the wine within, then, almost without looking, spun the cup and flicked it over his wrist. The saucer clanged against the bronze disc below.

"One to nothing," Hecate murmured. She lifted an eyebrow as she gazed in my direction.

I frowned. What was I supposed to do? Wendy was already three cups in. I couldn't direct her throw any more than I could change the direction of the wind.

Wendy held out her cup for a refill and the servant immediately complied.

"No getting ahead of us, now," I warned the younger woman as she started to take another sip.

She rolled her eyes and ignored me.

Whatever. She wouldn't be able to make another toss until Tempest and I had gone, I was sure. Well, I hoped, anyway. It was supposed to be three rounds after all.

"My turn," I said on that thought. Might as well get this game going. Drawing it out much longer would be futile.

Making sure to keep my left elbow pressed to the cushion, I considered the target. I thought about how I wanted it to fly straight and true. I held my breath and sent my dregs flying across the room. The droplet landed on the edge of the saucer and my shoulders sagged in relief when the sound of the cymbal rang into the air.

"One to one," Hecate announced. Underlying the words, I thought I caught the smallest sound of pride. Maybe I was hearing things.

A smile pulled at the corners of Bacchus's lips. "Vitus."

The blond champion twisted his neck from side to side but kept his elbow on the cushion. He swapped his cup to his left hand and rolled his right shoulder. After another few moments, he swapped it back and took aim. He let the dregs fly. They found their mark.

"Two to one."

I looked to Tempest. She'd finished her cup and dipped her chin. "I guess I'm up."

"You can do it," I encouraged. "Just remember to release it high, so it arcs, rather than straight like a baseball."

Tempest lifted an eyebrow. "Baseball?"

I forgot she hadn't been raised in the U.S. Hadn't been raised in the mortal realm at all, actually. Baseball would be a foreign concept. "Never mind. Just think 'rainbow.'"

She snorted in amusement, but then got serious. She aimed and let loose. The dregs hit the saucer and crashed into the cymbal with a resounding pling.

"Two all."

"Last point for this round," Bacchus teased. "I haven't missed a Kottabos throw in eons."

"Overconfident much?" I snarked back.

Bacchus simply smiled and made his throw, easily knocking the saucer off the pole.

"Three to two, round one goes to Bacchus," Hecate announced as all the cups were refilled.

We had to win the next two rounds, or I'd be doomed to calling Bacchus 'master' for the rest of my miserable drunken life.

"This time your team goes first." I didn't want to be stuck

playing catch up. Then, if they made a mistake, we could capitalize on it.

Bacchus dipped his chin in agreement. "As you wish. But first we must drain our kylix. Ya mas!" He lifted his cup into the air.

I glanced at Tempest, and together we copied his movement. "Ya mas," we repeated, and everyone took a sip.

"What does that mean, anyway?" I asked as I stared into the depths of the red liquid. It was obviously a toast, but I didn't know much about Greek or Roman culture, whatever Bacchus ascribed to in the current moment.

"It is simply 'to our health,'" Bacchus replied. "It is the hospitable thing to say. Like cheers or saluté."

"Or skaal," Tempest chimed in.

"Oh," I said, lamely. "Nice."

Bacchus smiled, indulgently. "We think so."

"And yet your hospitality doesn't seem to extend to the referee of the Kottabos match?" Hecate crossed her arms over her chest. "I certainly wouldn't mind a drink."

I snorted into my cup, then widened my eyes. Apparently, the wine was loosening my control. I had to keep it in check.

Bacchus narrowed his eyes. "Of course, dear Hecate, you would be more than welcome to join in our toast, except I'd hate to see your impartiality diminished along with your inhibitions."

"I hardly think a single glass of wine will in any way affect my impartiality. Or my perception of fair play."

"Very well, if you insist." Bacchus gave another flourish of his hand and one of the maenads skipped her way over with a cup. I couldn't help but notice that the eyes painted on the side of Hecate's kylix were bloodshot and thick-lidded. Age lines fanned out from the corners of each eye.

I glanced at Bacchus, who smirked in enjoyment at his own little joke.

Hecate lifted the cup to examine the design more closely. She lifted her eyebrows and shook her head. "Really? You are such a child."

"So you keep telling me," the god of wine replied.

"'M ready," Felix interrupted before more could be said.

Shocked, I looked at the dark-haired man again. We'd barely received our second cup. How could he have finished already? Even Wendy, who'd gotten her refill before everyone else, still had wine in her hand.

"Excellent. We can begin round two."

Hecate took a sip then gestured toward Felix, giving him the go-ahead. "Whenever you're ready."

Without missing a beat, Felix launched his dregs and nailed the saucer.

"One to nothing," Hecate murmured. I guess being referee required the regular score updates, but honestly, I could have done without the reminder of our underdog status.

"I'll go. I'm gonna make it this time, I shwear." Wendy blurted.

Given how she was slurring, I had my doubts, but we needed to score. *She* needed to score. If she didn't make her point, we were going to be behind again. We *had* to win.

I took a deep breath and held it as Wendy prepared for her toss. She took aim, let the wine fly. It wasn't going to make it. It was going to fall short.

No no no no no, I thought at the descending red splash. I arched my back, lifting up from my shoulders as if I could help the wine fly higher without actually pulling my elbow from the chair. The angle of the arc shifted ever so slightly as the droplet shrank on itself, gathering into a more uniform teardrop shape. *Faster* I urged. *Get there.*

The dregs flew true, glancing off the side of the saucer just enough to make it teeter. With a wobble and a crash, Wendy scored a point.

Eyes wide and mouth shaped into a surprised 'O,' Wendy turned to face me. "I scored." she said. Then repeated with more excitement and less shock, "I scored!"

"One all," Hecate agreed.

"I'm impressed." Bacchus gazed at me with narrow-eyed thought. "I didn't think she had it in her."

"I knew she could do it," I replied, covering the lie with a gulp of wine. I hadn't. Not at all. I thought for sure the droplet would miss and we'd lose. Apparently, she'd thought the same.

"Hmm," was all the response I got, but Bacchus drained his cup. Without any kind of announcement, he flicked his dregs at the saucer and scored.

"Two to one, Bacchus. Well done." Hecate pressed her lips together, the commendation in her words not reflected in her tone.

I held Bacchus's gaze as I drained the last of my wine. "Now it's my turn."

After taking a few deep breaths to calm my heart and center my mind, I let loose. The dregs flew with perfect accuracy.

"Two all."

"Last point, Bacchus. No pressure."

"Vitus has been playing Kottabos since before your grandmother's grandmother's time. This is nothing to him. To us."

"Big words lead to bigger falls," I replied.

Vitus curled a lip, but stayed silent as he spun his cup. The dregs launched through the air. I squeezed my eyes shut, wishing the dregs to fall short but listening for the clang of the cymbal. A breath of air swept past my face, lifting the small hairs that had freed themselves the loose bun on top of my head.

No sound came.

I opened my eyes.

Vitus stared, mouth agape, at the splash of wine that had landed on the floor.

I met Bacchus's frown with a grin. We had a chance. A one point opportunity.

"I missed." Vitus murmured. "I can't remember the last time I missed. Apologies, my lord."

"It's alright, Vitus. They won't be able to make all three points this round. They're merely mortal."

It was my turn to frown. *Merely my ass.* These elementals and their minions might have millennia of experience, but they weren't infallible. They could make mistakes, and they had. Now we had to capitalize on that.

"You've got this, Tempest," I encouraged. "Steady aim."

The blonde demigoddess dipped her chin in acknowledgment, then fired her wine toward the target.

Chapter 22

Clang!

"Yes!" I shouted, remembering at the last second to keep my arm glued to the chair. As much as I wanted to jump up for a victory dance, the game wasn't entirely over. We couldn't afford to lose a point.

"Two to three. The Daughters of Lilith win round two, which ties it up. Next round will decide the Kottabos winner."

The maenads poured our third glass of wine, and my fourth overall, and I was definitely feeling the bubbly warmth of a fun evening out. The party was in full swing now, the band rocking out to some sort of wailing melody while the maenads who weren't serving the game shook strings of small bells and lifted their arms above their heads in sinuous full-body movements.

I didn't want to enjoy the atmosphere, seeing as my future depended on a stupid drinking game, but honestly, the tune was catchy. Maybe I'd suggest using a tambourine or chimes or something in some of Silas's songs. It would certainly set them apart from the other California ska bands.

Silas. What would he even make of this place? I could easily imagine him jumping up on stage to jam with the locals and check out the unique instruments. But the writhing mass of ladies reminded me too much of the altercation in the Trident and the mayhem of his last waking moment.

I felt for the thread that connected us. For a solid three heart-beats I couldn't find it, and nearly panicked at the thought I was already too late, but at last I isolated its gentle song. It was buried deep and weakening, and the sound of the room around me nearly drowned it out. I clenched and unclenched my unencumbered hand.

Apep was the Great Devourer, the serpent who was the beginning and the end of all things. If Grams and Hecate were correct, Silas was now trapped and alone while his essence slowly drained away. His energy, the stuff that made him who he was, would fade into nothing, returned to the void that began all things. Everything he was would be lost. Everything we could have been would be a distant forgotten dream.

How long could he hold out against the serpent's strength? Would I make it to him in time? Would I even be able to free him once I found him?

There would be no light, no joy, without him in my world. I couldn't even comprehend the thought. We hadn't been dating that long, but even before that he was the person I looked forward to seeing the most at the Trident each night. I'd tried to hide it, to suppress my feelings, but I'd loved seeing him on stage, feeling his music energize the crowd and bring people together. He was the best part of my day.

And now he could disappear forever.

I shook my head with a frown and bit my lip, trying to rein in my dark thoughts. The numb tingle surprised me. I'd had three glasses of wine, but over the course of a good long while. I couldn't be all that intoxicated, could I?

I had to get my head on straight and focus. There was too much on the line.

"Lil, it's your team's turn to go first. Who will take your first throw?"

I glanced at Tempest. The other woman was slightly more

sober than the rest of us. Like me, she had spent her life working in a bar—granted it was a Aethereal mead hall and she'd been in charge of the boiler, but even still, she was used to drinking—but she'd also had one less glass of wine.

"I'll go," she offered, "but I need a minute."

"Take your time, of course, my lovelies. I don't want any hard feelings when you lose." Bacchus smirked at us as if he could read the swirling mess of thoughts in my head.

I grimaced in return. Everything felt loose and wiggly as I rested the cup on the arm of my couch. It was the best I could come up with to describe the noodle-sensation in my limbs. Nope, noodle was actually better.

I wished I had some water. Bacchus hadn't offered anything but wine, and I was afraid to ask for fear of losing a point or breaking some unspoken rule of Kottabos.

Startled by the clang of the cymbal, I brought my awareness back to the room around me. I'd been drifting without realizing, and I hadn't even noticed that Tempest was ready to throw.

"One nil, to the Daughters of Lilith," Hecate intoned.

I blew out a breath, relieved, and blinked hard a few times trying to bring myself back to the present. I couldn't be this drunk. I just couldn't. I pursed my lips and then smiled, feeling the movement of my cheeks and tongue. Everything felt relaxed and easy, but I knew intellectually nothing was actually relaxed and easy.

"Vitus, are you ready to redeem yourself?" Bacchus asked.

The champion's blond hair fell in front of one eye as he nodded. He blew the offending locks out of his face before taking aim.

I held my breath. The dregs flew. The cymbal crashed.

"One all," Hecate counted the score.

It was our turn again. Tempest shot me a significant glance, motioning with her eyes toward Wendy. The younger woman was now lying fully on the klinē, her head resting on the crook of her elbow while her wine cup rested on the cushion in front of her chest. She opened and closed one eye at a time, staring at the Kottabos pole. "Who added the second target?"

"Oh my," Bacchus laughed. "I fear you've overindulged."

"Not," Wendy argued.

She couldn't even speak a full sentence. Maybe I wasn't the one putting our team's success at risk after all. We'd need to give Wendy a chance to sober up, at least a little. In typical twenty-one year old fashion, she'd overestimated her drinking capacity and underestimated the strength of the wine.

I would have to be next up. I wasn't ready for it. I still had an almost full kylix of wine, and I wasn't going to rush drinking it. Shooting wine was not my favorite.

I took a small sip and relaxed as much as was possible. Honestly, the klinē was pretty darn comfortable. I could see why the Romans had enjoyed their symposiums so much. Or was that the Greeks?

I frowned and examined Bacchus with critical eyes. "So are you Greek or Roman, anyway?" I asked, then immediately clapped a hand over my mouth. I was probably being terribly rude, but as usual, my blunt tongue got the best of me.

Hecate snorted, nearly spilling her wine. "Yes, Bacchus, tell us. Are you Greek or Roman?"

"I could ask you the same, dearest."

"Bah, I've been around millennia longer than you. I was born on the eve of creation."

I lifted my hand into the air. "I already know Hecate's story. At least a little. But I don't know hardly anything about you, Bacchus. I mean, god of wine, obviously. And parties."

"And the euphoria of unfettered inhibitions." Bacchus smiled and lifted his cup into the air.

"What's that even mean?"

"Madness. He likes to make people crazy," Tempest supplied, helpfully.

"I help the individual free their mind, that is all," Bacchus countered. "I release them from society's pressures so that they can be who they truly are." He took a sip of wine. "Take you, for example. You spent your life hiding your abilities. Now you have them, and still you fear to use them. You suppress your skill to fit in with the common man, while yearning to be recognized for what you are. And now that you've found a sisterhood, you are forced to face, once again, your own insignificance. It's really quite entertaining."

"Thanks for the psychology lesson, but what does that have to do with freeing the mind?" I asked.

Bacchus leaned forward. "Release your power and find out. I can help you."

I squinted my eyes at the androgynous god of wine. "How?"

"Take a sip. Drink it down. Let go of control. Join the maenads in their dance and release your inner self."

I looked to Hecate, but the triple goddess simply lifted an eyebrow and took a sip from her own cup. What did that even mean? Did she agree with Bacchus? Was she collaborating with him? They didn't seem to have the best of relationships, but I didn't know how things worked in the Aether. Maybe the elementals didn't do friendship.

No matter. I couldn't ask in front of everyone, and I couldn't leave my klinē to dig deeper. I was stuck until the game was over. And I had to drink the wine anyway, to keep playing.

I took a sip without breaking eye contact with Bacchus. The god's full red lips pulled back in a wide smile.

The music changed ever so slightly, and the dancers began circling the room, keeping to the outside edge between our klinē and the walls of the space. A woman slid a hand across my shoulder, then twirled away as I turned to confront her. Someone squeezed my toe. I pulled my foot from their grasp.

The room began to grow fuzzy around the edges, or maybe it was my vision.

"It's your turn, Lil. Are you ready?" Bacchus's voice seemed to echo around me. The gowns of the dancers swirled, confusing my brain.

I looked at the bottom of my cup. An image of a naked woman standing proudly with her hands cupped in front of her. A six-pointed star hovered above her palms, the top and bottom rays of the star standing taller than the others.

That hadn't been there before, I was certain of it. It had been an image of the snake eating the boat.

My gaze turned up to question Bacchus, but his champions distracted me. Horns poked out from their curly hair and their feet had turned into cloven hooves. Thick fur covered their legs, which now bent in the wrong direction.

The blond, Vitus, who'd already scored his point, winked at me and smiled, a dimple pressing into the corner of his cheek.

"What the hell?" I asked no one in particular.

Your third eye is opening. Hecate's whispered words weren't spoken aloud but wrapped around me like a blanket. *Accept the gift of Bacchus's making. He thinks to confuse you, to shock you with your own power and bring you into the security of his embrace. Don't fear your individuality. Use it.*

My head turned toward Hecate. The goddess glowed with beauty, her tripled form standing back to back. The Crone faced me and smiled encouragement, like the grandmother I'd never known.

In my peripheral vision, Tempest burned with red fire that didn't touch her skin. My friend met my gaze, her eyes like banked coals, black as night with shifting red centers. I gasped and leaned away, barely remembering to keep my elbow on the cushion. Tempest tilted her head to the side and even with the strangeness of her form, I could see her concern. She had no idea why I was startled. Whatever was happening was only in my mind.

You are a Daughter of Lilith. Shape the Aether to your purpose as your ancestor once did. Hecate continued to speak without speaking.

I lifted the kylix to eye level and examined the cup. The eyes that had been painted on the side were sly. For some reason, it reminded me of my favorite mug, the one that Ezra had given me during my tenure at the institute. *Crazy like a fox.* That was me in a nutshell. It didn't matter if I was seeing things or not, I was going to use the skills I'd been given, even if I was still learning how to use them, to get us out of this unending situation.

I hooked my finger through one handle. Eyed the target on the pole. Swirls of energy wafted like fog between my hand and the pole. Fog not unlike the mist in the Temple of the Crone. Hecate's third and wisest form. The learned owl. The hunter in the night.

The kylix spun around my hand. Once. Twice. I gathered the threads of energy and formed them into a bridge between the dregs and the balancing saucer as I flicked the cup over the top of my hand.

Sure and true, the droplet of wine and sediment flew unerringly to the plate, following the exact path I had envisioned. With a resounding clang, the plate hit the cymbal.

"Two to one," Hecate spoke aloud. For a flash of a second the Crone switched with the Maiden who grinned with youthful exuberance. "Well done, Lil."

With my sight still fully bound in the Aether, I could only dip my chin in acknowledgement. Anything more felt like overstepping, like I would fall off the edge of the earth. Except I wasn't on Earth, I was in Aether, and I could feel the spirits dancing around me.

The maenads in their gauzy dresses. Gazing on them now, I could see the truth of their forms. Skeletal women, their flesh falling off their bones, their eyes darkened pits in their faces. They were not beautiful maidens, but vengeful demons, intent on protecting and serving Bacchus. I saw violence in their dance. Mania in their movements.

Before I could draw my attention back to Bacchus, the saucer had been reset and the god's dark champion made his play. Felix's toss was true, and I had no time to stop it.

"Two all," Hecate said aloud. "It all comes down to the final throw."

"Only if they can wake her without leaving their klinē," Bacchus smirked.

I looked at Wendy and nearly choked on my own tongue. The younger woman was curled on her couch in a fetal position, sound asleep, her body wrapped in a glowing blanket of woven white that seemed to pulse with each breath. Holes had been ripped in the weave, revealing a writhing gray mass of shadows trapped beneath the gauzy cocoon.

"What did you do to her?" My head throbbed and my hand tightened into a fist. I wanted to jump up and slug the supercilious bastard in his dimpled chin, but if I did that, we would lose the game for sure. And then what? I'd be bound as a maenad per our bargain and Silas would be lost to the abyss forever.

"Me?" Bacchus pressed a broad hand to his broader muscled chest. "I have done nothing but act as a gracious host. If she doesn't know how to hold her liquor, that's certainly not my fault."

My eyes narrowed, but I couldn't prove anything. I couldn't do anything from where I was sitting, either. Not unless I could reach her from a distance. But how?

I set my cup in my left hand and lifted my right toward Wendy's slumbering form. Without conscious thought, I rotated my pointer finger clockwise two turns. A loose thread of her blanket unwound from one of the holes near her feet and stretched toward me. I pinched the thread between pointer finger and thumb. The light eagerly wrapped around my fingers like greasy melted mozzarella cheese. My lip curled even as I tugged at the string, pulling the whole blanket askew to expose Wendy's head and shoulders.

Wendy startled awake, sputtering as if water had been dumped on her head. She blinked furiously. "Wha's that?" She asked incoherently as I tugged at the string. The hole in her covering widened, and three of the shadows wriggled their way free, only to flee beneath her couch. It reminded me of something . . .

"It's your turn, my lovely," Bacchus interrupted before I could pursue the thought. "Can you make your throw? Or will you condemn your mother to her fate?"

"'Course I can make my throw. 'S easy peasy."

Without preamble, Wendy let her dregs fly. With a thought for their path, the saucer fell.

"Three to two," Hecate murmured. "It all comes down to the god of wine in his own demesne."

Chapter 23

Unlike the rest of his court, Bacchus remained visibly the same even when viewed through the lens of my Aethereal vision. He retained the full lips and Roman nose of the androgynous youth. His long hair still curled around his shoulders, and his sandal-clad feet maintained all ten toes.

He shaped his demesne according to his own whims, based on his own desires. He chose to appear a beautiful, carefree youth, yet he surrounded himself with the inhuman and reveled in the taboo. He encouraged freedom from convention yet bound his followers into spiraling madness.

His very being was a contradiction that resisted comprehension, and I had to beat him at his own game.

Bacchus pushed his finger through the handle of the kylix. "Last chance," he smirked. "You can still leave now, return to your life in the mortal realm and leave Apep to his abyss. I would not begrudge you the choice."

I lifted an eyebrow. "If you score, it will only be a tie. There will have to be a tie-breaker." I would have to find a way to use that to my advantage.

Bacchus's dimples pressed deeper into his cheeks. "Alas, that's not how the game is played. If you don't win, you lose."

"That was not our deal." I felt my jaw clench as I realized once more how I had been tricked.

"It was precisely our deal. But as I said, I will give you this one opportunity to leave and free you from the binding of our bet."

I swallowed but shook my head. Bacchus was picking at threads, twisting the words of our agreement to his purpose. It was like the old heads or tails trick: Heads I win, tails you lose. Except, I'd also lose if I walked away.

I was glad for the prop of the cushion under my elbow: it hid the tremble in my arms. I felt powerful and yet powerless, filled with both fury and fear. I was a novice, thrown into a game far above my understanding, and yet I was coming to realize that my abilities were uniquely suited to this trial.

I was out of my depth, but I couldn't—I wouldn't—let Bacchus win. He held the key to Apep's demesne and the path to Silas, and I was going to get it. I was not going to remain here any longer than necessary after that.

I kept my gaze focused on Bacchus but propped my hand on my hip in defiance. At least, that's what I wanted him to see. In truth, I wrapped my hand around the grip of the athame in my hip bag. The handle seemed warm, even through the nylon fabric. The knife channeled fire. I knew that from Aegir's Hall. I didn't know if it could do anything else, but luckily, wine was mostly water. Maybe there was an opportunity here.

Bacchus's eyebrow lifted and his lips twitched. He thought he had us. He thought we were binding ourselves to his control. He was wrong. I wouldn't give him, or any of the elementals, any more power than they already had.

With a careless flick of his wrist, Bacchus let the wine fly. My gaze tracked the red drop. I clenched my hand. An orangey-red-colored gust of hot air blasted past my cheek, once more lifting the wispy hair from around my face as it intercepted the wine. With a pop and a fizzle, the droplet evaporated without meeting its destination.

The music stopped. The dancers froze. Bacchus's sly grin shifted into a furious snarl.

Hecate's gleeful voice broke into the momentary shocked silence. "No point. The Daughters of Lilith win with a score of three to two."

"Cheat! You've used your power to disrupt the sacred game of Kottabos."

"No rule was stated regarding the use of Aethereal skill," Hecate interrupted. "And if there were, you would have been first to break that rule. Adding influence to the wine hardly seems fair, either."

"It is my sacred wine, the same wine that all guests and visitors drink," Bacchus deflected.

"And yet, you do not deny that it has been altered to increase your influence. An influence you used to unlock the deeper secrets of the Daughters of Lilith, hoping to siphon their power for your own benefit. Hoping to turn them to the madness that leads to chaos."

"They walk the maze," Bacchus growled as if that were an answer. "They trespass through my demesne to reach the chaos snake and must pass the trials."

"You owe us the key," I interjected. I didn't care if Bacchus had tried to influence us. It wasn't the first time an elemental had tried to use me, and I had to imagine it wouldn't be the last. All these so-called gods seemed obsessed with power and control. The only true question for me was how we could use that to *our* benefit.

In fact, now that I was growing used to the weird glowing vision, it wasn't so bad. It wasn't all that different from seeing the demons hovering over people at the Trident. It was a tool I could use.

Bacchus's eyes narrowed and he tilted his head back thoughtfully. "Tell you what, my lovely. If you manage to make it back to your little drinking establishment, spread the game of Kottabos.

Bring it back to popularity amongst the sons and daughters of Eve, and all will be forgiven."

"You want me to teach people to play Kottabos?"

The god of wine pressed his lips together in a lopsided smile. "Mmm-hmm."

"It's the messiest drinking game I've ever come across. No one is going to want to get splashed with wine and ruin their clothes."

"It didn't bother the Romans. I think you'll find a way."

"And if we don't?" I asked.

Bacchus shrugged, relaxing back onto his klinē once more. "Think of it as a toll. You played my game. You won. But to my mind, you cheated."

Hecate stepped forward and opened her mouth to protest, but Bacchus was quick to lift a hand in peace.

"Therefore, if you wish to appease me and pass to Apep's demesne, you must give a small token to the gate keeper. It's not such an onerous task, is it? You work at a bar. You can surely come up with a way to include my little game."

"Fine," I replied, mirroring his earlier comment, but deciding to make the terms perfectly clear. "I agree to introduce Kottabos as a one-time special event tournament modified to be appropriate for the customers and menu of the Trident. After that, I'm under no further obligation to you or your demesne or any of your minions."

"Deal." Bacchus stood and extended his hand.

As I touched his skin to shake on it, a sizzle of electricity seemed to pass between us.

"And so it is bound."

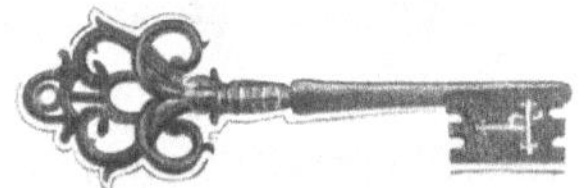

Chapter 24

I carefully stood from my klinē, bracing my feet while Tempest hurried to help Wendy. The apprentice was hardly able to stand upright. I wasn't entirely steady myself, but I made an effort to face Bacchus and bow as much as I dared without losing my balance. My mom had always taught me to be a good sport and a respectful winner.

"Good game, Bacchus." I straightened and dipped my chin toward the champions, each in turn. "Vitus. Felix. Good game. Thank you for teaching me something new."

I held out my hand for the key, but Bacchus just pressed his lips together in a slick smile as he and his champions rose from their reclined positions.

"The honor was mine," Bacchus replied. "Now let's get you on your way."

Bacchus kept one hand pressed into my lower back as he led us toward the gate in the wall. I glanced over my shoulder at Hecate, but the goddess only winked and once more dissolved into thin air.

"Hecate has other places to be, I'm sure," Bacchus murmured into my ear, sending uncomfortable shivers down my neck. "This is *my* demesne, and only *I* can lead you to the next trial on your path to the chaos snake."

"Next trial?"

Bacchus grinned wickedly. "You didn't think this would be easy, did you?"

My nerves ratcheted up another notch and I shot a glance at Tempest, but she was too busy trying to keep Wendy upright to notice. I couldn't even be sure she'd heard.

The satyrs followed close behind my friends, hovering but not touching or helping. Their hooves clacked on the terracotta floor.

I swallowed the sudden lump in my throat as I returned my gaze to the heavy wooden door before us.

Bacchus reached into a hidden fold of his toga and removed a bronze key. With a sly tilt of his head, he watched me as he turned the lock at the center of the forbidding gate. Just as in Hecate's crossroads, the mechanism clicked, and a gong sounded. The sound of the maenads and satyrs behind us faded as the door dematerialized in front of us, revealing a forbidding lightless hole. Air whooshed past my head as the gaping threshold sucked at everything within five feet of the opening. My hands grew sticky with cold sweat as my heart rate sped.

"Enjoy your trip. I do hope you make it home."

Bacchus shoved my back just as I was turning to face him. My mouth gaped open, and I fell backward into the abyss.

I was slightly more prepared for the fall this time, but it was still a shock. I gasped but held back a scream. Just as before, the wind rushed past my ears, but I couldn't see anything in the pitch black of the tunnel or path or whatever it was I fell through.

"Tempest?" I called. I pinwheeled my arms through the air, hoping to connect with someone or something. There was no response.

"Wendy?" Nothing.

I had been pushed in first. Had Bacchus reneged on the deal? Only allowed me to pass, and kept Tempest and Wendy behind? Would they follow? Could they?

The questions swirled through my mind and panic set it. My lungs heaved in my chest. I was alone. Isolated. Abandoned.

I hadn't been clever enough. Bacchus had tricked me, and I'd fallen for it. Literally.

A tear burned across my cheek. I wiped it away. Just the wind stinging my eyes.

I could be trapped here forever, and no one would notice. No one would care.

Apep was the abyss snake, after all. Bacchus had probably shoved me directly into his mouth. I would be lost in this endless black.

A whisper cut through the wind.

You'll never make it.

You're all alone.

I curled into a ball and hugged my knees to my chest. It was true. Without the light, without my sight, I was nothing. I didn't know what I was doing any better now than I had before ever venturing into the Aether.

Look at me. Trapped in an endless abyss.

You need help.

You're sick, just like your mother. She failed, and so will you.

The voices swirled around me, inside me, coating the back of my tongue and wrapping around my heart. I pressed my cheek into my knees.

You're the baggage someone else has to carry. The weight holding them down.

Give up.

Give in.

I couldn't catch a breath. Couldn't think.

You're not normal.

Someone has to look out for you, Lil. You can't look out for your-self, after all.

Those last words had been spoken by my father, years ago. Right before he pawned me off on the institute, where they would "take care of me." Tears coursed down my face, soaking into my knees.

You're a danger to everyone around you. Unskilled. Out of control.

Let go and join the darkness. Find peace in the shadows. You won't hurt anyone here.

It was so tempting to do as the voice said. I had let everyone down. I'd been unable to protect them from the dangers of the demons. I had failed, and Silas had paid the price.

"They're drawn to you, as if they're dying of thirst and you're the only oasis in the desert. You heal them." Silas's voice cut through the fog in my brain. He wasn't here. It was just a memory, but it was a potent one. One that I wanted to remember.

I clung to the thought and pictured the alley where Silas and I had argued. I stared at the memory as if watching it all play out from above.

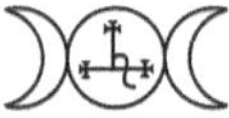

I'd tried to apologize, but instead I'd confessed. "I'm not normal."

"That's a bullshit excuse. There's no such thing as normal." Silas had replied.

"Fine. You want to know the truth? I can see demons. All around us. All the time. Sitting on people's shoulders and hovering over their heads, wrapped around their bodies, and telling them to do things. They whisper of sex and death, betrayal and sacrifice, vanity and pride. When I was twelve, my mom tried to kill me. She was being controlled by one of them and ever since that night, I've been able to see them. My dad thought I was crazy.

Everyone thinks I'm crazy, but I see what I see and I'm not making shit up." I had spilled it all, every crazy detail.

But where I had turned away before, I could watch Silas now. His eyes had softened. His smile had been understanding, but not pitying. He stepped forward, reaching for me. His fingers hovered a few inches from my shoulder as if he wanted to turn me around, but then dropped away.

"I believe you," he'd said.

"I don't know how to be around normal people. I don't know how to have friends. Other than Ezra, I've never had any kind of real relationship, of any kind, since I was twelve years old." I watched myself shrink, my self-loathing evident. I didn't want to be this way, but it was exactly who I was. Right?

"I believe that, too." He'd seen me, even then, even before the chaos. He'd been holding his trombone like a shield in front of his chest, but on those words, it relaxed to his side. He took another step forward. His gaze traced the line of my neck, and his eyes held adoration, acceptance, understanding, and dare I think it, *heat.* He *wanted* me. Wanted to be a part of my life. But I'd pushed him away. Again.

"I'm broken." It was the truth my past self spoke; one that a part of me still believed. I was baggage, dead weight. An outsider who couldn't be a part of normal society. I was too different. Worse, I put him and everyone around me in danger. He would be collateral damage to the demons that haunted my every waking hour. Like Apep. The chaos snake never would have targeted him if it hadn't been for me.

"That, I don't believe." The words were spoken so quietly my hovering astral body almost couldn't hear them, but I remembered. And I saw the truth in his eyes. The truth as he saw it.

"You should." I had still seen myself as my father saw me.

"No. You're strong. Stronger than anyone I've ever met, save Grams. Maybe. You put up walls, keep people out, and yet they gravitate toward you with every breath you take. They're drawn to you, as if they're dying of thirst and you're the only oasis in the desert. You heal them. Give them something they need, even if it's just a smile or a point in the right direction."

"That's the demons. Not me. I just satisfy their desire." It was all I really knew how to do. Appease the demons and they go away. Give them something to satisfy their needs and they would do no harm. I didn't defeat them. I hadn't even really defeated Aegir. The other gods had intervened.

My mother had intervened. Because she *hadn't* been sick. Delusional, sure, but not clinically. She had bound herself to the ocean god to fix what she had broken: our family. She embodied the myth of Rán in a twisted attempt to find love, but in the end it had backfired.

"You *see* people. Do you know how rare that is?" Silas was insistent. The intensity of his gaze bored into mine and I could almost see him willing me to understand, to believe. "Imagine how much more you could do if you let people help you. Let them in."

Silas's free hand came up to my cheek. His eyes were soft, compassionate. I wanted to drown in those eyes, and wished I could feel his touch now, as he brushed a hair behind my past self's ear, his thumb trailing across the skin of my neck.

"I can't. They'll run away."

"I won't." And he hadn't. He chose to love me as I was, as I am, unconditionally.

Chapter 25

Wiping my eyes with the back of my hand, I rubbed away the last vestiges of self-loathing and insecurity to reveal a sudden and profound clarity: I was enough. Imperfect, still learning, but enough. I saw myself differently through Silas's eyes. He didn't need me to change. I didn't need to be anything other than I am. It gave me the strength I needed to break through the insidious voices in my head.

Now I just had to figure out where I was, and what was going on, so that I could use that strength to free him in turn.

Stars blanketed the sky, providing the only light by which I could see. I breathed in the night air. The scent of fresh flowers—not cloying like roses, but light and fresh—wrapped around me. Behind me, water gently lapped at an unseen shore. I pressed my hands into the ground at my sides. Sand. Dry sand. *Warm* sand.

With one final centering breath, I stood and fully examined my surroundings. It seemed I had been dropped near a river, lush with water lilies and fronds of what I could best guess were papyrus. There was no moon tonight, but the birds seemed happy enough calling to the stars.

A rotting wooden boat was docked at a stone causeway that jutted out into the water about a hundred yards up shore.

Tattered sails flapped listlessly in the soft breeze off the water. The stern curved over the deck, but the decorative head had cracked under its own weight, the carved flower splintering at the neck and turning to dust.

Torches held by unmoving animal-headed statues wearing starched kilts burned in regular intervals along an ancient stone causeway that paved the way up the beach. The flickering light sputtered into darkness a few hundred yards offshore.

Soft sobs met my ears. I followed them to find Tempest curled up on the ground, much as I had been, rocking herself back and forth while tears streamed from her eyes. Afraid to touch her for fear of shocking her further, I crouched a few inches away and called her name.

She didn't respond.

I tilted my head to the side. Whatever magical aura vision I'd unlocked in Bacchus's demesne wasn't active now that we were in Apep's demesne. Or what I assumed was Apep's demesne. But it couldn't have just disappeared. It was an ability I had inside me. Right?

I closed my eyes and let my awareness drift inward. There, in the center of my consciousness, a swirling mass of energy curled and twisted on itself. I poked at it with a mental finger. It churned faster, then exploded outward, expanding beyond my internal awareness. I opened my eyes. The world was lit with Aethereal energy. No longer seeing only the physical manifestation of the elemental's desires, I could see the truth underlying the perception.

I turned back to Tempest, who was coated in a thick gray fog that wrapped her like a mummy. The misty threads wound around her body so tightly, I couldn't find the beginning or the end. She shivered, and I could almost feel the fear radiating from her body.

She was going through the exact same transition I had, but did she have someone like Silas to anchor her into her own mind?

Did she have a memory from Ezra to free her from the internal torture?

I didn't know, and I didn't know how to help without hurting her.

When I'd been kept at the institute, I'd had a roommate for a while who was a sleepwalker. We were locked into our rooms at night, so there wasn't any danger of her falling down stairs or into the pool or anything, but she would pace across the room until she ran into something, then turn around and walk back until she ran into something else. She was kind of like a Roomba vacuum, except she didn't clean up along the way.

In any case, the first few times it happened, I'd tried to ignore it. I would roll over and go back to sleep as best I could. It wasn't a big deal, she just wandered around. But each night it seemed to get worse and last longer. She would bang into things and knock them over. Then she started picking things up and throwing them. Books, pens . . . her stuffed plushy dog . . . I got sick of it.

I shook her shoulder and told her to snap out of it. She didn't register my presence at all. So I pinched her. I'm not proud of it. She wasn't the nicest of my string of roommates, but neither was she the meanest. She mostly kept to herself. But it had been several nights in a row, and I couldn't sleep.

So I pinched her. I'll never forget the reaction. Her eyes widened. She saw me for a flash of an instant. Then her eyes rolled back into her head, and she started having a seizure. I pushed the emergency button to call for help, but by the time the floor warden arrived she'd bitten almost all the way through her tongue and had banged her head on the floor so hard I was sure she'd have a concussion.

They rushed her to the hospital. She never came back.

To this day, I don't know what happened to her. I don't even know for sure that it was my fault she'd had the seizure. Maybe she would have had it at some point anyway. But I wasn't going to risk physically waking Tempest now.

Instead, I skootched in closer to her, as close as I could get without touching. Sometimes, the greatest friend is someone who will just sit with you when you're hurting to be present in your pain. I didn't try to hold her. I didn't try to hug her. I knew she'd feel me next to her regardless.

And then I started talking, rambling through whatever stories and memories might draw her out of her personal nightmare, whatever that was.

"The first time I met you, I knew you were going to be good for my brother. Ezra's always needed someone who can keep up with him both mentally and physically. Despite the wheelchair, he's an active guy. Way more active than anyone else I know, that's for sure. You seemed to get him, and that was good. Of course, I wish you hadn't delivered him to our mother as a sacrifice to Aegir, but then, nobody's perfect. You made up for it. And I think he's forgiven you. I know I have. You were doing what you had to do to protect your family, just like I was, just like I would have done."

I paused, examining the threads that still wove around her figure and wiggling myself another inch closer. I hoped she could feel my warmth. Could hear me talking, even if it didn't make a whole lot of sense.

"We're a lot alike, really. Both mama bears when it comes to those we love. It's a small circle of people we trust, but our brothers are our rocks. Our anchors. I know Dion would do anything for you, just like you did for him. Ezra's the same for me. And now Ezra is tied to you which means I'm tied to you, too. It's a small but tight web we weave. Not unlike the threads I see around you now, except instead of tying you in knots, the threads of family and friends reach outward, expanding our experience instead of contracting around us."

I thought back to my mother and her new situation in Aegir's Hall. "My mother made the mistake of binding herself to Aegir, to the Aether, where he could control and use her. His threads were like the strings on a puppet. They force her to move to his whims. I think they were the same for you when you were bound to him and to his purpose. I bet if I could go back there now, I would see threads everywhere, with Aegir at their center, the spider in his web.

"The threads I see around you now are wrapped around you like the linens on a mummy. They keep you isolated, alone. Trapped in your own mind, in your own misery. I'm afraid to touch them or do anything to them because I'm afraid they're growing from your own mind. If I damage them, will I damage you? The mind is strong, but also fragile. I won't risk it.

"Of course, you probably wouldn't see them, even if you were me and I were you. I don't think sight is your skill. I think you're a Daughter of Lilith with the strength of scent. Not unlike Brigitte, really. Grams said she has the sniffer of a bloodhound. After what you did in Hecate's temple, I think you do, too. You sniffed out our destination, even when we had to pass through Bacchus's demesne to get here. That's pretty impressive really."

Tempest let out a groan and her eyelids flickered. She shuddered, her shoulder bumping into mine. The wrappings around her aura shifted and loosened ever so slightly.

"That's it. What do you smell?" I asked. Maybe if she could tune into her power as a Daughter of Lilith, she could break free of Apep's trap, but I needed to keep talking. "The unidentified flower is a lotus, by the way. Either that or papyrus, but the lotus smells stronger to me. Of course, I can't smell as well as you can. But I can see everything. We're sitting on the banks of a river and the sand still feels warm to the touch. I wonder if Apep allows daylight here, or if the sand is warm because he wills it to be warm? I mean, he's a snake, and snakes are cold-blooded, so warm sand might be a draw."

My gaze drifted up the beach. "He's going all in the on the Ancient Egypt motif, by the way. There's a boat that looks like an Egyptian royal barge, and animal-headed statues wearing starched kilts and everything." I peered into the black above the shoreline, looking for any indication of what the causeway led to. I could just barely make out a slightly darker shadow against the night sky.

"I think there's even a pyramid. Maybe, once you wake up, we'll follow the yellow brick road to find Oz. I bet that's where he is. For a guy who was never worshipped, he certainly dialed into a single ancient culture."

I sniffed, trying to pull anything else out of the air that might help Tempest. "Do you smell the river? I can smell a bit of that musty murky green stuff that all rivers seem to accumulate in the shallows where the water runs slower. I bet for you that scent is strong."

Tempest's tears stopped falling. She sniffed, whether to control the snot or smell our surroundings, I couldn't be sure. She wasn't an ugly crier, but everyone got a runny nose. Right?

The gauzy Aethereal wrappings unwound a bit more, the frayed ends drifting and blowing away from her body. I decided to keep trying the scent angle to draw her out.

"Can you smell the smoke coming off the torches running alongside the causeway? Is there any incense wafting out of the pyramid? I haven't seen any people; no worshippers or souls of the dead like in Bacchus and Aegir's demesnes. I have to imagine that back in the day, in the real Ancient Egypt, the B.O. must have been overwhelming. No deodorant, just perfumes and incense. Did Apep include that on his demesne wish list?"

Tempest inhaled deeply through her nose. The last of the threads wrapping her figure loosened and drifted away on the wind, like steam blowing off a hot cup of coffee on a cold day. Her shoulders relaxed and she blinked a few times, finally turning her head to look at me.

I grinned. "There you are. I knew you'd make it."

"What happened? Where are we?"

"I do believe we are in Apep's demesne. Bacchus kept his word."

"Where's Wendy?"

I frowned and shook my head. "I haven't seen her. I found you shortly after I woke up, and I haven't had a chance to look for her yet. But if her experience was anything like ours, we should try to find her quickly. Apep's trap is in the mind, and she was already pretty far gone thanks to Bacchus's wine."

My gaze drifted up to the shadow that blocked out the stars. "If Apep is here, he'll be in there." I pointed up the causeway. A heavy weight settled deep inside my gut as I stared into the pitch black void at the end of the road. "That's where we have to go."

Chapter 26

Tempest leaned on my shoulder as we trudged through the sand to the stone causeway. I didn't think she was physically hurt in any way, but the mental strain seemed to be wearing on her. Her aura had dimmed from the fiery red in Bacchus's demesne to an ashy gray punctuated only sporadically with the embers of her flame.

She was tired. Depleted. Apep's test had weakened her, but still she strode on, as determined as I was to see this through.

"This is madness," Tempest grumbled. "We're being herded to our deaths like livestock to the slaughter."

Then again, maybe she wasn't as on board as I thought.

"I'm not leaving Silas."

"Of course not," Tempest snapped. She pushed upright to walk without support, then almost immediately slumped at the shoulders. "I wouldn't expect you to. I just . . . I miss Ezra. We barely won that Kottabos game. If we'd lost, we would have been trapped in Bacchus's service."

"The bet was only for me," I interrupted.

"Are you kidding? You think he would have been satisfied with you alone, when we were all playing the game? He would have found a way to twist us all to his purpose, just like Aegir tried to do, just as they *all* do. If Bacchus hadn't missed, I might never have seen Ezra again."

"About that," I paused. There was no reason to hide from Tempest, not anymore, but it still felt odd to admit to any ability that wasn't totally 'human' in nature. "Bacchus wasn't wrong. I *did* cheat. Somehow, I influenced some of the throws in our favor."

Tempest's eyebrows lifted almost into her hairline. "You manipulated the Aether?"

I slowly lifted my shoulders and squinted a hesitant smile. "Yes? Something happened during the game. I could see the threads of energy around us, and I used that to make sure we scored and to stop Bacchus."

"Holy mother of creation," Tempest murmured. She chewed on the corner of her lip. "I didn't know that was possible."

"Me, either."

"No wonder the gods are lusting after you."

"Lusting hardly seems a fair term."

Tempest snorted derisively. "Look, if they're sending hordes of minions after you, they want you *bad*. It takes a lot of energy to create spirits that can cross the veil, and even more to open the path to Earth. Having you on their team would set any one of them miles above the rest."

She stopped walking to face me, taking both of my hands in her own. Her aura had grown stronger in the last minute or two, the embers igniting a low burning flame that brightened the space around her body. Her eyes, blue in the regular light of earth, had darkened to near black that pierced my soul with an eerie intensity. I couldn't look away.

"Apep is stronger than Bacchus already, which makes him a dangerous foe. If he knows what you are, what you can do . . . well, this could have all been designed for the very purpose to trap you to his cause."

"I have to do this," I whispered. I knew she was right, but I couldn't change course now. I could feel Silas's song in my heart. I checked the thread that bound us. It led unerringly toward the pyramid. He was in there somewhere, and the others, too. I couldn't leave them to be collateral damage in whatever game the elementals were playing.

"I know." Tempest squeezed my hands. She opened her mouth to say more, but a shout from the riverbank interrupted whatever she was about to say.

"Lil! Tempest!" Wendy waved at us frantically as she jogged down the causeway to meet us. "There you are! I've been looking everywhere for you."

Tempest let go as we turned to cross the last few steps up the slope to the causeway on sliding sand. Wendy met us at the edge of the rough paved stone.

"Are you okay?" I asked. "What happened?"

"'M fine," Wendy answered.

I examined her with a critical eye, slightly surprised the sheltered twenty-something had been able to break free of the mental prison Tempest and I had suffered.

With the Bacchus-granted sight still in full force, I finally saw what I hadn't been able to understand before. Wendy wasn't wrapped in a blanket so much as cocooned in some kind of softly glowing armor that shifted with her every movement, but just a fraction of a heartbeat too late. I had connected with that shell in Bacchus's demesne, using it to wake the sleeping girl. But beneath it, visible between rents in the glowing fabric, lay a pulsing edge of darkness.

It almost looked like she carried two auras, an inner one built of shadow and the outer built of light. Was that even possible?

"I remember going through the door and falling," she continued while I mentally debated. "Then there were some really terrible dreams. And then I woke up on the boat."

"You were on the boat?" I glanced over my shoulder at the dilapidated structure. It looked ready to sink, like if you put one toe against the deck it would crumble to bits.

Wendy nodded. "I looked for you, but you weren't there. So

then I thought maybe you were already in the temple and headed that direction, but I spotted you before I went inside. Where'd you go?"

"Temple?"

"Dusty old place at the end of the road." She waved a hand toward the shadow that blocked out the stars, her gaze intensely focused on my face. "Where were you?"

I tore my gaze away to watch my feet on the uneven stone as we hiked the path toward the pyramid, explaining what had happened along the way. The torches held by the twenty-foot tall Egyptian statues lit the road but seemed to do more harm than good. Their flickering light made the shadows dance and the gaps and ridges in the pavers harder to see. I stubbed my toe on an edge and nearly fell on my face.

"I think Silas and your mom and the others who Apep has stolen are in there." I nodded toward the pyramid as I concluded my story. "It's the only thing that makes sense. I'm sure we're in Apep's demesne, now."

"You're right," Wendy replied, a touch too cheerfully. I glanced at her from the corner of my eye, but the younger woman was marching with her head down, watching her feet as much as I was. "I mean, about this being Apep's demesne. There's a giant snake carved into the door of the temple."

"You keep calling it a temple, but Apep was never worshipped. That's what Hecate said, anyway."

"It's a mistake to believe her. She's as devious as any of them."

Wendy sounded so certain of herself, but I chalked it up to a lifetime spent under her mother's tutelage, learning to fear the elementals and their powers.

"Maybe," I replied noncommittally, "but all the same, I'm not so sure it's a temple as much as it is a tomb."

Wendy shrugged. "Temple. Tomb. Tomato, tomahto. I'm sure my mom is in there, and I bet your boyfriend is, too. Let's go find them."

I glanced again at Tempest, who was once more leaning on my

arm. Wendy supported her on the other side, but even with our help her aura was dimming with each step.

I paused our trek and swallowed. I didn't want to make the offer. I didn't want to be stuck here with just Wendy, but I couldn't keep Tempest here any longer. She was too tired, and this really wasn't her problem.

"Tempest, maybe you should go home. You're drained. I can see it. Grams always says time works funny here, and it's dangerous not to rest. You should go back. Wendy and I have to continue on, have to find Silas and Brigitte, but you aren't obligated to be here."

"I'm not leaving you, so you can quit that line of thought right now." Tempest straightened to walk fully on her own once more and the flame of her aura momentarily brightened. "I might be tired, but I'm not done yet. I can do anything you can do better."

I grinned at the reference to my inside joke with Ezra. "And you can even reach the top shelf," I teased.

"He can, too. He has that grabber thingy," I could hear the fondness in her voice, even if I couldn't see the smile on her face.

"But he's waiting for you at home. You don't need to face the void."

"We need the triple form," Wendy protested.

I furrowed my eyebrows and snorted with incredulous amusement. "I thought we shouldn't believe Hecate?"

Wendy shrugged without looking my direction.

"It doesn't matter, anyway. I'm not going anywhere," Tempest insisted. "Ezra would never forgive me if I left you here alone. He's worried. He said he could feel it, almost like a change in temperature or weather pressure. He told me before we even got to the Trident last night . . . or whenever that was . . . that you needed help and he asked me to go with you, wherever it was you were going to go."

"So he can see the future now?" I asked, keeping my voice

light even as I chewed on my cheek with worry. The Aether had changed him.

Tempest was quick to shake her head. "He's a son of Lilith. I know that on the Earthly side of the Between, you all like to think it's only the Daughters that have power, but the sons are strong, too. They can't cross through the veil between worlds without help like you do, but neither can I. And I know Dion has always been able to connect with the energy of the Aether. It was why he was Aegir's favored host. The other sons had power, too."

"You seem to be growing stronger away from Aegir's Hall," I said after a few moments contemplation. I glanced at Tempest from the corner of my eye. Her aura was still dim, but she wasn't fading now that she stood on her own two feet. "Maybe more in tune with your own heritage?"

Tempest's lips twisted into a troubled frown. "I don't know. I've never been away from Aegir's Hall for this long but being on Earth feels different. It's changing me." Her voice softened and threads of anxiety laced her words.

"I think we're all changing." I rested my hand on Tempest's back, offering what comfort I could. "All the time."

"I can smell *everything,*" she whispered.

"You're a Daughter of fire," Wendy interjected. "Like my mom."

Tempest's nose wrinkled but she started walking up the path again, leading the way as Wendy and I followed a step behind. "I'll have to ask how she controls it. There are a lot of unpleasant smells, let me tell you."

I laughed. "You've obviously been introduced to Ezra's post-workout gym bag."

"You have no idea."

"I knew him when he was a nasty teenager without a girl coming to visit. I know *exactly* what you're talking about."

Tempest chuckled and the atmosphere lightened a little. I was glad for that. We were walking into the abyss andwe'd need as much light as we could muster.

We paused at the end of the causeway, in the last circle of flickering light before the hundred yard dash to the front of the building. We stood and stared.

Unlike Hecate's maiden temple with its white marble columns and pastures of green, there was nothing inviting about this place. Everything about it screamed "run away," and yet my feet were rooted in place.

My gaze traveled the distance from the edge of the torchlight to the wall and I shuddered. The ground seemed to be writhing with shadows. As I watched, a wave of darkness crested across the stone, eroding the light as it broke against its shores.

"Do you see that?" I asked.

Tempest jerked her chin down in a nod. "Apep is the Great Devourer. The abyss snake."

"God of chaos and destruction," Wendy murmured.

I snuck a glance at the younger woman out of the corner of my eye, the reverence in her tone setting me on edge. I didn't quite know how to respond, so I tried to make a joke of it. "I didn't realize he was a black hole."

I chuckled, but it sounded hollow even to my own ears. When Tempest didn't respond, my nerves ratcheted up yet another notch. "He's not a black hole, right?"

"This is the Aether. Physics don't apply," Tempest replied.

"I saw him at Aegir's feast. He was a snake. A big red snake with hypnotizing eyes. He was not a black hole." But I had stared into the abyss that resided in his gullet, and even I knew my words were false.

After a moment's pause without a reply, I drew my own conclusions. "We're going to be eaten."

I couldn't tear my eyes away from the writhing darkness that washed against the imposing edifice in waves.

"It's a distinct possibility."

"It's just an illusion," Wendy contradicted. "Like everything in the Aether, it's not real."

"How did your mother get captured, then?" I asked. The little know-it-all didn't know everything.

"You broke the circle. It's your fault. None of this would have happened if you hadn't drawn Apep's gaze. Now you need to fix it."

My eyebrows lifted. "I need to fix it? *I* do? You're in this, too, you know."

"I wouldn't be here if you had done what you were supposed to do."

"And what might that be?" I demanded.

"Quit it, you two." Tempest snapped. "You're worse than all my sisters combined. The stark truth is that we can't let Apep grow more powerful. We have to find Silas and Brigitte and stop him now, while we can."

"Right."

"Which means we have to go in there," she continued.

"Right." I gazed into the darkness, measuring the inky, undulating distance from the torchlight to the tomb entrance with my eyes.

This was gonna suck.

Chapter 27

"Stupid Egyptian statue," I grumbled. I did not want to walk into the light-eating mass of shadow serpents without something to push them back, but the torch did not want to leave its holder.

The male statue had to be twenty feet tall and had been positioned with its feet spread, one in front of the other. Its head was shaped like a lion, its snout carved into a vicious snarl. It held the torch in one hand, its gaze trained on the pyramid entrance. Like a big cat on a tree branch, I was lying flat on my stomach, stretched out across the man's arm, trying to reach the burning stick without lighting my hand on fire.

Tempest gazed up at me from the ground, her arms crossed over her chest.

"The torch isn't going to help," Wendy protested. "They're eating the light. We just need to go already."

"I'd rather they ate the torchlight than our energy. It'll give us a bubble of protection to walk through."

"I'm not sure it works like that," Wendy sniped.

"How would you know?" I pushed another inch down the statue's arm. "Just a little farther," I whispered, ignoring Wendy's continued complaints.

At last, my fingers reached the post. I gripped the metal, but the torch wouldn't budge. I jiggled it from side to side. Dust rained down on Tempest's head. She sneezed.

"Hey!" She complained at the same time I said, "Bless you."

"Bless me for what?"

"The sneeze. It's polite or something. My aunt always made me say it."

"It's weird. I'm not blessed. You got dust up my nose."

"Sorry." I jiggled the torch some more, sending more sand and dirt drifting to the ground. I guess I wasn't that sorry after all. I wanted the damn torch.

Tempest glared, but moved out of the way as I finally wiggled the torch free from the stone hand. It was a lot heavier than it looked.

"Here," I said through gritted teeth as I tried not to fall off the statue. "Take it."

Tempest reached up as I reached down, and we somehow managed to avoid burning anything.

"I think this is stupid," Wendy stood with her hip cocked to the side and her arms crossed over her chest, refusing to help.

"Think what you like. I'm not going in there without light." How Wendy thought she'd be able to navigate her way through the temple without a torch, I didn't know, but I didn't care. She was being contrarian just to be contrary. Without a light, we would be fully at the mercy of the abyss snake.

I held the torch in front of me and headed toward the temple one slow step at a time.

"Here goes nothing," I muttered, watching the shadows carefully as they danced around the edges of the light.

They were clearly non-sentient but drawn to the light or the energy or something. Like moths to a bug zapper, they crowded around our little circle of illumination, pushing against the edges, then pulling away, only to return moments later.

"Stay close," I urged, but Tempest was already hovering as close as she could to my shoulder without actually touching me,

Wendy on the other side. We were like children huddled under a single umbrella.

The farther we got from the boat and the river, the darker our surroundings became. Even the stars seemed to shrink in on themselves, their light becoming weak and feeble. About ten yards down the wide avenue, we passed another set of statues, but their torches were dark and cold.

I frowned. "Why aren't they lit?"

Tempest inched closer. "Maybe we should light them?"

I glanced back toward the river and the statues that guarded the causeway. Their light was strong, stronger than the flickering torch in my hand.

"We can try." I wasn't convinced the torches would light, but maybe we could build our own yellow brick road.

I held my torch up to the dark brazier above my head, then squealed and jumped back as shadows scattered like cockroaches when the brazier took the flame. They had covered the torch, unseen in the dark but smothering the glow. Despite Wendy's bravado, she and Tempest stayed within the new circle of light as I made my way to the opposing statue. It felt like I was walking through mud, the shadows pressing back against the circle of my torch. I didn't know if they were trying to prevent me from growing the light, or if they were eager to eat its energy, but sweat was running down my temples by the time I lit the new flame.

Breathing heavy, I returned to the other women. Already the flame over their heads was being squeezed by the shadow snakes.

"I don't know if we're helping or hurting our progress," I murmured as I looked toward the temple, still at least fifty yards away. I could see at least one more set of statues between here and the entrance, but the darkness beyond that was absolutely impenetrable.

"I told you the torch wouldn't work," Wendy griped. I ignored her.

"You think they're feeding on the light? Growing stronger from it?" Tempest asked.

"Maybe. They're definitely affecting it, swallowing it up. I don't think the torches were left unlit. I think they were put out. The shadows are moving toward the water."

"Apep is expanding his influence." Tempest's gaze was trained on the temple in front of us. "Breaking free of his restraints."

I blew out a breath, bracing myself for whatever might come our way. "Let's hurry." I felt the need for urgency in my bones. Whatever was happening in there, we needed to end it, fast.

Our bubble of light tightened around us as we stepped back out into the dark. The closer we got to the temple, the faster the shadows absorbed the light and the harder it was to walk forward. Our torch flickered as if we were walking into a gale force wind. Heads down, we pushed on, keeping the flame in front of us like a shield.

"Bad idea. This was a bad idea." Tempest moaned.

We lit the next two torches as we passed, hoping that the expansion of the light would push back, or at least slow down the advancement of the dark. It didn't seem to make a difference for our progress, however. The closer we got to the temple, the slower we moved.

The yawning black gate loomed large. The stars winked out overhead. We approached the final statue, standing at the steps to the pyramid entrance. This figure didn't hold a torch. Instead, the half-man creature held some sort of two-pronged copper spear above his head as if ready to throw.

Unlike the other statues we'd passed, this one didn't face the causeway. His gaze was trained on the pitch black that yawned wide between two stone columns. Tall squared-off ears pricked up in interest like a dog on the hunt, while his long curved snout pointed toward the ground, following the path of his gaze. He was a warrior, ready to fend off whatever emerged from the temple.

I shuddered at the thought of what such a creature would need to defend against. And we were going in there.

Chapter 28

A low moan howled out from the endless dark of the temple's entrance.

"Was that the wind? Please tell me that was the wind," Tempest whispered.

"It was the wind," I lied. I had no idea what it was, but it didn't sound natural. Then again, nothing in the Aether was natural. "Let's go."

Tempest gripped my arm. "If we go in there, I'm not sure we'll come out."

"We're Daughters of Lilith," Wendy snapped, as if that answered everything. It didn't. But she wasn't entirely wrong.

"If it's too dangerous, if we're too late, I'll cut our path home." I was reassuring myself as much as Tempest, but it was a lie. I wasn't going to leave Silas in the void. I wasn't going to allow Apep to grow any stronger than he'd already become. The snake could not be given free rein to roam the shadows of Earth.

"I don't like this."

"Neither do I. Let's go." I swallowed the last of my fear and put my foot on the first stair. The moan grew louder. I ignored it.

"I am a Daughter of Lilith. No one can stop me. I am a

Daughter of Lilith." I whispered the words quietly to myself. Mantras were normal, right?

I took another step.

"I am a Daughter of Lilith. The gods have no power over me. I am a Daughter of Lilith."

The torch in my hand flickered and dimmed, its light suppressed by the shadows weighing on its power.

"I am a Daughter of Lilith," I repeated the mantra. "I have no fear of the dark or the wilds. I am a Daughter of Lilith."

I gripped Tempest's hand, urging her to find her strength. We reached the entrance to the temple, and I peered inside.

"I am a Daughter of Lilith. I will not be tamed. I am a Daughter of Lilith."

I stepped inside the temple, dragging Tempest and Wendy behind me. "Do you smell that?" she whispered.

I shook my head, though I wasn't sure she could see the movement.

"It's like the smell of rotting coffee filters and dried fish. Something is here with us."

"You're paranoid," Wendy replied. "I don't smell anything."

I still couldn't see much of anything past the immediate torch light, and even that was getting smaller and smaller with each passing moment.

"I am a Daughter of Lilith. The creatures of the night know me and protect me. I am a Daughter of Lilith."

The creatures of the night. Like the owl perched on the statue of the Crone. Owls could see in the dark. Grams always said I had eagle eyes, but now I wished I could see like an owl.

Heat warmed my back, and I remembered the athame in my hip bag. I wasn't alone. Not physically, and not spiritually.

"Hold this." I gave the torch over to Tempest so I could unzip my little carryall. The knife was blazing hot and the triple moon with Lilith's sigil glowed in the dark. I pressed my thumb to the image. "Give me the sight of the owl."

Nothing happened. I wasn't sure why I thought that would work, but weirder wishes had come true in the Aether.

I took another step forward. My foot hit resistance, something firm, yet moveable, that sounded like crackling paper.

"What is that?" I asked. I crouched down and poked it with my knife, then promptly gagged on the scent of stale urine and desiccated meat.

Tempest bent next to me, revealing the object in the dimming torchlight. "That's where the scent is coming from."

"You were being too kind when you described it," I replied, trying my damnedest not to breathe.

Despite her dismissal of Tempest's sense of smell, Wendy was the smart one and stayed back, her arms crossed over her chest as she scanned the room around us.

Annoyed, I ignored her and poked the thing again with my knife but held my nose this time.

The object was translucent white, but wide enough to be a blanket. The long end disappeared into the dark, deeper into the temple. There was a pattern to it. Almost a weave. My mind had trouble making sense of what I was seeing.

And then I saw it.

Scales.

Apep had shed his skin. It was massive, bigger even than I remembered from Aegir's Hall. The chaos snake had grown. And if he'd grown physically larger, he must also have grown more powerful.

As if on that thought, the torchlight shrank even tighter around us, barely illuminating our feet.

"The light's almost gone," Tempest choked. Even she couldn't take the smell. Or maybe she was afraid of the dark. Either way, we needed to move.

The sound of sand sliding across stone reverberated around us. I looked back over my shoulder toward the entrance to the temple. Blank stone wall greeted us. We were trapped.

Tempest's hand trembled, the torchlight jiggling in response.

"Welcome, Daughterssss of Lilith." The voice was deeply sibilant, the echoes making it impossible to tell where it was coming from. "Welcome to my demesne. I've been waiting for you."

My hand clenched around the handle of the athame, the warm wood somehow comforting. I wasn't alone. I just had to keep repeating that to myself until I believed it.

I gripped Tempest's elbow and together we stood from our crouch. Her whole body trembled, but she stayed with me when I took a step to follow the dead shed skin. I felt Wendy move up behind us, her body warmth close, but not touching.

"Yesss, please come inside."

Ghostly columns appeared out of the darkness as we crept forward, following the snakeskin as it wound its way through the pillars. Flaky scales, some as big as my palm, wafted in the breeze of our passing. It was as if Apep had rubbed against the stone to relieve the itch.

"I have a good lotion recommendation, if you need it," I said, trying to lighten the mood. Anything to push back the fear.

"Lil," Tempest hissed in reprimand. I ignored her.

"Or maybe a dandruff shampoo is more appropriate? Anything to keep the itching and flaking away, am I right?"

A hiss was my only response. I still couldn't tell where it was coming from. Our only clue to Apep's whereabouts was the skin itself.

The torch extinguished in Tempest's hand. Smoke wafted around us, blessedly concealing the smell of Apep's discarded hide, if only for a moment.

Tempest's trembling grew stronger. She dropped the useless torch and wrapped her hands around my arm. "I can't see anything!"

I swapped the athame into my left hand and held it at arm's length, as if to ward off the unseen forces of the night. A slithering sound came from the right, and I spun to meet it. A low hiss passed behind my back and Tempest flinched.

"Follow your nose," I whispered. "Like you did in the tunnels."

Tempest sniffed and pushed me forward gently. "That way," she whispered.

Wendy put her hand on my opposite shoulder and squeezed. "No, this way," she said, pulling me to the left.

Meanwhile, Bacchus's gifted sight grew brighter as the endless dark persisted. Tempest burned with the embers of a banked fire while Wendy's cocoon armor shone like a glow-in-the-dark star—visible only if you didn't look at it directly. The snakeskin, on the other hand, shimmered with a soft, sickly green, barely visible even to my enhanced vision. It was just enough to lead the way.

"Thissss way, ladiesssss," the snake hissed.

The sibilant voice drew me forward. I held the athame in front of me, pointed outward, while I felt for any obstacles with my feet. For several steps there was nothing but air on the left and the crinkly soft snakeskin on the right, then my hand brushed against what felt like a flat wall.

"Yesssss," the snake hissed. "Come."

My hand found the edge of the wall, a corner. I pressed forward, keeping my hand to the stone for direction. Tempest switched sides, trying to get away from the stink of the snake while keeping one hand on my shoulder. It didn't work. The tunnel was barely wide enough to fit. I was able to touch both walls and the ceiling, and I couldn't help but brush against the foul scales.

Struggling not to gag and forced to walk in single file, we entered the narrow space. The angle of the floor changed, and we descended down into the depths of the pyramid.

"Where are we going?" Tempest whispered. "What is this place?"

"The inner sanctum," Wendy replied from her position at the back of our little procession. "This is the source of the chaos, the center of the void. We're entering the abyss."

"That can't be right," I replied. "The abyss is within the snake." I'd seen it. I'd experienced the terror of the void.

"This is Apep's demesne. Everything is him and he is everything," Tempest murmured. "We're at his mercy."

# Chapter 29

An eternity later, the wall ended, and my hand thrust out into open air. The blackness around us was absolute. I stopped moving as I groped around for something solid to connect with, some indication of the boundaries of the room, but there was nothing in front of me, and nothing to either side. Only the wall of the tunnel behind me. I couldn't reach the ceiling anymore, either, so the space opened up overhead at least beyond my fingertips.

Tempest gripped my shoulder, the subtle trembling of her fingers belying the mental weight that pressed down on our heads. I could feel the snakeskin curving away to the right, but I stopped, unwilling to move forward into the unknown cavern.

"Welcome to my fortress." The snake's voice sounded like it was inches from my nose, and I jerked back, my head smacking into Tempest behind me, who grunted in surprise and pain.

"Ow," she whispered, her voice sounding nasal.

"Sorry," I whispered back.

"Keep walking!" Wendy commanded. Tempest lurched into my back, forcing me another two steps forward. Wendy must have pushed her.

I rolled my eyes, not that anyone could see, and took two careful, hesitant steps into the room. Something brushed against my legs. I squealed and shook my leg, but Tempest was still behind me. A shuffle and a shove later, I was pretty sure all three of us were in the cavern. I pointed the athame in front of my face, waving it back and forth in case something else approached that I couldn't see.

Fingers snapped behind me. Flames burst to life in braziers all around us, the shadows that had been absorbing their light and energy peeling back from their feast.

I gasped. Apep's snout was no more than a foot in front of my nose. His tongue flicked out and nearly licked my cheek. I swung the athame toward him. He recoiled and I missed by a wide margin. The abyss snake grinned and rose up loom over us, the top of his wide head at least twenty feet in the air.

"Welcome to the absyssss."

Time slowed.

Apep's mouth opened impossibly wide. His jaw unhinged. Fangs glistened in the flickering light of the braziers.

A shove from behind. I whirled, stunned. Wendy grinned, her eyes gone black as the shadows around us.

Tempest screamed as she turned her eyes up to the snake.

All thought stopped. I closed my eyes. Looked for Ezra. Listened for the sounds around Grams's cabin. I braced. Lifted both hands. I pressed my right palm to Tempest's shoulder and shoved her sideways, out of the way of the snake and Wendy both. At the same time, I used the athame in my left hand to cut the path through the Between behind her.

Still screaming, Tempest's body lurched. Her arms windmilled, as if she'd been pushed off the side of a building. Eyes wide, she cried out, but it was too late. She was safely back in the mortal realm.

I had a split second to see Wendy snarl as Apep's fangs snapped down around me.

Chapter 30

If I'd thought the darkness of the temple had been absolute, I had been wrong. The abyss was the absence of all things. No sight. No sound. No taste. No touch. No smell. Nothing. It was a sensory deprivation chamber, but worse. At least when you were floating in the water you could hear your own breathing. I couldn't even feel myself breathing.

Wendy had betrayed us.

Shock and terror waged a war for supremacy in my soul.

She had led us to his demesne and fed me to Apep.

She had been the one to keep us moving forward. She'd taken the first step through Hecate's crossroads. Had been the first to volunteer to attempt Kottabos. She'd never hesitated.

I thought back on the first time we met. She had even been there when the shadows first arrived at the Trident, had watched them feed on Ferghus. It was *her* fault the Trident had been overwhelmed with demons. Not mine. Her innocent facade had been just that: a mask.

All the signs had been there, I just hadn't seen them. I hadn't recognized them for what they were.

And then there was the events at the coven circle. Apep had been hovering just outside the edges of the meeting, watching and waiting for his opportunity. He hadn't been attacking Wendy; he'd been working with her. She'd probably given him the location of where to find us. Could she have done something to sabotage her own coven sisters? Her mother? Had she intended for Brigitte to be swallowed by the abyss?

I shook my head. I couldn't know her intentions, only what had actually occurred. She had been at the Trident. While I was stuck in the center of the pentagram being interrogated, she had stood at her mother's shoulder. However the circle had been broken—which I still didn't think was my fault—Apep had used the opportunity to swallow Brigitte.

She had been herding us toward Apep with every step on this journey.

And now that we were here in his demesne, she had pushed me into the abyss.

At least Tempest was home safe. I hadn't drawn her into this after all. She'd played her part in helping get us here, but she hadn't paid the price for my misplaced trust.

Still, I had a purpose for being here, and a mission to complete. I may have been swallowed by Apep already, but at least I would be with Silas. He was in here somewhere, floating in this same void, lost in the Aethereal coma that Apep's shadows had trapped him. Ben was here. And the Zombie girls. Brigitte was here. Probably countless others, though I didn't know their names or faces. Some may have already succumbed to the void, their energy seeping away and dispersing into the endless nothing. But I still retained some notion of self, and I had to believe my friends had, too.

I pictured Silas in my mind's eye. His scruffy five o'clock shadow. The battered old fedora worn on a jaunty angle. His rich brown eyes that expressed every emotion to its full depth. The quirk in his smile and the little crease in his cheek when he teased me. His lips, soft and sweet, wrapping each syllable of his songs with purpose. The haunting melody of his trombone when he poured his soul into each note.

I could almost see him there in front of me, the swirling energy of his existence twisting and fading, then reappearing closer. Blues and purples shot through with sparks of neon white outlined his achingly familiar face, not unlike the visions I'd had in Bacchus's symposium, but without the physical body beneath.

The thread of iridescent light that bound us grew brighter, thicker. It connected with my vision of Silas.

Not vision. The *essence* of Silas.

Gently, ever so carefully, I tightened the slack on the line. Grams had said it was fragile, but I couldn't move in the space. There was no resistance to push against. The only way to bring him near was to use the string. Hand over hand, I slowly dragged us together in the endless void.

"Silas?" I called.

The essence of my anchor spun, sparkles of light scattering from his form like pixie dust and fading into the nothing.

"Lil?" Silas's gaze searched the darkness but didn't connect with my own. "Is that you?"

Like tin cans on a string, his words vibrated down our connection. He couldn't see me, but the Bacchus-vision let me see him. He could feel me though. He could hear me. That would have to be enough in this place.

"I found you!" I gathered his energy toward me. More of his sparkles drifted away on the breeze. "I can't believe I found you!"

"I knew you would," his voice softened. "I tried to keep everyone together, but I lost them in the dark. I don't know if they're still here or not."

"We were tricked. Wendy sold us out."

"Who's Wendy?"

So much had happened in such a short time, he hadn't ever met the woman Surfer Jeff had termed my "karma sister." If she was karma, I must have done something truly terrible in a past life.

"Never mind. We have to find a way out of here."

"I'm not sure I can." With every movement, every word, Silas lost a little more of himself to the void. "I feel like I'm fading. I held on as long as I could, but there's not much left."

"There's plenty left, Silas. You're here. I'm here. We're going to find a way out."

"This is the endless abyss, Lil. There's no way out."

"I'm a Daughter of Lilith. I'll find a way or make one."

Silas's essence smiled, but the twist of his lips was resigned. "I just wanted to see you one more time." A ghostly hand swept up to touch my incorporeal face. "You were the best part of my day, every day. From the moment I met you, I knew you were the melody I'd been missing. Everything up until then had been chords without purpose, but you turned my life into song."

Tears I couldn't feel welled in my nonexistent eyes. I'd made it just in time to see him disappear. It wasn't fair. It wasn't right.

"This song's not over. You're not going anywhere."

But Silas's light continued to fade.

"Tell Grams I love her. She's a tough old broad, so she'll be fine."

"No. You tell her yourself. I'm cutting us out of here."

I thought of Grams, tried to picture her face, but the image wouldn't come. I listened for her canyon but couldn't remember the sound the birds made.

Ezra. Tempest. They were there, too, but I couldn't remember. The memory, the connection wasn't there. It was as if the abyss had eaten it all away. All that remained was Silas. Somehow our connection had been strong enough to pierce the edge of the abyss and cross the Between.

"Goodbye, Lil. Wish we'd had longer." Silas's voice had grown weak. Our line flickered and dimmed.

"No!" I surged forward. I wasn't going to let him go quietly into the night. "You haven't told me what my melody sounds like. I need to hear it."

"It's not finished, yet."

"I don't care. I need to hear it."

Silas's essence coalesced into a vision of his upper body, the rest of him fading from view as he consolidated his energy for the music. I felt along the connection between us and imagined pushing energy down the line like water through a hose. Our bond thickened into a rope of glowing power. His color grew stronger, his outline more defined.

He closed his eyes and tilted his head to the side, as if listening for the song. A pulse of light swept from his chest up through the outline of his face and lips. He began to hum.

The tune was soft at first, almost hesitant, but grew bolder with each new line. The notes wrapped around me, supporting me in the darkness and shedding light all around. I kept feeding Silas my energy and he lit the void.

"Keep singing," I whispered. "It's so beautiful."

I didn't care if I gave him all of my essence, I didn't want his song to end.

A few measures later, a new light appeared, this one a green sparked with yellow. A drumbeat popped into existence, building a rhythm beneath Silas's melody.

"Ben?" I whispered. It had to be. I didn't have the connection to the drummer that I had with Silas, so I couldn't hear his words, but Bacchus's sight couldn't be wrong.

More lights arrived, drawn by the music, the only sense in the void. Pinks, blues, whites, and yellows, a nebula of colors I'd only ever seen in pictures from space. They gathered together, mingling and collecting strength from each other.

Silas's figure grew larger, re-forming into more of his physical form. A trombone appeared in his hand, and he lifted it to his lips, the vibrant melody louder and richer than before. The essences of the others were feeding him, boosting him just as his music returned them to themselves.

Heat in my hand. A glowing impression of Lilith's sigil in the triple moon. The athame was still with me, even if I couldn't feel its weight.

I mentally scooped up the sigil and swam through the darkness to the nearest floating figure. Yellow and pink, a swirl of mist that suggested long hair, and I hoped it was one of the Zombie girls. I reached out to the figure and pressed the sigil into the woman's energy. The light swirled around the central full moon like water down a drain, disappearing from view but leaving the sigil in place.

A flash of a hospital bed. The beep of a heart monitor. Blue eyes opened. She'd gone back to her body. I'd done it.

I moved to the next figure. And the next. Half a dozen later and I reached Ben. Time for him to go home. The drumbeat stopped.

Silas would be the last. His melody still played, the trombone ringing through the vast darkness.

Chapter 31

"It's time to send you home," I murmured. The music paused and I wrapped what energy I had left around the dust-motes that comprised Silas's form. I would give him one final hug before I used the athame to cut the path through the Between and return him to his body.

"Not a chance," Silas replied. His voice was stronger than it had been just moments ago. He sounded more himself, as if the music had revived his soul. Maybe it had. "I'm not leaving you here alone."

My energy lagged. I couldn't feel my body, but if I could have, I would have sagged in place. "I think you're better off without me. I don't fit in your world. I only bring trouble."

"You don't bring trouble. You defeat it. You're a seer, Lil. You feel what others avoid. And I don't want to not feel anymore. I want to live, and I want you to live with me."

"I don't know how to get us both out of here. I think I can send you back to your body, but my body is here. Sort of. All of me is in Apep's belly, not just my spirit."

"Then we figure out how to get him to vomit you up."

"What, like Pinocchio in the whale?"

"Exactly."

"It won't work," a frail voice called from the void.

I searched through the dark and between the distant pinpricks of starlight but couldn't pinpoint the speaker. How could I even hear her? I wasn't connected to anyone or anything but Silas in this empty abyss of nothing.

"Who's there?" I demanded. "Reveal yourself and I'll send you home."

The woman chuckled, her voice grating. "It's not that easy, this time."

A fire blazed to light in a furious inferno, outlining the figure of a woman, then immediately dimmed back to the ashy gray of a cold fireplace, barely visible against the solid black that encompassed us. I thought I recognized her curvy figure.

"Brigitte?"

"I'm surprised you're here." The figure sniffed, which had to be an affectation given that there was nothing here to smell, but confirmed that the voice belonged to Brigitte.

"Wendy betrayed us all," I replied.

"The shadows finally consumed her, then." The woman drew closer, and I cringed. Her skin had blackened to char and peeled away from the bone. Embers flickered away into the night, taking bits of hair and ashy fabric with them. She was a campfire come to life, her body the log that fed the last flickering flames of her essence. "I suppose they'll destroy us all eventually, now that the balance has been tipped to Apep's favor."

"Wendy wasn't being consumed. She was being smothered. Cocooned in armor of light."

Brigitte shook her head, scattering burning bits to the winds of the void. "I did what I could to protect her, to draw her to the light, but her strength lies in the darkness. She could never be part of the coven. Never one of us. Not a true Daughter of Lilith. Not like you, bright as you are. It was only a matter of time before Apep found her and bent her to his purpose."

"So it was you who bound her?" Brigitte had done the opposite of my own mother. Where I had been disconnected from the

Aether to avoid any bindings, Wendy had been wrapped in it to prevent the use of her power.

"If she gained her full strength, she would spell the doom of the coven." Brigitte laughed without humor. "Then you came along and unbound us all, doing her work for her."

"Excuse me? What's that supposed to mean?" I demanded.

"Who are you talking to?" Silas asked.

I waved a hand toward Brigitte, as if he could see her, but realized he still couldn't see me, so how was he supposed to see someone he wasn't connected to?

Then again, how was it *I* was able to hear her? I wasn't connected to Brigitte. I hadn't bound myself to her coven . . . right?

I examined the space around us, looking for some clue as to how it might be possible, and at last I found it. A thread no thicker than a single fine blond hair ran from what I considered the center of myself—not that I could see myself here in the void —to the center of her burning darkness. It would be easy to sever the line. Simple to cut her away and leave her to disintegrate in the void.

"You see?" Brigitte demanded. "I warned you. Binding yourself to a son of Adam is useless. Now you're both stuck here in the endless abyss, both forfeiting your lives and your purpose, and for what?" She spat the question with violent disdain. "He would never have been drawn here if you hadn't attracted Apep's attention. He would have been better off without you, and you him. Your skills could be put to better use in service of the coven, in protecting the balance, but you were too *self-centered* to see that. You couldn't be bothered. Now you'll pay the price. Now you will wither as I do, as you descend into the void."

"Descend?" I turned in a circle. "There is no up or down in this place."

"Lil?" Silas's essence pulsed purple as his concern raced down our connection.

"The beginning is the end, and the end is the beginning," Brigitte replied, cryptically.

I decided to leave that one alone. Digging deeper into the illogical thoughts of the condemned didn't seem a prudent use of time. Not when we had bigger fish—or snakes—to fry.

"There still has to be a way to get us home. All of us." I was determined to find a way. It may have taken me twenty-eight years to find my true self, but I wasn't going to waste it here, now. "We're Daughters of Lilith, dammit. This isn't our end."

Brigitte curled in on herself, her aura crackling like a log being turned over in the grate. "I told you already. There's no way out."

"Who are you talking to?" Silas asked. "Who's here?"

"Brigitte. Another Daughter of Lilith."

"Not just a Daughter. First Sister of the West Coast Coven," Brigitte interrupted.

"Then why don't you act like it?" I snapped. "You're way more knowledgeable than I am. Why are you sitting here wasting away in the darkness?"

"I have failed. My own daughter turned on me. What's left for me out there?"

"I dunno, life? The rest of the coven? Where'd they all get off to, anyway. How come they're not here looking for you? How do you contact them?" The questions came tumbling out of my mouth, unfiltered.

"They know better than to try to face down Apep. None are strong enough to withstand the gods on their own."

The woman was deranged and clueless. She feared the gods and yet wanted to control them. I'd already faced down Aegir—yes, with help, but still—and sent Apep packing the first time. He was scary, to be sure, but not all-powerful.

"Then aren't you glad I don't know any better." I made it a statement. She could think what she liked; I wasn't leaving any of us here in the void. "So." I returned my thoughts to Silas and his plan, ignoring the witch who had spent so much time living in a box of her own making she couldn't see past its walls. "Let's get Apep's gag reflex working. What do we do?"

The void was black and empty. The darkness absolute. Apep was the Great Devourer, the god of chaos and destruction and the cold nothing of the endless abyss. He thrived off of negative emotion. Drove his victims to depression and self-sabotage. His shadows ate at their energy, pulling them into the depths of despair before devouring their essence.

So. What would make him feel sick?

Art. Creation. Imagination. Heat and flame; joy and passion. The most powerful elements of what it meant to be human were the things that would make the snake hurl.

Silas had grown stronger through his song, an act of pure creation. In that creation, he'd drawn more light, lifting the spirits of everyone around him. Rather than fueling the dark, dispersing into the black hole of Apep's bottomless stomach, he'd consolidated energy into something new.

I wasn't much of a singer. My cocktails were my art. Through juice and liquor and garnish, I created something new. I brought order to the chaos, lifted my customers' spirits through delicious camaraderie.

"Brigitte, what's your happy place? What is your art?"

"What are you talking about?" the woman croaked. "Art? I am a Daughter of Lilith."

"Right, but everyone creates something. Silas works in song. I work in cocktails. My brother, Ezra, creates in computer code, building apps and programs that people use to do other things."

"What does this even matter?"

I would have rolled my eyes if I could. "Apep is the god of destruction, devouring the world. His opposite is creation. So what do you create?"

"I create nothing. I add nothing to the world. My only creation was my daughter, and she is corrupt, a shadow worker." Brigitte's ball of despair popped and hissed as more of her figure blew away into the abyss.

Rather than answer her directly, I decided to do what I did at the Trident. I slipped the athame back into my hip bag and imagined myself behind a polished wood bar. I envisioned a rag in my hands, and all the bottles at my fingertips. I began pulling my ingredients together.

It couldn't be too sweet or she would reject it. It couldn't be too smoky or it would make things worse. She needed a swift kick in the pants, a shot of adrenaline and a wakeup call.

"Silas, could you play something fun? Give us a little energy with an improv bar tune?"

A shot of coffee liqueur, two ounces of rye. Silas picked up a syncopated rhythm on the trombone.

Colors began to bloom around us once more. Dust motes gathered and puffed into clouds.

"What are you doing?" Brigitte asked. Her voice sounded small and distant, but I wasn't going to let her fear drive her away.

"Making you a drink. I think you need one." I replied as I added two dashes of orange bitters and stirred.

"We're floating in the nothing. There's nothing here to make."

I poured the drink into a chilled coupe. It was a departure from my usual Tiki fare, but it felt right. Almost.

"You said it yourself. This is the void. The end and the beginning. Everything we need for creation is waiting for us right here, at our fingertips. All we need is the spark of an idea to start something new."

Thunder rumbled in the distance as I flamed an orange twist over the top of my imaginary glass. "This is my idea. Maybe, if you let it, it will spark something in you."

I pushed the drink toward her. It might have been made of nothing but moon beams and fairy dust, but it had taken form in my mind and held that shape as it passed to the shadow woman.

"I smell . . . coffee?" Brigitte sniffed, awe ringing out in her voice. "I haven't smelled anything in so long, I'd forgotten what it was like to see the world through scent."

"What else do you smell?" I asked, curious if she could pick out all the ingredients I'd shaped for her.

Brigitte gathered the energy of the abyss toward herself, breathing deep. Silas continued playing, his trombone calling to all the infinite corners of this place to bring together the last fading echoes of the memories of the lost and forgotten.

"There's whiskey and orange." Brigitte's figure filled out and the flames jumped out of the embers, as if finding new fuel to burn. "The smoke of a burnt match."

A flash of lightning pierced the air, searing the cloud of energy over Silas's shoulder. Thunder boomed overhead. A vibration rattled my molars and I gasped, tasting copper on the back of my tongue.

"Keep going," I urged Silas and Brigitte both.

I mixed another drink in my mind, this one for myself. Inspired by Silas's off-beat song, it was a version of a sour, with lemon and maple syrup, a touch of mint, and a lovely whiskey I'd once tasted on a trip to Colorado.

The rumble in the air grew louder, jittering my imaginary bottles. I didn't let it stop me. I didn't let it scare me. I had no fear of this place; it was mine to control.

The nothing around us began to heave, which I wouldn't have thought was possible since it was the nothing, but it felt as if the very air bent and twisted through the space like ripples on a still pond. Each act of creation was a rock hitting the surface of the water. Each rock created its own ripples, and the ripples intersected, creating even more, until the vibrations ricocheted around us, tossing us from side to side like a paper boat on the water.

I used my tether to Silas as a lifeline, my anchor in truth, but my connection to Brigitte was too fragile, too thin to grab onto. It snapped. Her figure tumbled away, still holding the martini glass shaped ball of energy I had given her.

I hoped she would survive.

"This is it!" I shouted to Silas. "Keep playing!"

I mixed another drink in my mind while still holding tight to our connection. We couldn't give the snake even a moment of rest. If we paused, the nothing would tear us apart, one dust mote at a time.

The air squeezed around us. Pressure built. My eardrums popped. A vise tightened around my chest. I couldn't breathe. Yet still, I mixed my drinks and pulled the rainbow into a heavy cloud around us.

The colors began pressing together, bleeding into one another. I felt my throat close. I kept making new drinks. Silas kept playing.

The rainbow compressed. Narrowed into a pinprick of bright white light. With a final heave, we were pushed through the eye of the needle and out into the world.

Chapter 32

I lay panting on the warm stone floor of Apep's temple tomb. Silas's ghostly image lay on its side next to me, trombone in hand. He wore the same clothes as his last night in the Trident, down to the battered fedora that I loved to hate.

He grinned at me as we caught our breath, or at least, as I did. "We did it," he said.

"You will regret it." The copper-red snake rose above me, his hood spread wide. Venom dripped from his fangs. Or maybe it was vomit. I couldn't be sure.

I dragged myself upright. A moment of déjà vu overtook me. I'd been here before, but in Aegir's Hall, facing down the chaos serpent.

"How did you . . . ," Wendy came around from behind Apep. "This isn't possible. No one returns from the void. The abyss is endless."

The armor she'd worn as a mask had cracked and split into flickering shards of sickly yellow light, like an old incandescent bulb hanging in a haunted basement. Beneath that failing facade lay the truth of her soul: a writhing, pulsing morass of tar-like shadows.

"Your mother says hello," I said. "I couldn't hold onto her; I didn't have enough of a connection. She got sucked away."

"Another of your failures, then," Wendy replied. "I told her you weren't special. I told her you couldn't be trusted. I warned her. But did she listen? Of course not. She never listens to me. Instead, she called that meeting to bind you into the inner coven and you hadn't even apprenticed."

"I didn't even want to be a part of it. I just wanted to find Silas. Now I have, so I think we'll be on our way." I turned to my trombone player, palm held out to send him home.

"I don't think so." Wendy thrust her arm toward Silas. Shadows launched from her fingers to dig into his spirit like harpoons, pulling him out of reach. "Once in the void, forever shadow bound."

Silas's eyes widened in shock. His mouth opened as if to say something, but no words came out. The shadows ate through his figure like termites in a rotting log.

"No!" I shrieked.

A thick scaled coil wrapped around my arms and waist before I could do more. Apep lifted me into the air, his body squeezing and binding better than any rope. "You are too troublessssome by half."

"Stay with me, Silas. Play something!" I screamed, gaze never leaving the spirit of the trombonist who held my heart. The music would bind him. It was part of his soul. If he could play, he could hold himself together and I could send him home.

Apep twisted me around to face him, his eyes shining in triumph. "You still think you can win thissss battle, but I will not be denied my prize. With this one at my side I will be unsssstoppable. We will unmake the world."

"Everyone will know the same isolation I have felt for years," Wendy added. "Starting with you two."

Her shadows grew stronger, bigger as they ate through Silas's energy. Bound by Apep's coils, I couldn't move, could barely breathe. The snake held me aloft, just out of reach. "I want you to watch him fade and fuel the abyssss. It is the consequence of your failure to act. Your failure is my victory, and my vengeance. Never again will anyone dare defy me."

Tears dripped down my cheeks as I gasped for the air that Apep squeezed from my lungs. "Please, Silas." The words came out barely above a whisper. "Fight him. Create." I wheezed. "Close eyes. Play. Only way."

My trombone player gaped at me, holes appearing within his essence, thinning his spiritual form. His arm lifted, carrying the image of the trombone that was as much a part of him as the hand that held it. He pressed the mouthpiece to his lips. No sound came out.

"You cannot win this battle," Apep, hissed. "But I will give you a choice. Join my ranks and serve the shadowssss, and I will sssset him free. Fight me, and I consssume him, one fearful memory at a time."

Still holding me in the air, away from Silas, Apep lowered his head to meet Silas's gaze. The snake would hypnotize his victims before swallowing them into the abyss. I knew. I'd seen it. I'd experienced the terror that would paralyze, knew that Apep's greatest strength was our fear.

The world was going dark around me, but I fought to stay conscious. I'd been here before. I wouldn't give up. I wouldn't give in. Silas needed me. He'd stayed to protect me, to bring me out of the abyss. I wasn't alone, and neither was he. I wouldn't let the snake take him, now.

The athame was back in my hip bag, unreachable with my arms pressed to my sides. I couldn't use the goddess-given blade to break free from Apep's coils. I had to find another way.

"Choose," Apep hissed.

Energy. The essence of the Aether was simply energy. Bacchus had given me the ability to see the underlying form of the energy all around us. Like a sixth sense, I could do more than the average human. I could do more even than the sisters of the coven. I was *the* Daughter of Lilith.

I closed my eyes. Opened my senses.

The blue and purple sparks of Silas's being were shot through with black, the shadow worms drawing the light away from him bit by bit. The iridescent thread of our connection grew fainter with every moment that passed.

Wendy's heartbeat rattled her chest, her body hidden beneath writhing waves of slick black shadows. That would be my fate if I gave in. My destiny to be shrouded in fear and loathing, an agent of chaos and destruction.

The snake's scales shifted against each other as he twisted around me. Shadow worms raced up his length toward me, twisting and weaving together into the ropes and cloth that would bind me to Apep's service. To become his minion. They waited on the edge of my essence for my decision.

I couldn't serve the snake. I couldn't sacrifice Silas.

Apep was right. There was no way I could win this battle.

"Let him go," I whispered, the words barely able to escape my lips.

Apep's coils loosened a fraction, just enough for me to draw a breath. "What did you sssay?"

"Let him go," I repeated. "Send his spirit back to his mortal form. Wake his body from its coma and let him go. I choose Silas."

"Assss you wisssssh." The snake flicked its tongue at me in gleeful victory. The shroud of Apep's binding draped over my head, obscuring my vision in a haze of gray.

Wendy snapped her fingers. The shadows that had consumed Silas raced to her command, fleeing his pockmarked form.

"I love you," I whispered as darkness descended. "Go create something beautiful."

Chapter 33

Dimmed by the shadows that shrouded my body, I felt numb and disconnected, no longer able to sense the Aether, only the void. Apep was the serpent that encircled the world, the black hole that sought to tear it all apart. Wendy was the personification of rot and decay, her body the ooze left at the bottom of the rotten bag of spinach. What she touched was driven to despair.

I was the cold nothing, devoid of emotion, the ice that dulled the senses. Color had drained from the world, leaving all things gray and lifeless.

But Silas . . .

The moment Wendy's shadows retreated from his form the trombone burst to life. A single crystalline note filled with the passion of a pure soul split the gray nothing. The air vibrated with its intensity, that one piercing sound breaking through the haze.

My gaze was drawn to the bell of the trombone. A beam of iridescent light containing all the colors of the rainbow and some I couldn't name flowed from the end of the horn. It was the only color left in my existence, and I couldn't look away. Powerful in its vibrancy, it simultaneously cut through the shadows and called out to the beauty of the Aether. Wave after wave of sound pulsed around us, reminding me that though I was isolated, I wasn't alone. I had been forced into Apep's service, but I wasn't a puppet to do as I was told.

Apep's coils loosened. "What isss thissss?"

"Ignore him," Wendy demanded. "Send him home and fulfill the bargain."

As if in slow-motion, my head turned to the woman who would be my sister. My karma sister. My thoughts were sluggish as the chaos snake pressed his will into my mind. Yet her words triggered hope.

I hadn't been bound. Not entirely. The transaction wasn't complete, our deal remained one sided. Until Apep returned Silas to his body, he was not my master.

Silas clearly comprehended the situation better than I did. He stepped farther away from Wendy, turning his attention to the god of the abyss.

And then he began to play. *Really* play.

The song started slowly, in a decrescendo off that first blinding cry, a bluesy scale that softened into a low bass heartbeat that resonated within my belly. Silas held the rhythm.

Apep hissed, his eyes glued to the bell of the trombone. The snake began to weave side to side. His tongue flicked out, tasting the air. The hood at the top of his neck flared wider and he arched overhead, dancing to Silas's tune.

My body bobbed with the trombone's pulse, taking its cue from the music before my brain could catch up. The beat grew louder. Faster. High pops of improvised sound randomly accentuated the syncopated rhythm, each one jerking my shoulder to the side as if I'd been hit.

The veil covering my soul thinned. With my sight still covered in hazy gray, I watched as Silas solidified in front of me. The shadows that had eaten his soul were gone. He was whole and he was glorious, glowing with the power of his song.

Faint threads of sparkling white light twisted around us in billowing whorls, melting the ice that encased my form. Bits of light shone through my mental fog like grass beneath the snow in spring.

The trombone dipped and danced through the air. Apep's head followed each movement, and his dark red eyes tracked the slide.

With clenched fists, Wendy stamped her foot. "I said ignore him! Better yet, eat him! Swallow him whole. Send him to the abyss where he belongs. Where they *both* belong!"

Like a cobra in a basket, Apep's focus never wavered from the snake charmer in front of him. He hissed but remained transfixed on the brilliant light emanating from the bell of the horn. When Silas jerked his instrument up and to the side, the snake fully released me.

With a frustrated screech, Wendy threw a new set of shadow snakes toward Silas. I lurched forward, fighting the dread gray that covered my thoughts, in a poor attempt to reach him.

I needn't have worried.

Silas swept the bell of his horn across their path and the snakes disintegrated. Light opposed the dark. Courage opposed fear. Neither could exist without the other and yet they couldn't exist in the same space at the same time.

If Silas could face the snake, so could I. I needn't fear losing him. Not if we stood together.

I shook out my shoulders and the last of the shadow threads drifted away. I was a Daughter of Lilith. I would not succumb to the whims of the so-called gods. They had their place, but it was not as my master.

Wendy lifted both hands toward Silas. Between one breath and the next, I stood at his shoulder, the athame in my hand and my arms held wide to shield him from the shadows. Light burst from within my soul, the same iridescent rainbow I had seen in the center of the coven circle. As my mother had taught me in Aegir's Hall, I formed the energy into a wall between my arms. I no longer doubted my own strength.

Wendy's shadows fizzled like spent matches as they crashed

against my shield. With my vision clear and tuned to the Aether, I faced down my enemy, the servant of Apep.

"Get out of my way," the woman growled. No longer the mousy submissive creature I'd met in the bar, she stood tall and unencumbered. Shoulders back and chin up, fingers stretched wide as they prepared to launch her destructive element at the man I loved, she had come into her own. A warrior of the void.

I pointed the athame toward her heart of darkness.

Chapter 34

A retching sound distracted me. Distracted us all. Ripples cascaded up the chaos snake, and the serpent began to heave. Keeping one eye trained on the servant, Silas stepped behind my shoulder and turned his bell on Apep. He blew what could only be described as a call to arms. The horn rang through the tepid air of the Great Devourer's tomb, shifting into a martial tune that brought to mind a column of medieval knights riding into battle.

The snake's jaw unhinged. His mouth opened wide, and pupils dilated. Viscous liquid dripped from his fangs. He lurched forward with an odd sucking sound as a lump pushed up his throat. One final loud gag and a ball of shimmering multi-hued energy erupted from the belly of the serpent.

I pounced on the opportunity. Using the athame to focus and direct my thoughts, I pulled a thread from the edge of the sphere and threw it at a distracted Wendy. The blade lit from within, drawing on and channeling the energy I commanded.

The cotton-candy-pink section of string lifted from the ball of energy. I giggled, thinking of the old Disney Cinderella cartoon. I waved the athame like the fairy godmother's wand, and the string danced through the air to Silas's tune.

"Kalamazoo and calamity, too," I whispered. The string landed on Wendy's outstretched arm and stuck, clinging to her aura like a cobweb. Where it touched, the shadows bubbled and frothed, the two elements mixing and nullifying each other in a cosmic battle of opposites.

Wendy shook her arm, trying to dislodge my Aethereal net, but the more she flailed, the more it wrapped around her aura, weakening her energy as it dissolved into the mess of her being. Keeping slack in the line, I fed more and more of the essence toward the shadow warrior, using the athame as the guide. The ball of energy unwound and shrank as the elements counteracted one another.

"What is this?" Wendy demanded. "What are you doing?"

"Maintaining the balance." Palm out, my left hand maintained my shield while the athame in my right spun the thread of Aethereal energy toward the woman. Grams and Brigitte had argued over the meaning of balance in the Aether. Brigitte's definition called it control. Grams on the other hand . . .

Wendy pointed her unencumbered right hand in my direction. Shadow snakes whispered their lies in my mind as they raced across the stone floor toward my light. They bounced against my wall of energy, testing the boundaries for weakness. I could feel each attack like a spatter of oil from a hot pan. I grimaced, fighting against the stinging pain but ignoring their taunting cries.

I didn't need to stop Wendy entirely, I only needed to counteract her influence. Not destroy, but diffuse. Not control but restrain.

Apep started gagging again, but this time I didn't turn to look. I pressed my light against Wendy's dark, doing everything I could to protect Silas, who still stood at my back playing for the abyss snake.

Wendy caged her hands in front of her chest, drawing the shadows from her aura into the space between her fingers. The threads twisted and swirled together, growing larger with each heartbeat, congealing into a sphere the size of a lemon, then a grapefruit, then a cantaloupe.

Wendy twisted her wrists and shoved. I braced for impact. Her shot flew high. Time seemed to slow. She wasn't aiming for me. She was aiming for Silas.

Tugging on the thread of energy that wrapped her left wrist, I pulled it from her aura and threw it like a lasso toward the ball, snagging it as it started its descent toward Silas's head and yanking it away before it could land.

That was what she had been waiting for.

With a primal scream of fury, Wendy rushed forward and barreled into me, tackling us both to the ground and tripping Silas.

Silas stayed standing, but the Aethereal trombone was torn from his lips. The music paused.

Wendy and I grappled on the floor, our auras sizzling wherever they touched. She knocked the athame from my hand, sending it skittering across the floor.

"Thisss isss your end!" the snake hissed.

"The knife!" I shouted at Silas. But he didn't have a physical form, and the knife was a physical object. I'd carried it with me when I crossed the Aether, and though it channeled the substance of this realm, a spirit couldn't touch it.

I watched in horror as Apep's pupils narrowed into focus. His sinuous body rose up over Silas's form, his mouth gaping wide in preparation for a strike.

Silas stood, mouth agape, eyes wide, transfixed by the yawning abyss. Somehow I knew, deep in my bones, that if the snake took him, this time there would be no coming back. Silas had weakened him. The snake was starving. He wouldn't stop to savor this meal. Apep would tear him apart and consume his essence before Silas could even think to play a beat.

I did the only think I could think of. I head-butted Wendy in the chin. The woman yowled and let go just enough for me to bring my knee up and push her off. I scrambled for the dropped athame. My fingers wrapped around the handle.

Apep launched forward like a spring.

I pointed the blade and channeled everything I had at the snake. A beam of condensed light erupted from the end of the knife, striking the serpent in the side of the head, and knocking him off course.

My trombonist miraculously jumped out of the way. The snake missed by inches but would be quick to recoil and attack again.

Trance broken, Silas lifted the trombone to his lips once more.

"Shut your ears! Don't listen!" Wendy screamed, but it was too late.

Apep was once more under Silas's spell, and there would be no escape. Just as we had suffered through the heavy darkness of the abyss, the light would burn away his shadows. He had no defense against the pure act of creation that was the improvised song. His was the realm of destruction, tearing apart what was good and beautiful in the world in favor of the empty nothing.

Wendy blasted a handful of shadows in my direction. I scrambled away as the snake once more vomited up the congealed contents of the abyss, this ball of Aethereal energy larger than the first. The snake seemed to shrink as the ball of life rolled away.

I grabbed a second thread before the ball rolled too far, throwing loop after loop toward Wendy while I tried to stay out of reach. Wendy matched my every move, the biting insects of her shadows eating away at the shield of my aura. Fury laced every erratic toss of her hand.

But where I could use the regurgitated energy to my advantage, Wendy only had her own strength to rely on. Each throw weakened her. Fewer shadows left her hand, even fewer reached me. So long as Silas continued to play, I had the advantage.

Seeming to realize her predicament, Wendy turned and fled, retreating deeper into Apep's tomb.

With a grin of imminent victory, I followed.

Chapter 35

Wendy left a lingering trail of shadows as she raced ahead of me down deep passageways and secret tunnels beneath Apep's tomb. My aura lit the way, sparking against each cast off worm and making it easy to follow her path.

It also helped that I could hear her feet pounding on the stone floor and smell the fruity watermelon of her deodorant. Or, at least, I assumed that was her deodorant. I hoped it was.

My breath heaved in my chest as I chased down my quarry. The mousy-no-more woman led me through twisting pathways and down ramps, ever deeper until I thought there was nowhere else to go, but she kept running. Pressure built in my ears and the weight of the world pressed down on my head and shoulders.

Wendy had tricked us, trapped us, allied herself with the Great Devourer, and threatened the fabric of Aether and Earth alike. If she had her way, we would all, every last person on earth, succumb to depressed isolation and cold nothing. Numb to world, without the ability to fight off the shadows that whispered their lies of our innermost fears, the world would be left gray and lifeless until it all fell apart.

There would be no balance, no light to offset the shadow, no joy to counteract the sadness. It had begun in the Trident, but it would spread.

And only I could stop it.

I hadn't understood until now. Hadn't realized what I was. How could I? I'd needed the coven to expose my truth and Bacchus to activate my sight. I'd needed help, no matter that I eschewed the idea. I'd needed the community.

But not conformity. If I'd bound myself to the circle as Brigitte had wanted, I would never have visited Hecate's temple or Bacchus's symposium. I would have hidden myself away, just like the others. Different and yet the same as what my mother had done.

That wasn't me. Would never be me. Not anymore.

Apep had done his part as well, the snake revealing my fears so that I could face them—could stand against them and choose to rise above. I was stronger for his attempt to subdue me. I had made it through to the other side.

My aura burned brighter, fueled by my sudden self-awareness.

Just in time.

I skidded to a stop inches from the edge of a sheer drop to my death.

It looked like we'd emerged from the pyramid, but the pyramid had no bottom I could see. It was a smooth slide along the cut stone blocks into a pool of viscous black liquid. One more step and I would have fallen into a swirling mass of shadows that would have eaten through my light like acid.

This was the true abyss, the source of Apep's power. Like the primordial waters beneath Aegir's Hall, Apep watched over the living nothing, the ocean of darkness at the end of the world.

Wendy was nowhere to be seen. Her footsteps had gone silent, and her shadows no longer sparked against my aura. Yet there was nowhere else she could have gone. The tunnel was too narrow, and I hadn't passed any branches or side chambers in at least two hundred yards. I'd been following her too closely for her to get away entirely. She had to be here, somewhere.

As if on cue, a head rose up from the ebony pool, followed by shoulders. The liquid clung to Wendy's figure, refusing to let her go.

"Isn't it wonderful here?" She asked. "Peaceful. No more voices in my head telling me I'm dirty or wrong, that I'm not good enough or strong enough, that I'll never be accepted or valued. Here, I am perfect. I am *free*."

I backed away from the edge of the cliff. "Are you though?" Of all the chaos shadows I'd seen since we'd begun this little journey, these were the most solid. Almost sentient, they caressed Wendy's body like lovers.

"She never saw the truth, you know. She thought you were perfect, the daughter she always wanted but never had in me."

"Who?" I asked, but I already knew.

"She tried so hard to mold me into one of them. Day after day, alone, she forced me to work with the elements, trying to draw out my 'true' nature. But I never smelled the Aether like she did. I couldn't hear the voices on the wind or feel the vibrations of the environment. All I could see were shadows. All I could hear were the voices leading me into the darkness. Leading me here."

Wendy rose up higher out of the pool. Her arm emerged and she twisted her wrist so that her palm faced up as she extended her arm to the side. The living nothing wrapped around her hand and arm like a smaller version of the snake upstairs, sliding up to her shoulder with a hiss of scales on skin.

I backed away another three steps.

The woman's serene smile as she gazed at the serpent sent shudders down my spine. "*This* is my true nature. This is where I belong." She turned empty black eyes in my direction. "There is no pain here, no rejection. I am the avatar of the void. Accept the nothing and know peace."

She threw her hands up into the air. A tidal wave of living nothing crested above her head. With a snarl that would have made a lion proud, and hands spread like talons of an eagle, she launched it in my direction.

There was no way my aura—no matter how powerful I felt or brightly I glowed—could stand up to that.

I ran.

I sprinted as fast as my legs could carry me back through the tunnels and passageways, the darkness lapping at my heels. Wendy cackled in glee as she surfed the wave, chasing me back to her master and bringing the void with her.

Gasping for breath, a stitch in my side, I wished I'd kept up with Ezra's training regimen. If I made it home, I would tell him that. No, not if, *when*. I could just hear him now, saying "I told you so."

But first, I had to make it to Silas. I had to send his soul back to his body, and I had to cut my way home through the Between. All while avoiding being swallowed or torn apart, molecule by molecule.

I turned left. Then right. Up the ramp. Back to Apep's chamber.

Silas still played for the snake. I could just hear his song over the pounding of my footsteps and the gasping of my lungs. I turned the final corner. My eyes widened.

Apep, once so large you couldn't see the end of his tail, had shrunk to the size of a normal boa constrictor. Still bigger than I'd like to see on earth, but a fraction of his previous self. Balls of glowing energy large and small lay scattered around the room.

Silas turned and smiled at me around the mouthpiece of his Aethereal trombone, shooting a wink in my direction, just like he did on stage at the Trident. He'd been at work all this time, gathering the creative energy of the void and pulling it from Apep's gullet.

But then he saw the force riding in behind me and his eyes widened. Our work wasn't done.

I didn't know how to defeat her, but I knew I could harness the glittering orbs in the same way she exploited the dark. I had to. She was my opposite, but no different than me. No more skilled, no more powerful. We were the same underneath.

I raced to the nearest sphere and grasped it between my hands. Dense with energy, it pulsed beneath my palms, reaching for my aura. I welcomed its warmth. Flinging the energy out with a flick of my wrists, I unraveled the weave and wrapped it around my shoulders like a toddler playing superhero.

In a flash, I was at Silas's side. The blues and purples of his aura were bright and powerful, restored by the creative forces he'd used against the snake, but I knew it wouldn't be enough.

Wendy was right there, the crest of her wave curling over our heads. I had mere moments to brace for impact. I curled my body around Silas's soul and pulled my cape around us both.

With a final, evil laugh Wendy crushed us beneath the black.

Chapter 36

For a few bittersweet moments we existed in an iridescent rainbow bubble of our own making. Outside its walls, the persuasive negativity of the living nothing roared around us. The endless black pounded against my shield and demanded that we succumb. But inside, for a heartbeat, we were safe.

Silas's Aethereal form gazed at me with warmth in his eyes. The corner of his mouth lifting into a wry grin.

"Quite the predicament," he said.

And here I was trying to get all romantic. As if hiding under a blanket while being pummeled by dark forces could be romantic.

"At least you managed to minimize Apep," I replied. "Not that it'll do much good since I failed to take care of Wendy. She's even stronger now. She'll feed him and they'll be even more powerful than before."

"What happened?"

My shoulders slumped as I explained the deeper caverns of the pyramid and the vast living nothing writhing at the back gate. "I thought I had her cornered, but once again she tricked me. I followed her right into the trap, and she sprung it closed around me. Around us."

The nothing pounded harder at my protective bubble, and

the rainbow flickered. I looked up. A hairline crack formed above our heads as Wendy continued the barrage. I closed my eyes and focused, pulling the bubble closer around us and reinforcing it with what energy I could spare. Gritty and sore, my eyelids didn't want to reopen, but I couldn't give in now. I turned back to my trombonist, feeling the weight of exhaustion on my shoulders.

Silas watched me with an intense, unreadable expression carved into his shimmering purple and blue aura. His soul was a vibrant force that burned with life. I didn't want to let him go, ever, but I knew that I couldn't hold out against Wendy much longer. I had to send him home before it was too late.

I lifted a hand to his cheek, reveling in the tingling warmth that radiated up my arm from the touch. "I have to send you back." All it would take was a thought and a push. And the last of my strength.

"You're coming with me." He made it a statement, but I quickly shook my head.

"I can't. Wendy will come after me, after us. She called herself the avatar of the nothing. She'll unmake the world."

My shield cracked again, wider this time. The void serpents oozed through the gap, reaching for Silas's soul.

I focused on the radiating lines, but this time it was too much. I couldn't fix it alone. My thoughts were as fragmented as the bubble, maybe worse. I needed help.

Still holding the athame, I pressed my thumb into the handle. My jaw clenched as I fought to trace the sigil with my mind's eye. I kept losing the thread. But Silas's essence was at stake. If I didn't hurry, they would tear him apart, and my heart along with it. I couldn't lose my heart, even if I had to give it away.

My arm shook. My legs couldn't hold my weight. I poured energy into the blade, using it like a laser to burn away the dark and seal the broken edges of my bubble.

"And if you use the last of your energy to send me home and are crushed beneath the weight of the void, who will stop her? Who will be left?"

"I can't let her take you. You have to exist in the world. You have to create." It was my last chance.

Silas lifted my empty hand to his lips and kissed my knuckles. Where we touched, warmth and joy blossomed. A trickle of energy bloomed within my core. We crouched there in the glow of the Aether, holding hands beneath our blanket of light. Our gazes connected and I couldn't look away. He pressed his lips into a beatific smile and closed his eyes.

"You are my sunshine . . ." he began to sing, but rather than bright, the melody was mournful, transposed into a minor key that lifted goosebumps on my arms.

As if responding to the song, the shadows that thrashed against the bubble slowed their frenetic movement. The pressure on the shield relaxed incrementally, giving me the space to breathe.

". . . each night, I dream of you my darling . . ." The lyrics were different. Nothing I'd ever heard before. And the song was *sad*. I wanted to lay down and weep, to wallow in my misery. To sit with it and suffer in the sorrow.

And yet, with every breath, the shadows eased.

"What are you doing?" I whispered, in awe of the depth of vulnerability Silas shared and yet unable to believe it was working. It seemed like this was the opposite of what we needed to do. We should be fighting the negative with positive, right? Defeating sadness with joy.

Silas ignored me. Instead, his voice grew stronger.

". . . I'll never leave you. I'll always love you, through darkness and light . . ."

There was comfort in the communal misery. Support in each other, to sit with each other in our pain. Like I had done with Tempest. We didn't have to suffer alone; we didn't have to solve all the world's problems in a single moment. There could be no shadow without the light, no joy without the pain, no order without the chaos.

A hiss reverberated against my light. Red scales slid into view, then faded into the dark of the living nothing once more. Apep was listening.

I tightened my grip on Silas's hand and the athame. Shivers raced down my spine and I worried at my lip. The snake was coming for us. Wendy was coming for us. I needed to send Silas home before it was too late.

I couldn't let go. I didn't know if he was making the lyrics up on the spot, but the song called to my soul, the emotions so overwhelming I almost couldn't breathe. Tears welled in my eyes.

Apep slithered past our view again, and I could have sworn he was larger than before, once more large enough to swallow a fully grown adult.

"... now and forever, you are my darling, my life and my heart ..."

The snake slammed against our bubble, right behind Silas's head. I shrieked, but Silas held me tight. His eyes opened and he held my gaze.

"... you are my sunshine, you are my shadow, I'll share your happy and your sad, we'll be together, now and forever, 'cause you make me whole."

Fangs bared and dripping, mouth gaping wide, the snake stared into our little sanctuary, then rotated to slither its way around our bubble. With each sinuous curve of his tail, Apep carved a path through the shadows that encased us in a black shell. The shadows themselves, tiny serpents that they were, seemed drawn to Apep. The Great Devourer sucked them into his gullet growing stronger with each new addition.

Silas restarted his song.

"Stop!" I urged, finally realizing what was happening. In his sadness, Silas was feeding the snake the light he'd previously stolen plus its own essence. The shadows that formed the vast nothing were being drawn back into the void that existed within Apep's dark soul.

But if the snake regained his strength, he would once more be able to feed on the energy—on the light—of the world.

Right?

Silas spared me a sad smile, squeezing my hand in reassurance, but I wasn't reassured. Warmth flowed up my arm. He wasn't just feeding Apep. He was returning my shared energy to me.

"Please, Silas. You have to stop." Tears poured down my cheeks. I would send him home. I had to.

". . . I'll take your darkness, I'll share my light, we'll be together, now and forever . . ."

The writhing blackness around us was thinning, but so was Silas's aura. He was literally taking my darkness and sharing my light. I lifted the athame, ready with Lilith's sigil in my mind, once again able to focus.

The snake reappeared, this time sliding around the base of our bubble. The shadows were all but gone, and soon the snake would attack our enclosure. I was sure of it.

I closed my eyes. Listened for the beat of the heart rate monitor in Silas's hospital room. Looked for the thin blue blanket covering his hospital gown.

A kiss pressed to my forehead. I opened my eyes. Silas's aura hovered over me, the last of his energy contained in his smile. I sliced a path through the Between, connecting his soul with his body. With a mental push, I sent him back to Earth. The song ended, but he would be safe.

Chapter 37

Engorged red-scaled flesh encircled my bubble. Pulsing in a steady slow rhythm, Apep's body slid past my view. Flickering torchlight overhead lit my space brighter than I'd yet seen. The Great Devourer must have eaten every shadow in his tomb.

I waited for him to turn on me. Silas had shared enough of his energy that my bubble was whole and unbroken, the shield thick and strong. Its pure white incandescent light radiated into the tomb. Surely that would attract Apep. He was the Great Devourer, god of chaos and destruction. I was his catnip. He'd gone to great lengths to draw me to his side, attacking the Trident, enthralling Wendy, and swallowing Silas. He'd trapped me here; I was his prisoner, stuck in a bubble of my own making . . .

So why didn't he eat me? He was certainly large enough to accomplish the task if he wanted. Yet he didn't make any aggressive moves at all. Just a steady pulsing slide. He wasn't even squeezing my shield.

I couldn't see much over Apep's girth, but there was no sign of Wendy, either. It was as if she had just given up. No more shadows, no more of the living nothing for her to manipulate against me. The snake had eaten it all.

Needing to understand, to see more, I cautiously pulled my shield back into a solid, rainbow hued ball that hovered over my hand. My lips twisted as I waited for something, anything, to happen. The snake kept up his patrol. Not a single shadow serpent made an appearance.

Still holding the athame, and with the energy of creation at the ready, I slowly rose from my crouch. My legs ached from being bent in an awkward position for so long. My left foot had fallen asleep. I shook it out as my wide-eyed gaze took in the room around me.

For the first time, the tomb was fully visible. Four of the torch-wielding Egyptian statues stood facing inward toward the center of the room, one in each of the four corners of the space. The walls had been painted with vibrant murals depicting Apep in all his glory and multiple forms. In one he swallowed the sun. In another, the anthropomorphic Egyptian gods stabbed him with spears, fighting him off their boat. In a third, his coiled body sat in contemplation of a parade of humanity, his cobra hood spread wide above them.

I turned a slow circle, in awe of the artistry of the space. And yet, the snake himself continued his slow pace, not changing direction nor speed nor squeezing tighter around me.

And then, as his head came into view, I understood. The snake had swallowed his own tail. His body curved around me, his eyes wide and unseeing as his head traced his body's path. At the center, he crossed over himself and changed the direction of the curve, creating a slithering figure eight on the floor. The end had become the beginning and the beginning had become the end, an infinite loop of creation and destruction.

On the opposite side of the room, Wendy huddled within the snake's coil, a dark mirror of my position. Her arms wrapped around her knees and her face pressed into her arms. The snake had consumed her ocean of shadows along with the light Silas had pulled from the void. All that remained was her own innate power. Like me, she'd used the last of her energy to protect herself from the snake's voracious appetite.

Relief washed over me. Silas's final song had done what I couldn't: He'd tamed the chaos snake. Like the pied piper, he'd led the serpent away from us, but instead of drowning him in the river (which, honestly, I might have preferred had it been possible) he'd tempted him with a feast. In his greed, Apep had swallowed his own tail. It seemed impossible, but it was the truth.

A laugh erupted from my throat. I startled at the sound, hand shooting up to cover my mouth. I could go home.

I lifted the athame to cut my way through the Between. Closed my eyes. I pictured Silas in his hospital room. He'd just woken up. Grams was there. Ezra and Tempest, too. They sat at his side, Grams holding his hand. I knew they waited for me.

I was about to step through the gap when a gasping sob distracted me. I lost the vision. Pulled back into the tomb, I frowned, frustrated. This was done. Apep and Wendy were both neutralized. I could go home.

So what kept me here? Why couldn't I leave?

Wendy's hunched shoulders shook. Fear radiated from her form. Whatever had happened in those last few moments before I sent Silas back to his body, she had lost the strength she'd used to chase me through the pyramid tunnels. She'd reverted to the mousy girl I'd first met in the Trident, only now, she was stuck in the mental purgatory we'd arrived in. Or, at least, that Tempest and I had arrived in. Given that Wendy had tricked us, trapped us, maybe she'd been spared before, but not any longer.

Served her right.

Except, I couldn't help but empathize. She'd spent her entire adult life trying to live up to others' expectations. Forced to hide her power, to mask her true identity, she'd never had the chance to become the woman she could be. It was no wonder she'd jumped at the opportunity to find a new path.

Apep had tempted her with stories of power and revenge, had convinced her that he was the only one who would accept her as she was. I could understand that need for community, for support and guidance. She feared being alone, and yet couldn't be like the others. They didn't see her value.

Except, she had inherent value. It didn't matter what anyone else thought. There could be no light without dark, no life without death, no earth without sky, or creation without destruction. To carve a sculpture, you have to first tear the stone from the ground.

She and I were two sides of the same coin.

She was my karma sister. The yin to my yang.

I couldn't leave her here, like this, unbalanced and alone. No matter how fair it might seem.

I took a deep breath and blew it out with a sigh. Silas believed I saw people, that I healed them and made them better. I didn't know if that was true, but I knew I had to try. Wendy deserved a chance to become the person she was meant to be.

I had more work to do. Silas was safe. His soul was back with his body, and both were in the capable hands of Grams and the hospital. He would be fine. Besides, everyone kept insisting that time was irrelevant here in the Aether. All that mattered was energy.

I didn't have much to spare, but I could make this work. I had to.

First thing's first, I had to exit the snake's coil without disturbing him. I imagined myself trying to climb over his tail, but I knew I'd get stuck and end up riding him around the circle like a kid on a carousel horse. Worse, he might wake from his trance and let go of his own tail. That was the last thing I needed. It would just start the whole mess over again.

So what to do?

I stared at Wendy and the swirling black shell that covered her form. If only I could pop the bubble. What would she do? Would she try to attack me again? Wake the snake? If I startled her, would she give me a chance to explain?

Probably not.

How had I helped Tempest? I'd sat with her. Talked to her. Helped her find the inner strength she needed to fight off her own demons. That's what I needed to do for Wendy, but I needed to do it from a distance, and hope that she would be willing to listen.

Hope. It was a perilous and fragile emotion.

Chapter 38

I took a lesson from one of my former therapists and chose to meditate. I didn't need to see Wendy with my physical eyes, I needed to connect with her spiritually. It had all been a little too woo-woo for me at the time I was learning it, but now that I'd been here and could actually *see* the Aether, it was all too real.

I crossed my legs and rested my hands on my knees, palms up, the athame held loosely across the fingers of my right hand. I shut my physical eyes and opened the Bacchus-given sight.

The tomb was devoid of color—Apep truly had eaten everything—but it wasn't pitch black. Instead, everything around me existed in shades of gray. Everything except the bubbling light in my hands and the writhing ebony of Wendy's armor, which seemed to absorb the light around it.

Interestingly, Apep had become a pulsing network of both light and dark that followed the path of his body. They chased each other up and down his length, like cars on the highway. The iridescent light of creation flowed toward Wendy and broke apart bit by bit until nothing was left but the living shadow of destruction, while the darkness wriggled its way back to me, shooting off sparks that coalesced into ribbons of brilliance.

I smiled. Yin and yang, just like I thought. This felt right.

Balanced. And wasn't that what the Daughters of Lilith were supposed to achieve?

Wendy's strength lay in the darkness, in the shadows, in destruction and decay. She had used that gift against people, but it didn't have to be that way. Like the physical elements, there wasn't anything inherently evil about the dark. Water could drown, but without it there would be no life. Fire could burn, but without it there would be no warmth. Tornadoes and rockslides could kill, but where would we be without air and earth?

What had been used for evil could be turned to good. It was all a matter of perspective.

I pulled a thread of bubbling joy from the energy that swirled around me. Heat to counteract the cold. I imagined my station at the Trident, the bottles glistening in the multi-colored light of the pirate and mermaid themed wall behind me. Wendy needed a little warmth and a bit of spice in her life. Two different rums went into my imaginary shaker. A dash of Allspice Liqueur. Cinnamon syrup. Vanilla. I shook my version of the classic Nui Nui over one shoulder then dumped it all into a highball glass with a cinnamon stick and orange peel. It had to be the coziest Tiki drink I could make.

Now, where was a server when you needed one?

The snake wrapped around us continued his slow, steady journey circling our positions. His body was the channel between light and dark, creation and destruction.

I grinned. He could bring her the drink. He could feed her my energy. Just enough to wake her up.

On a whim, I lifted the athame from my lap and dipped it into my creation, imbuing it with the blessing of our shared ancestor, Lilith. Like a star come to life, my imaginary cocktail burst forth with blinding energy. Squinting against the glare, I set the drink on Apep's coil, and the snake carried it to my nemesis, my karma sister.

As if smelling the oncoming bounty, Wendy's armor reached for the energy with tendrils of black destruction. Tentative at first, they licked the edge of the glass, taking small sips like a woman tasting her date's drink. The color leached away, particle by particle, disappearing into Wendy's shell.

The shadows grew thicker, twisting around her huddled form, protecting her. I frowned. It wasn't working. I didn't want to strengthen her shield. I wanted to wake her up.

I watched my drink fade from view and sagged. I'd given my energy to that creation, and it felt like a waste. I was tired. So tired.

And then, as if on cue, the armor swallowed the drink in one giant gulp. Wendy shot up, eyes wide open. She gasped. Her arms swept out to the sides and her back arched. A bubble of writhing black energy erupted from her chest and shot straight for me.

I lifted my hands, but there was nothing there except the athame. I didn't have a shield. I'd given too much of my own aura to protect against her strengthened power.

I closed my eyes and braced for impact. This was it. I'd made a huge mistake. I only hoped Silas would forgive my battered soul.

The blade in my hand sizzled. The handle froze solid, so cold it burned, yet I couldn't uncurl my fingers to let go.

Wendy's shadows slid along the knife edge, but the steel absorbed the power. Pain lanced up my arm. I cried out, but there was nothing I could do. The pain wasn't my own. The knife acted as a conduit, transforming Wendy's pain into something I could use. I swallowed her darkness just as she drank my light.

A new bond formed between us, a twisted string of glittering shadows. Images flickered through my mind like lightning across my brain, searing my mental pathways in icy fire. Visions of sweat and tear-filled hours spent drilling magic she couldn't control. Days spent isolated in empty desert campsites, her mother gone on coven business or venturing out into the human world she so disdained.

Wendy had been so alone, for so long. She hadn't had a brother like I had to keep her grounded as a child, or an anchor like Silas to support her as an adult.

Now, she had me. It wasn't perfect, and it wasn't pretty, but it was the first real connection in her life that wasn't tightly controlled.

As the memories faded, my aura grew stronger. My flagging energy boosted, just as Wendy's had done.

When the last of the shadows had been drawn into the athame, the pain ceased. My body slumped. I twisted my head to the side to stretch my neck and pressed the heels of my hands to my eyes. When I felt the last echoes of misery drain away, I opened my eyes.

"What happened?" Tears glistened on Wendy's cheeks as her head turned to take in the room. Her eyes narrowed when they met my gaze.

Reality hit me, then. She still thought she was my enemy. She still saw herself as the avatar of Apep, the agent of destruction and master of the living nothing.

I pulled some of the energy from the snake into my hands, wary of her response, but determined to stay hopeful that she would understand and see my true purpose.

"Welcome back." I held her gaze but kept a gentle smile plastered across my lips. "You were lost in the dark, alone. I brought you back."

"Why?"

I lifted an eyebrow and twisted my lips to the side with a shrug. "You're my karma sister. I couldn't leave you behind any more than I could leave Silas."

Wendy's head snapped around, looking for my trombonist.

"He's gone. I sent him home. I'm about to go, too, but I thought I'd offer a ride."

"What are you talking about? I tried to kill you. Swallow you whole. Just like my mother." She paused and her eyes widened into saucers. "She's not here, is she?"

I shook my head. "I don't know what happened to her, exactly, but she never reappeared, even with Silas pulling as much energy out of Apep as he could. Last I saw, she was tumbling into the abyss, holding onto one of my cocktail creations."

"Good." I could she her jaw working as she clenched and unclenched her teeth. She stared at the ground, thinking, as the snake continued its slow figure-eight journey around our two positions. "She never understood."

"No, she didn't."

"But you do?"

"I'm trying. Like I said, you're my karma sister. Look around you. Apep has changed. He's the same, but different. The beginning and the end. The ouroboros. He's converting your shadows into my light and tearing my light apart to reveal the shadow within. We're not so different. Two sides of the same coin and all that jazz."

"You don't hate me, after what I did?"

I paused and bit my bottom lip, considering, and letting Wendy know that I was taking the question seriously, too.

"No. I don't hate you. I don't like what happened. I wish you hadn't betrayed me to the snake. But I understand how you were tempted. I was tempted, too. The serpent knew our innermost fears and used them against us. If it hadn't been for Silas, we both would have been lost. So no. I don't hate you. It'll take a while to trust you, but I'm willing to try, if you are."

"What will that look like?"

I chuckled. "I don't know, but one thing I do know, we have to get out of here to even begin."

Wendy looked at my skeptically. "How do we do that?"

"Stop. Look. And listen."

Wendy's chin dropped and her brow furrowed. "Seriously?"

"Yep. Stop what you're doing physically and calm your thoughts. Close your eyes. Visually imagine the place you want to go to, your anchor. I imagine for you that's your camper, but only you know what will work best. Once you have the image in your mind's eye, in perfect detail, listen for the sounds of that place. Let them carry you through the Between and back to Earth."

Wendy's expression didn't change.

"Give it a try. I'll wait."

I stayed seated with my hands on my knees and watched as Wendy reluctantly closed her eyes. For several heartbeats nothing happened. Then her image flickered in my sight. She started to fade, and then returned to solid form.

"It's not working," she whined. "You don't know what you're talking about. My mother never did this."

I shrugged. "It's what works for me, but maybe Brigitte had a different ritual." I pressed my fingers to my mouth, thinking through the implications. "Her strongest sense was smell, correct?"

Wendy nodded.

"For Grams it's her hearing. My mother visualized everything. So maybe you need to tap into your strongest sense."

"I'm a shadow dealer. No sense is stronger than the others."

"What about emotions? You spotted Ferghus's sadness from a mile away. Maybe you need to tap into the emotional resonance of the place you want to go."

Wendy snorted, but closed her eyes even as she rolled them again. Within moments, her breathing slowed, her body flickered in and out of view, and with a pop of displaced air, she disappeared.

The snake continued his endless turning, his body still reflecting the push and pull of both shadow and light. After one last glance around the chaos tomb, I closed my eyes, envisioned Silas in his hospital bed, listened for the beeps and bustle of the machines and people, and left the Aether behind.

Chapter 39

I landed on Silas. Literally. Though not entirely.

My upper body sprawled across his chest while my lower body draped over the side of the bed with my feet still crossed at the ankles. It almost felt as if the floor of the Aether had dropped out from under me, and I'd caught myself from landing on the hospital tile by catching myself on my trombonist.

Silas grunted, but immediately grinned, wrapping his arms around my back and shoulders before I could straighten up. His eyes, warm like melting pools of chocolate, gazed into mine. Time slowed.

"There you are," he whispered.

A chair squeaked. Grams murmured, "We'll leave you two alone for a bit."

Two sets of footsteps and the squeak of rubber wheels on linoleum floor left the room, but I didn't watch them go. My heartbeat pounded in my chest. I couldn't look away. The deeper I looked, deep into the swirling depths of his pupils, I swore I could see the blue and purple sparkles of Silas's soul.

I bit my lip to control the trembling. He was here. He was safe. My trombonist who had been my anchor and had risked everything to tame the serpent, to give me the chance to soothe Wendy's battered essence, was going to be okay.

With a shaking hand I swept the hair off Silas's forehead and lingered. My thumb brushed against his skin.

"You're safe." I studied his face to be sure. There was no sign of any physical damage, and no demons lurking around his aura.

"It wasn't a dream." It wasn't a question. His words sank into my bones, soothing my trembling heart.

I shook my head. "You tamed the snake. Apep was the god of chaos, of the endless abyss. Now he's something different. Something almost new, but ancient, too. You changed him. How?"

"The thing I love about music, the heart of it all, is the emotion it evokes. A good song can make a sad person happy, or a happy person sad. It can amp up the energy or calm the mob."

He paused. Pushed a loose bit of hair behind my ear while his eyes traced the lines of my face. I waited, transfixed.

"The best songs, the ones that change the world, they come not just from the heart, but from the soul. Emotion made real. And if that emotion is powerful enough—"

"Powerful?" My voice came out husky, even to my own ears.

Silas's lip quirked to the side. "Like, say, love," he paused again as his eyes once more caught mine. "And you're forced to choose . . . well, let's just say joy and despair don't often walk hand in hand, but when they do, it's transformative."

Silas's hand grew heavy on the back of my head. I leaned forward as butterflies danced in my belly. His gaze searched my face, asking permission. The beeping heart rate monitor of the machine he was still attached to accelerated.

Our lips met. Light exploded behind my eyelids. The iridescent colors of the Aethereal rainbow, swirled with the blue and purple of Silas's energy. His tongue swept across the seam of my lips, asking for entry. I deepened the kiss, pouring every fear, every joy, every longing look, and every hopeful touch into our connection. Silas met me every step of the way.

It wasn't as if we hadn't kissed before. Then, it had been like teenagers exploring the temptations of the other person. Now, it was more meaningful, more memorable, more impactful . . . just . . . *more.*

Without separating, I slid my body onto the hospital bed, straddling Silas on top of the blankets. Both hands cradled either side of his face. He pressed a hand into my lower back, holding me in place while his other hand massaged the back of my neck.

This was it. This was home.

Silas had walked with me through the shadows, or at least huddled with me under their onslaught. He'd stayed when he should have left, given himself to save me, and I'd done the same for him. He'd seen my darkness and accepted it. Offered solace in my despair. We were more when we stood together.

I wasn't alone.

"Now just you wait a minute," Grams's raised voice broke through the haze in my brain. "He doesn't need any more tests. He needs his rest."

I lifted my head with a gasp and pressed my fingers to my lips. Eyes wide, I couldn't help the giggle that threatened to erupt from my chest. I'd been *this close* to tearing off his blankets and the thin little hospital gown and taking things further. Too far.

Silas's shoulders shook. He bit down on his lips trying to hold it in, his hands clenched on my hips.

I snorted. It broke the dam and between one breath and the next we were laughing so hard we couldn't stop.

Silas pulled me down onto his chest, in a bear hug, our bodies shaking.

"Who's in there?" A woman's voice I didn't recognize called out from behind the door.

"Never you mind, dear. Like I said, he's fine," Grams replied.

That only made us laugh harder. Soon, tears were streaming

down my face. I laughed so hard I cried, and the tears turned into sobs.

Silas stroked the back of my head as the thin blue cotton beneath my face soaked up my tears.

"I was so afraid I was going to lose you." I gulped. "When the shadows—"

"Shh." Silas pressed his cheek to the top of my head. "It's okay. It's all okay now."

I curled my fingers against his shoulder. "I don't know what I would have done. If I couldn't find you, if Wendy had won . . ."

"But she didn't."

"No." I'd saved her, too. Or I thought I had. In truth, I had no idea where she was or what she would do next. I had given her a piece of my soul and taken a piece of hers. I hoped she understood that from now on, she would never be alone, either. "We're karma sisters."

"You are my sunshine, you are my shadow, I'll share your happy and your sad, we'll be together, now and forever—" Silas lifted my chin with a gentle finger and forced me to look at him, "'cause you make me whole."

Chapter 40

The door burst open. I scrambled off Silas as a heavyset nurse in purple scrubs stomped into the room, followed by Grams, with Ezra and Tempest bringing up the rear.

"You shouldn't be in here." She jabbed a finger at my chest. "He needs his rest and there's no hanky-panky in the hospital."

"Are you sure? I've seen Grey's Anatomy," I replied with a smirk even as my cheeks blazed with heat. I tugged at my shirt.

"Fiction and nonsense," the nurse replied without missing a beat. She scanned the machines attached to Silas.

Ezra rolled over to give me a sideways hug around my waist. "Glad you're back safe," he whispered, only loud enough for my ears. Well, and probably Grams's, too, but the nurse didn't blink or turn.

"Me, too," I replied, just as quietly.

It had been an adventure I didn't want to repeat any time soon . . . or ever. My eyelids drooped and I could feel my energy draining away with each breath. I couldn't even calculate how long I'd been awake, but it was too long, that was for sure.

"Can I go home now?" Silas asked. He reached for my hand, pulling me a step closer back to his bed. I couldn't tell if he just wanted to keep me close, or if he was afraid I was going to fall down, but either way, I appreciated it.

"You've barely been awake an hour, young man. The doctor's gonna have to run some tests first, and you'll need to be under observation for at least one more night. You don't just come out of a coma with no follow up."

"I feel fine. Great, even. Energized. I think I just needed a nap."

"For three days?" The nurse snorted. "Actually, that sounds pretty alright to me, too. But no, you and your friends can't go home 'til the doctor says. You're gonna be stuck with me for a while."

"What about the others?" I interrupted. I hated to admit it, but I hadn't even thought about Ben or the Zombie girls, not since I sent them home at any rate. "How long have they been awake?"

The nurse turned, her fists going to her wide hips as she lifted one incredulous eyebrow in my direction.

"Who did you say you were again?" she asked.

"She's my guest," Grams replied at the same time Silas said, "My girlfriend."

"I want her here," Silas continued. "She gets to stay."

"Hmph." The nurse's face pinched as she considered me. "I don't know where you've been or how you got past me in the first place, but to answer your question, your friends have been awake a few hours. I can't give you any more information than that."

"I've been talking with Virginia," Grams drawing our attention to the foot of Silas's bed. "So I'll tell you what the nurse won't: They're fine. No lasting *damage*." She emphasized the last word, which I took to mean that the demons weren't bothering them anymore, and the abyss hadn't altered them in any obvious way.

I dipped my chin. "Good. That's good." I still felt responsible that I hadn't acted sooner to stop the shadow wraiths in the first place, but at least the Zombie girls hadn't actually turned into zombies. That would have been horrible.

"Alrighty then, if you're staying, you better listen to the rules." The nurse remained focused on me. Apparently, I was the troublemaker in the room. She wasn't entirely wrong, but still. "Rule number one is no hanky-panky. You're not allowed to share his bed or get him hot and bothered in any way. His body—" she turned a sharp eye toward her patient, "—no matter how he says he feels, needs to heal something bad." She turned back to me. "So if I catch you up there again, you're out."

Ezra started laughing. "Yeah, sis. You're out."

I rolled my eyes, hoping the blush in my cheeks wasn't visible. "Got it."

"Rule number two," the nurse continued, "no more than two visitors at a time. Y'all can take turns, but there's not enough room in here. The doctor will be coming soon, and we'll need to be able to examine the patient without squishing around you."

"Not a problem," Grams replied. "Only Lil will be staying for now. I'm going to check in with the others again, and Ezra, I think you can take Tempest home now, too. She needs to rest."

I looked at the blond woman closely for the first time. Dark blue-black shadows hung beneath her eyes and her normally perky posture slouched at the shoulders. Even her hair hung lank in its typical ponytail.

If she looked that bad, I must look horrendous.

"You, too," Grams added. "Pull up that comfy chair there and sit before you fall asleep where you stand."

"Now hold on a sec," the nurse lifted a hand in the air. "There's no redecorating. The chair needs to stay where it is so we can move around the bed."

Grams flicked her fingers and a tendril of rose-gold energy drifted toward the other woman. "Come now, she can stay in the corner there where she can still reach his hand. Touch is healing, after all."

The nurse's eyes softened, and she sighed out a deep breath.

"Oh, I suppose," she replied. "So long as she's not in the way of the machines."

"I won't be." I yawned. I had a feeling I'd be asleep as soon as I sat down. The only thing keeping me awake now was the fact that I was standing upright.

Ezra moved out of the way so Grams and I could push the chair closer to Silas's bed. As soon as it was in place, Grams pushed me into the cushions and Silas handed me one of his thin little pillows. I propped my head against the side of his bed and closed my eyes.

Grams patted my shoulder. I couldn't even generate the energy necessary to open my eyes or smile in thanks. The calm darkness was calling.

The nurse's shoes squeaked on the floor. "She might be worse off than this one." Her voice trailed out the door.

Silas brushed his fingers through my hair, the weight of his hand soothing and warm. "Well, it's not quite what I had in mind when I said we'd cuddle on the couch, but you're here. That's all that matters."

"Through darkness and light . . ."

Chapter 41

Sometimes, it was the quiet hours just before opening that I loved the most. The Trident was fresh and clean—or as fresh and clean as it ever really got—and there were no demands on my time. I could slice my garnish and contemplate the world under the ever watchful gaze of the mermaid figurehead mounted on the wall above my station.

Today was particularly refreshing since I'd spent the last twenty-four hours awkwardly sleeping on a hospital chair. I hadn't been able to tear myself away from Silas's side, and quite honestly, he'd seemed hesitant to let me go. I waited until the very last possible moment to leave, giving myself barely enough time to grab a ride home, change, and get to work. As it was, Chaz was going to be pissed that I'd logged in five minutes late.

He could suck it. He was lucky I was here at all.

I sliced the lime with a little more force than intended, my knife digging into the plastic cutting board beneath. My hand shook. I dropped the knife and clenched my fingers into a fist.

I'd almost lost him. I'd almost lost myself.

But I hadn't. We were home, and the doctor was going to release Silas in a couple hours. At least, that's what they said. All the medical professionals seemed befuddled about what had happened, or what had caused the mass comas—they assumed it was some kind of party drug, but the toxicology had of course come back clear. There was no explanation, but no reason to continue to keep Silas and the others in the hospital.

Grams had insisted.

I smiled, thinking of the determined older woman and her method of persuasion. There was no arguing with her. She never raised her voice, never lowered herself to a verbal fight, she just set her feet and plowed on.

I'd hate to be on the other side of that equation, but it was nice to have her at your back.

I picked my knife back up and continued breaking down the fruit for tonight's service when there was a knock on the still-locked front door. I wasn't expecting Gabi for another thirty minutes, and she had a key. All the shades and shutters were still closed, and the door was solid wood except for the port hole window, so I couldn't tell who it was until I walked over and checked.

Grumbling, I wiped my hands on my towel and headed over, slightly shocked to find Wendy outside, shifting nervously from one foot to the other as she glanced over her shoulder.

I unbolted the lock to let her in.

"Hi," I said, keeping my tone neutral as I awkwardly stood between the door and the frame. I couldn't exactly say it was good to see her, but at the same time, I couldn't turn her away. I hoped she remembered what happened in Apep's tomb and didn't hold anything against me. Even if I hadn't been able to save her mother.

"Can I come in?"

I twisted my lips to the side but only hesitated for a second before opening the door wider and stepping out of the way.

"Thanks." Wendy shoved her hands in her pockets, then pulled them out to cross them over her chest. Her eyes traveled around the room, taking everything in. "It looks different in daylight with the lights turned all the way up."

I made a non-committal noise in the back of my throat as I shut and locked the door behind her.

"Hollow. Anticipatory," she continued.

I shrugged. "I guess." I followed her into the room, trying to see the space as she did. Assuming I had been right about her greatest sense, she could probably feel the emotions embedded in these walls. I wondered what that would be like. This was my home away from home, so to me it felt cozy and peaceful, but the customers came in with expectations and drama all their own. Did Wendy absorb all of that information? Did she know everything that had ever happened inside this room?

I shook my head. It didn't matter. Not right now. "What do you need?"

Wendy winced.

I squinted. "Sorry. That came out wrong." I hugged my arms across my body, mirroring her position. "Just, what brings you here?"

The younger woman stared at my toes, as she pushed her glasses back up onto the bridge of her nose. "I guess I wanted to thank you. And apologize. Mother was right. I fell right into Apep's temptation. I should have known better. I should have been stronger."

I snorted. "If you got any stronger we'd all be in trouble."

Wendy shook her head vehemently from side to side. "No. I'm weak. Weaker than you. I see it now. It was no wonder Mother wanted to bring you into the coven, even without training."

"Let's be clear, I never wanted to, nor would I have voluntarily joined her coven. She couldn't see the truth if it bit her in the nose. The circle wasn't balanced. That's how Apep got in, in the first place."

"What do you mean?"

"I've been thinking about this a lot. When I was being interrogated by the West Coast DoLs—"

Wendy snorted. "That's funny."

"I wish I could claim it, but Grams said it first," I replied with a smile. "Makes me think of pink jackets and perms. In any case, when they were setting up the circle, I noticed a hesitation in the colors of the magic."

"Colors?"

I waved away the question. "I see the Aether differently, visually, as colors. That's beside the point. There was a hesitation after Brigitte pricked her finger. It was like the design was waiting for something more. Something different. As if your mother didn't have the power she needed to offset the rest of the circle."

"She wasn't naturally attuned to spirit."

"That's what I thought. But I think there's more. I think you *should* have been a part of that circle. As a shadow worker."

Wendy shook her head. "There are only five points in a pentagram. There's no room for shadows."

"I shrugged. I don't know much about the symbols and mysticism of the coven, but I do know that your abilities aren't evil. They are as much a part of the elements as fire and water."

"It goes against everything I've been taught."

"Maybe so. Maybe it takes an outsider to see the flaws in the system, to bring about change. I don't know. But I'll tell you this: you're not alone anymore. We're connected."

Wendy's smile was hesitant, but it was there. "Thanks. For everything. For saving me from myself."

I reached out and pulled her into a hug. "You're welcome. I'm glad we all made it back." Well, most of us, anyway.

A clang from the back room had me letting go of Wendy and quickly ushering her toward the door. "That sounds like my boss, so you'd better get going. He's been pissed at me for weeks and won't be happy to see me 'slacking off' again."

"Okay."

"Do you have a place to go? Do you know what you're going to do?"

"For now, I'm staying at the Morro campground. I have the

camper, and we booked our campsite for another week. After that, I don't know."

"Stay in touch then. Come back tonight during regular hours, or later this week. We'll figure out next steps."

"Thanks. You're too nice, you know that?"

I laughed. "Hardly. But I know how you're feeling, and what you're going through. It sucks. But I can help, so I will." I paused just before the door shut behind her. "Besides, according to Surfer Jeff, you're my karma sister. We need each other."

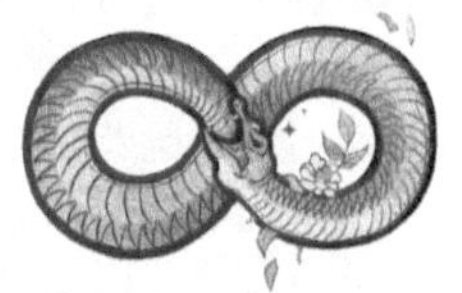

Epilogue

Hecate watched the snake chasing his own tail and laughed. She couldn't help it. This had all turned out so much better than she'd hoped.

"Poor Apep. I warned you not to interfere, but as predicted, you couldn't leave well enough alone." The stone walls of the cavernous tomb reflected her voice back to her, drawing her attention to the ancient art that adorned the space.

Mostly ancient, anyway. A new image glistened with wet paint. She walked around the room to examine it more closely.

A woman stood over the snake eating its own tail. A six-pointed star hovered over her cupped hands, the top and bottom-most points standing taller than the rest. Feathered wings spread protectively from her back while rays of light emanated from her form.

Hecate touched the wall, tentatively. "Lilith, my friend. At last."

261

A Note From the Author

Thank you so much for reading *Aether Crossed (The Rise of Lilith, Book 2)*. I hope you enjoyed reading the story as much as I enjoyed writing it!

Want even more? **Join Haskell's Heroes**, my approximately bi-weekly email newsletter where I share progress updates, short stories, current inspirations, reading recommendations, and anything else I think of.

Plus, just for signing up, you'll receive *Lilith Born,* a free short story that is the creation myth retelling for *The Rise of Lilith* series.

https://bf.meganhaskell.com/lilithborn

In addition, if you're up for it, I could use your help. Independent authors like myself are at a huge disadvantage because we don't have a big publisher pushing our books out to their networks. We rely on readers like you to share our books and spread the word. So if you have a moment, could you leave an honest review? Even a star rating and a few words about what you liked or didn't like could make all the difference.

Some great places to leave reviews are on the website of your favorite bookseller, Goodreads, or BookBub. And don't forget to follow me while you're there!

Want to read more from Megan Haskell? Turn the page! The first chapter from *The Last Descendant (The Sanyare Chronicles, Book 1)* begins after the break!

Chapter 1

With a deep breath, Rie left the pretensions of the High Court and its glittering throng behind her. The portal stretched and squeezed, drawing her cell by cell from the hard marble hall onto soft sand touched by gentle waves. She rested her hand on the cool sandstone that arched above her head, gathering her bearings as her heart rate calmed.

Centering herself, Rie pulled the salty stink of fish deep into her lungs before beginning the two-mile walk to Lord Garamaen's beachfront estate. The beach was hushed, as if setting the stage for the first appearance of the sun above the hills. Even the birds held their breath. It was too early for the tourists and dog-walkers to be out, and only a few surfers lounged on the calm waves in the distance. Rie savored the quiet, even if her two tiny companions didn't.

"The human realm is so boring," Hiinto said, spittle landing on Rie's cheek.

She wiped it away, careful not to swat the two-inch pixie holding onto her ear, but made a show of flinging the spit off to the side.

"Why can't we go somewhere new and fun?" he continued.

"Please. You wouldn't know what to do with yourself. You'd

hide in Rie's hair the whole time," Niinka replied from her makeshift swing at Rie's belt. She lounged upside down, appearing as nothing more than a trinket on a chain hanging out of Rie's pocket, while she sharpened her claws to a precise point.

"Not true!"

Rie clenched her jaw, biting back her irritation. They were her friends, but sometimes she wished they would act like adults, rather than siblings.

"It is true, and you know it," Niinka said.

"Quiet," Rie snapped, patience gone. A headache throbbed behind her forehead. She needed to focus.

Two men stood on the beach, directly in her path. Still at least fifty yards away, they seemed out of place without the surfboards or exercise attire of the usual early morning crowd. Rie paused, assessing. The blond one crouched, taking something out of a bag in the sand. He flipped it once, a shard of light glinting into Rie's eyes. The throbbing in her brain burst in white-hot light, leaving her blind to the real world as she entered a vision.

The blond man stands, facing her. He pulls his arm back, a knife whistles toward her. Blood streams from her belly, her shirt soaked in seconds, the sand absorbing the overflow. The sky is all she sees, expansive gray-blue dotted with thin wispy clouds. A small hand taps her face. Niinka's wide black eyes float into view. Then darkness.

Rie gasped, coming out of the premonition. The blond man rose from his crouch, facing her. His arm pulled back.

Sending her thanks to the gods for the warning, Rie spun left as a knife passed through the air where she had stood. Dropping into a crouch, she scuttled behind a large rocky outcropping, just as another knife hit the sand at her feet. She picked it up, testing the weight as adrenaline surged and her heart rate sped. Fear twisted a knot of dread in her gut.

Curuthannor's training kicked in. This might be her first life or death fight, but he had prepared her well. She took a cleansing breath, washed away the fear and replaced it with determination. The pixies let go of their hiding spots, chattering in the clicks and whistles of their native tongue. Rie ignored them, focusing instead on her surroundings, and her options. Stairs wound up the cliff to her left, heading toward the street above, but a hundred feet of open space stretched between her rock and the first step. No matter how fast she moved, she'd be an easy target. If she ran back toward the arch, she'd be similarly open to attack.

Rie grabbed a handful of sand with her left hand, while her right hand reached behind and traded the unfamiliar throwing knife for one of two eight-inch khukuri blades in the horizontal sheath at her lower back.

"What are they doing?" she asked Hiinto.

The little pixie crawled atop the rock, his translucent wings pulled back and naked skin camouflaged to match the color and texture of the sandstone. "They've split up, one on each side. They're creeping along now, not sure what you're doing, I think. What *are* you doing?"

"Which one is closer?"

"The one near the cliffs."

"How close?"

"Fifty feet, coming closer."

"Are you two hungry?"

Hiinto grinned, revealing a mouth full of sharp, serrated teeth, while Niinka rubbed her hands together. "Humans taste almost as good as the elves and greater fae," she whispered.

"Wait until they are close. I will deal with the cliff-side man. You two take a bite out of the one on the ocean-side."

"Yum." Hiinto licked his lips.

Sliding a foot or two to the left, closer to the cliffs, Rie listened for the man's footsteps in the dry seaweed. When she guessed he was within a few feet, Rie lunged sideways out from behind the rock and threw the sand into his face. He sputtered, dropping his weapons and scrubbing at his eyes. Rie dodged into range. Her right arm snapped out and up across the man's body, drawing a horizontal figure eight across his torso, the razor-edged khukuri knife sliding through the soft tissue of his unprotected belly like a spoon through pudding. She pulled back and away, but not before a loud pop echoed off the cliff face.

Rie's right leg crumpled beneath her. She fell to the ground, blood saturating the cloth around a hole in her upper thigh. She rolled away from the dying assassin. Sand exploded from the impact of another round. Rie tucked in behind a driftwood log, waiting for the second assassin to make another move. Blood seeped into her leggings, staining the blue denim a dark burgundy. The wound wasn't fatal, but the blood-loss was already making her feel faint.

Rie peeked out from behind the log. The pixies were nowhere in sight. The man drew closer, carrying his gun out and away from his body, held loose as if he had all the time in the world to deal with his target.

"Thanks for taking care of Grant," he said, a wicked grin on his face. "I hated his constant bragging, and now the bounty's all mine."

Rie kept silent, thoughts frantic for a plan.

He took a deep breath, exhaling on a groan. "You smell delicious. I can't wait for my first taste." His tongue slicked out across an extended fang. Blood sidhe, otherwise known as vampire. Shadow Realm hunters of humans.

Ten yards, and closing. There was no way out, nowhere to go, not with a wounded leg and open beach. She crouched, body weight centered on her good leg, the assassin's throwing knife drawn and ready. She would have to be fast, stand up and flick the blade end over end to hit her target.

The man screamed, gun firing two rounds in quick succession. Rie flattened against the log, but the rounds weren't aimed at her. Poking her head above the wood again, Rie gagged, the contents of her stomach threatening to spill onto the sand.

The pixies were hard at work. A fine red mist gathered like a cloud around the assassin's head. He swatted at empty air, turning in circles, but never close to touching Rie's friends. His cheeks disappeared first, hollowing out as the pixies stole chunks of soft tissue. Only visible as a flash when they paused to strike, the pixies made fast work of the man's face. With little meat left on his cheeks and Hiinto harassing his eyes, Niinka tunneled into the skin beneath his jaw. His scream abruptly cut off, Rie assumed when Niinka bit through his vocal cords.

The assassin faced her, mouth gaping like a fish. Lidless eyes glared, whites showing all the way around the chocolate colored iris. He stepped forward, lifted his gun for a final attempt on Rie's life. Hiinto landed hard on his wrist, clawing his way into the tendons and veins, sending the weapon to the ground along with a hard spray of arterial blood. Having eaten most of the man's tongue, Niinka crawled out through his mouth. Rie stood, aimed. A flick of her wrist sent the knife spinning through the air, once, twice. The third round connected the pointed blade deep into the man's neck.

The pixies continued to feed as the assassin fell face first into the sand. Blood arced from multiple wounds, slowing along with his heart rate. The pixies, bloated with blood and flesh, flew to Rie's side, bobbing drunkenly from side to side.

"Sorry we were late," Hiinto said, his head tilted to the side. Blood and gore streaked his face and body from eyes to bellybutton. "We got a little distracted when you cut the first one."

"They were blood sidhe, not human. A more complex flavor, more depth to savor," Niinka added, dragging her fingers one by one through her mouth, licking off every drop of red liquid she could find. Despite her trip through the gunman's throat, she was already clean, only a few spots of red marring her smooth white complexion.

"We survived. That's all that matters."

Adrenaline long gone, Rie's limbs hung heavy with fatigue. She shivered, whether from shock or dread, she didn't know. Her leg was still bleeding. Making a tourniquet out of a strip of her shirt, Rie tied a knot above the hole in her leg. The blood loss slowed, but she knew it was a temporary measure.

"We'll have to take their heads." Rie leaned heavily against the driftwood log. As badly damaged as they were, the assassins might find a way to feed and heal. Decapitation was the only way to ensure they didn't rise again.

Using the driftwood for support, Rie dragged herself to the gunman. Niinka's work, plus the knife protruding from his throat, made it easy to take his head. It was nearly detached already. The second assassin was harder, in part because she kept having to chase off the seagulls that wanted his guts for lunch.

Through it all, Rie existed in a cloud of detachment, as if the entire incident had happened to someone else. She didn't even regret killing the blood sidhe, the first sentient lives she'd taken. She hoped it was the shock, and not some sign of a malfunctioning conscience, but she didn't have the energy to worry about it. It was all she could do to finish her assignment and get home.

"Lord Garamaen will send someone to take care of the bodies," Niinka said. A deep yawn cracked her jaw. She climbed her way up Rie's shoulder to cuddle in the crook of her neck. Hiinto tucked himself into the pocket of her shirt.

Using the last of her waning strength, Rie hid the bodies as best she could under some loose driftwood, and stumbled in the direction of Lord Garamaen's hall. Salt and sand coated her mouth and throat, the gritty texture grinding between her teeth. She spit to the side. With a dry mouth, it didn't do much good. She prayed for enough strength to make it to his door.

Hooked? Keep reading!

You can purchase *The Last Descendant* in any format at www.MeganHaskell.com or on your favorite book retailer. www.books2read.com/lastdescendant

LILITH BORN
A SHORT STORY

A Creation Myth Retelling
From The Rise of Lilith Series

Between Chaos and Order stands Lilith

In the beginning there was nothing. Then came Desire.

In the battle between chaos and order, life and death, Seen and Unseen, Man and Woman must choose sides.

This is a retelling of the pre-biblical creation myth, as imagined for _The Rise of Lilith_ urban fantasy series by Megan Haskell.

Sign up for my newsletter to get your FREE copy!

https://bf.meganhaskell.com/lilithborn

Special Thanks

Books come from the soul. At least, mine do. They take hundreds of hours of loving work to write, edit, design, and bring to the world.

There's no chance I could do it all alone. I owe so many people so much gratitude, these words won't be enough. But I'll do my best.

First, to my husband, for supporting my dreams and giving me the space, time, and energy to write. Without your care and understanding, I would never have even begun this journey.

To my sister and editor, Kim Peticolas, thank you for your thoughtful criticism and attention to detail. You're always there when I need to bounce ideas or get a second opinion on something. Thank you!

To my non-fiction partner in crime, Greta Boris, thank you for keeping me motivated, talking things through, and letting me vent! Together, we're going to make The Author Wheel into something awesome.

The Rise of Lilith series is set in part in a bar. I've never worked in a bar. Luckily, I have a friend who has spent more than 17 years in the industry. Not only a bartender, but also a cocktail historian, Cush helped bring the setting to life and created the cocktail recipes to go along with the novels. Thank you Scott, from the bottom of my heart. Everyone else, go visit Cush's YouTube channel at www.cushtender.com. You won't regret it.

Also, please forgive any remaining mistakes in the bar scenes. They are one hundred percent my own.

A huge thanks go out to J. Kurnas (www.jkurnasdesign.com). She's the artist who designed the chapter headers, as well as the Elemental Pentagram sticker (available for sale on my website!) that really leveled up *Aether Crossed*'s interior. She was amazing to work with and I can't wait to hire her for even more beautiful book art.

I also couldn't be where I am today without my beta reader team, Jen, Katie, M'lissa, and Thomas. Your feedback is imperative to the quality of my books. I'm so glad to have you in my corner.

The original launch of *Aether Crossed* was an experiment. I'd been hearing a lot about Kickstarter and how indie authors were finding great success bringing their books to the platform. They were able to do more than just write a book, they were able to give their readers an experience to remember.

I wanted to do the same.

I opened the campaign on July 7th, 2023, and was blown way when it funded within one hour.

To all my Kickstarter backers, thank you! You made this book successful before it even hit the (virtual) shelves. Your support allowed me to hire J. Kurnas to make the chapter headers and expand beyond the book.

Dedicated thanks go to Nereida Green and Heather H for their support of the "Experience" tier!

Also by Megan Haskell

The Sanyare Chronicles

The Last Descendant

The Heir Apparent

The Rebel Apprentice

Guardian: A Companion Novella to The Sanyare Chronicles

The Winter Warrior

The War of the Nine Faerie Realms

Forged in Shadow

Quenched in Secrets - Coming Soon!

The Rise of Lilith Series

Aether Bound

Aether Crossed

The Author Wheel

About the Author

Escape into Myth, Magic, and Mayhem

I've been a fantasy reader for as long as I can remember. I've always loved joining extraordinary adventures in the written word, imagining myself alongside heroic men and women, fighters and warriors who strive to improve the world, or at least kill the bad guy. Ensconced in the safety of my bedroom, I explored strange lands with dangerous creatures. It was an addiction I was happy to accommodate, especially when my mom wanted me to do my chores.

A West Coast native, I'm living the dream of writing while raising two daughters in Orange County, CA with my husband and our ridiculously energetic dog.

Join me, and let's fight some bad guys together.

Shop my store for signed paperbacks and swag! **https://www.MeganHaskell.com/shop**